THE ASSASSIN'S TRIAL

THE ASSASSIN'S TRIAL

SKHARR DEATHEATER™ SERIES BOOK 08

MICHAEL ANDERLE

DISRUPTIVE IMAGINATION

Copyright © 2021 LMBPN Publishing
Cover copyright © LMBPN Publishing
A Michael Anderle Production

LMBPN Publishing
PMB 196, 2540 South Maryland Pkwy
Las Vegas, NV 89109

Version 1.00 October 2021
ebook ISBN: 978-1-68500-569-6
Paperback ISBN: 978-1-68500-570-2

THE ASSASSIN'S TRIAL TEAM

Thanks to our JIT Team:

Rachel Beckford
Diane L. Smith
Jeff Goode
Dorothy Lloyd
Peter Manis
John Ashmore
Angel LaVey
Kelly O'Donnell
Jackey Hankard-Brodie

If I've missed anyone, please let me know!

Editor
SkyHunter Editing Team

To Family, Friends and
Those Who Love
To Read.
May We All Enjoy Grace
To Live The Life We Are
Called.

— Michael

CHAPTER ONE

The smell must surely be intentional. There was no telling how the hags knew it would both mask their scent and make all those who approached the area feel an intense dread with every step they took. As a defense went, it wasn't particularly common, but most creatures avoided any location that smelled actively of death.

It was interesting but ineffective. The robed figure continued down the overgrown path. Very little of it was left that wasn't covered in thick vines and a carpet of leaves that the wind somehow refused to touch as well.

One needed to pay attention to the ground one walked on to realize where the hut was. At first glance, it was a hill covered by trees and bushes, although there were signs that not all was well. While the plants were thick, green, and truly healthy, there was no sign of any birds or even insects anywhere near the little hill.

Wisps of smoke and steam began to rise from a handful of trunks, although it added a little softness to the area and made it look like a soft mist was filling it. As the hooded visitor approached, however, it was immediately clear that this was the source of the foul smell.

The figure moved around the base of the knoll and followed the path that began to wind deeper into a trench and led directly to a small, wooden door. There were many reasons to avoid this place and the foreboding increased as it stretched a gloved hand toward the handle.

It would not be stopped and the door opened without any effort or so much as a squeak from the hinges. The figure slipped inside, knowing the door would close behind it. In the confined space, the smell was almost overpowering and the moment of darkness passed as the sound of a crackling fire was heard within. This was the only source of light in the room, although it burned fiercely and tongues licked against the cast iron cauldron.

Whatever was inside it had a bitter, acrid scent that stuck to the roof of the mouth and made it difficult to focus on anything else. The figure remained where it was, hidden in the shadows and utterly still, and watched the three hags who hovered over the large pot.

They muttered and chanted in a language forgotten by time, although the flames and the contents of the cauldron certainly reacted to it. Steam roiled within and spilled over to coat the floor in the same foul-smelling mist that had emanated beyond the hill as the figure approached. Even when they spoke individually, the sound was as one voice and made it impossible to differentiate between the three. It was like listening to three parts of the same whole.

"Its arrival is not unexpected."

"Not unexpected, no."

"We expected it."

"That is what I said."

"Why would you repeat what I already said?"

"Idiots, we said it at the same time. It doesn't matter that our visitor heard it separately."

"We should ask what it's doing here."

"We already know."

"Manners require that we ask our guest instead of telling it that we already know why it has arrived."

"Manners dictate a warm drink and a seat as well."

"Does it want a warm drink?"

The figure had no idea which of the hags had asked the question, and as they raised the ladles they had submerged in the liquid, it raised a gloved hand to decline the offer. There was no telling what they had added to their stew but the chances were that whatever it was could kill almost any mortal creature in the world.

Their voices were cracked, hissed, and high-pitched at the same time, which made them grating and difficult to listen to. It listened all the same, however, and hung on every word.

"What does it want?"

"We could ask it."

"We are asking it."

"No, the asking comes in a moment."

"It already knows what we want to know. It wouldn't be here otherwise."

The hags turned to face the hooded figure. Those who judged them by their diminutive stature were sure to regret it. Even though they were barely tall enough to bump their elongated, wart-covered noses into the chest of the average man, their size was no indicator of the danger they posed to any creature that posed any threat to them.

Very few beings that posed a threat to hags were left alive in the world, which was an answer in and of itself.

After a moment, the figure realized that the hags had already asked their question and were waiting for it to answer. Its hood remained low to cover its face as it took a step forward.

"I...need to ssssee into the future and in the sssshadowsssss..."

Its ability to speak was not in question, but the words felt uncomfortable as they tumbled from its mouth like speaking the common tongue was something that did not come naturally to it.

Still, the figure dropped to its knees, bowed before the hags, and lowered its head even more.

"The Assassin has not needed to see into the future for many moons."

"How many moons?"

"Many. Who the hell counts the moons?"

"Humans do."

"Humans don't live long enough to count many moons."

"Maybe elves, then."

"No, elves like looking at the stars. The moon holds no interest for them."

One of the hags approached the Assassin, still on its knees.

"What brings about this interest in the future? Since when has the future held any interest for the Assassin?"

The figure's head lowered even further, almost like it did not want the hag to look it directly in the eyes.

"Opportunitiessss…arisssse. My name has been losssst to legend, rumor, and mythsssss. But the death of one man—one man—would ssssee it become reality oncssse more."

"One man?"

"How can killing one man be the makings of a legend? I could kill one man with a snap of my fingers."

"Not merely any man, idiots. A special man. Killing the emperor would see one's name be heralded by the world again."

"The Assassin won't kill the emperor. It's not the emperor's fate to die at the hand of the Assassin."

"We can't tell it that!"

"It already knows. And we already know who the man the Assassin is to kill. A man."

"Such a man."

"A barbarian."

"The barbarian."

All three hags approached the Assassin now and stood over it.

"Skharr the DeathEater."

"Not the DeathEater. It is not a title, merely a name."

"It can be both."

"It is both."

"Skharr DeathEater. The Barbarian."

"The Barbarian of Theros."

"Slaughterer of the Seas."

"The King that Never Was."

"Death of Undeath."

"Dragonslayer."

"Emperor Maker."

The hags had heard the names. They knew who the Assassin should kill and spoke of it with something akin to reverence. All it meant was that the choice of the target had been perfect. One death would bring the Assassin's true name to the lips of mortals and immortals alike. They would fear him.

"The emperor will want to intervene."

"He can't. It's not his destiny."

"Whose destiny?"

"The emperor. He will want to stop any assassin from killing the DeathEater—a symbol of his power, he thinks. He can't be involved. Nothing can undercut the emperor's power."

"Not now."

"It's not his destiny."

"A challenge for the Assassin."

"You know our price."

"One of the few left in the world who remembers."

"Not many in the world know to ask our prices."

"It is better that way. We like our privacy."

"We don't need people wandering through our home looking for visions of the future."

"Does it know our price?"

"We already told it our price."

"No, we're about to tell it."

"It already knows. It would not have come to us if it did not have our price to pay."

The Assassin knew what the price was and it had been many moons since it had been paid. It was always more than what could be paid and worth it every time.

A gloved hand drew the leather pouch from inside the cloak and handed it all over. There was no point in haggling with the hags or trying to find another way. If they wanted it, they would get it. They could take it too, but something in the way they viewed the world insisted that everything given had to be freely given.

Fortunately, what was freely given in payment didn't need to be freely given to the one who paid them. The pouch contained an assortment of rings, necklaces, earrings, and studs, mostly silver and gold but also bronze. Emeralds, diamonds, and rubies were bundled together with glass and cheap crystal. The value of each piece was more than what they were worth, however. Those who had once owned them had felt something for each one and all were left with the touch of those who had loved others through them.

There was no way to tell why the hags loved these so much, nor was there any point in asking.

They swarmed over the purse and drew out each item while they whispered, chittered, and spoke in the language that would send chills up the spine of every person who heard it.

Of course, there would be no point in pressing them for what he wanted. The hags would say what they wanted to say when they wanted to say it. It was always interesting to deal with creatures who lived in so many different times that they could never be sure which one they were speaking from.

Finally, their attention turned to the Assassin and their claws clutched the hoard that had been paid to them.

"In the days of the godlings, will a man of the north challenge their tests?"

Their voice was different—changed and deeper, and although they spoke together, it still sounded like only one voice.

"Seven trials a sinless man will walk, seven trials will he acquit himself."

"Seven days to find his accuser and seven nights will he rest."

"And in the end, seven heads will roll."

It was more of a riddle than an answer and the Assassin didn't get what he paid for. Or, at least, that judgment could not be made on one's own. Little would be gained by making accusations about the hags. His head lowered in deference despite the outcome before his frame slowly rose from the mist that covered the floor. There was no means of recourse and the path was set. All the Assassin wanted was to know what the future foretold for the contract.

His boots moved through the mist to plow openings through the gentle clouds. The smell was somehow less pungent and a little more tolerable. Anyone who tarried would become utterly used to it. Those who remained longer would eventually need to breathe it in as much as they needed air.

Lingering would not end well. Pushing for more words from the hags would not end well. Few in the world remembered that much.

The trees were left behind and the soft earth gave way to hard stone as the Assassin wandered along the paths that turned to tunnels and finally opened into the chill of the mountains. The world opened before him. Finding the hags would never be easy. It was only for those whose lives required it, which demanded that one put one's life on the line. And there was no certainty that one would leave alive.

Or leave at all.

The Assassin vanished into the icy wind that washed over the mountains.

"War is brewing. The Sareenans have been looking for any reason to justify declaring war before their ephors, and Skharr might be exactly that. They have a history of bad blood with the barbarian clans and given how often their border is plagued by the DeathEaters, none can blame them. If he were to be involved in their problems, it would be all the excuse they needed to associate him with you, and their gods would bless a War of Cleansing against the empire."

Tryam looked up from the reports that had been piled on his desk. He had not been emperor for long and having Elric there to explain what the reports from the spies, diplomats, military officers, and others meant was certainly a help. Unfortunately, the news he generally translated for the young ruler was rarely good.

"I think I understand." He pushed from his seat and picked up the silver goblet still half-full of the chilled, watered wine he'd come to prefer as the summer heat began to become unbearable. "The Sareenans find themselves threatened by the empire's expansion to their eastern border so use their enemies to the south as a reason to justify threatening war. They know that if I act against this, it will cut away a threat I hold over others. Skharr is considered a pawn in my machinations."

"That is what I think, yes."

"Why do I have machinations?" He seemed intrigued by the idea although a hint of mockery colored his tone.

"The empire has machinations. But as it is a beast of many arms, it is easiest to blame the emperor for it all."

The young ruler scowled as he sipped the chilled libation. "I don't suppose I could tempt you with something to drink?"

"I cannot while working, Your Grace. It would not suit the lord commander of your Elite Guard."

People had begun to act like that since they'd put a crown over his head. Skharr was one of the few who still saw him as the young boy trying to prove himself. Perhaps that was why he liked the barbarian so much.

Elric cleared his throat to move them past the slight discomfort of the offer and collected one of the papers from Tryam's desk. "If we maneuver into the area with a large contingent of warriors, it will only cause more people to think you are declaring war. It would result in many good people dying for little to no reason. I say this for only your ears and mine, but I think Skharr might be willing to jump into a fight merely for the fun of it and reasonable words would likely fall on deaf ears. While he is here in the capital, we might face the very definition of a diplomatic incident."

"Agreed." As much as the emperor hated to say it, Skharr was the type to charge into battle because he was bored. "See to it that my horse is readied and arrange for a small escort to join me. Nothing too overt—I don't want the streets stopped for us to move through. My comings and goings need not be the talk of the city."

"I—what?" The guard commander took a step forward. "I did not intend to suggest that you go to him yourself."

"But it was your wisdom that pushed me to the right path, my friend." Tryam smiled and patted the man on the shoulder. "You should be proud of it."

"I...well, I did not see death by barbarian as the most likely way this morning would turn out for you, is all."

He smirked. "We both know I am more than capable of defending myself, but an emperor must project a show of force everywhere he goes. You and two others will accompany me. That should be enough, don't you think?"

"Yes. It should suffice."

It had been a long time since he'd felt this way. The world spun, his fingers tingled, and everything in him fought to simply remain conscious.

Clouds covered his eyes and he knew that the moment they dissipated, it would be safe to close his eyes. Until then, every time he tried, Skharr feared he would never wake.

Perhaps it was the result of something in his ale as drinking hadn't caused him to lose his wits for many years. The barbarian knew of only a handful of elixirs that caused this kind of reaction in those who imbibed them. They were usually produced for a few monasteries on the islands that dotted the continent where there was a need to reduce the body's temperature to near-death so the heat of the summer could be survived. The effect was to bring humans to the verge of hibernation.

It would have to be ingested in the correct amount and with nothing else that might alter its effect on the body. In addition, each person required different doses. Too much or too little could either kill the person drinking it or send them into hibernation from which they would likely never wake.

He only knew of it because it was the type of merchandise he had been paid to transport from place to place in the days when the seas saw a great deal of his presence. Those days had long since passed and he couldn't recall any further details.

For now, all he could do was fight it. He truly needed to find something more powerful than the little amulet he wore to reduce the impact of the poison that coursed through his body. Someone had dripped it into his drink and made sure it was a little too much—only enough to kill him. He would be found dead and the logical deduction would be that his heart had died and left the rest of his body to fend for itself.

The amulet was there, however, and held him in place and kept him alive. He wasn't sure how long it had been but from the way the sun cast shadows through the slats in his window, it seemed reasonable to assume that two days had passed.

"Trust me."

Skharr started and felt his body recovering from the attack it had sustained, but the voice was certainly not the kind he habitually heard. He knew that because he heard it not with his ears but in the back of his head.

"Trust me."

It had said that for hours, but he only recognized the fact now.

"Trust me."

He dragged in a deep breath and released it in a slow exhale that rattled the confines of his chest in what could only be described as a growl.

The voice whispered repeatedly in his head—as if it thought if it said it often enough, he would agree.

"Trust me. Walk the path that comes to find you."

It was like those words were enough to send heat into his body again. The barbarian sucked in another deep breath and held it for a moment. Power returned in a shaky measure to his limbs as he pushed slowly from his seat. His whole body ached, although that was likely more due to the fact that he had not moved in two days than the fight it had taken to regain control of his body.

After only a week since his return to the capital, folk were trying to kill him again. He had made enough enemies to stop him from wondering why, but it was interesting that they had tried poison instead of the usual violence.

Perhaps these were the types who had some proficiency and knowledge of what it would take to eventually kill him outright, but not this day and not this time.

"Fucking godsbedammed slime-sucking shits will die." Skharr hissed, rolled his shoulders, and filled his lungs as much as he could before he breathed out slowly. He relished the sensation before he turned toward the door.

It was surprising that they hadn't come to finish the deed while he was recovering, but it was their mistake.

He reached for the sword on his bed but paused short of drawing the blade and instead, drew the dagger. The room was small and made smaller still by a barbarian his size. It suddenly occurred to him that he would have to find something to help Horse hide the effects of the amulet he wore. While it made the beast younger and more virile—exactly as he'd intended it to do —it would raise certain questions.

After a moment's thought, he decided it couldn't be the amulet sewn into his harness. Skharr had worn it himself and while beneficial, it was nowhere near that dramatically effective. It must be the harness, and that had been made in the capital city of the empire—a city that was perhaps not the best place for him to be at present.

How the fuck was he supposed to know the boy was hosting the Sareenans? The two did not communicate regularly, and since the barbarian had parted ways with Cassandra, he and Horse had made themselves even more difficult to find.

He still had some of the dragon treasure but not much. He would soon have to make plans to replenish his dwindling horde.

Now, however, he was more concerned about two pairs of footsteps that ascended to his room. If they meant him harm— even if only to confirm that the poison had performed as intended—he would make them pay for it.

"At least let me knock!" the lord commander protested in a sharp whisper.

Tryam's eyebrows raised as the door opened a second before they reached it and a massive hand reached out to grasp Elric before either man was prepared to meet the barbarian. The guard commander was dragged inside and the sounds of a scuffle followed. The emperor couldn't help a massive grin that slid onto his lips when Skharr realized that the two who had come to his room were not assassins.

Or, at least, not any who intended to assassinate him.

"Sorry," the giant muttered as he yanked Elric back to his feet. "I wasn't sure why anyone would sneak in here."

"Did you honestly think I would let you visit the city without calling on you?" the young man asked as his eyes adjusted to the darkness in the room. An odd, sweaty smell lingered in the confined space, although he couldn't tell if it was because the warrior preferred to stay in the cheaper rooms of the city or if it was too much time spent covering his scent. "Of course, if you had sent a message to tell me of your arrival, I could have arranged for better accommodations, at least."

"Pity, that." Skharr growled, moved to the window, and lifted the slats to let fresh air and morning sunlight in. "And here I expected you would hold a parade in my honor."

Tryam smirked and Elric continued to roll his neck. The warrior had not attacked him with anything close to the intent to kill and as evidenced by the unsheathed dagger tucked into his belt, it looked like he had known that assassins were not standing outside his door.

"You knew we were coming, then?" The emperor sounded disappointed that they hadn't been able to surprise him.

"Two deaf rocks would have been woken by your whispering." The barbarian grinned. "If you had been assassins, it would have been a poor career choice and rather short-lived at that."

It was best for everyone that Skharr did not try to act the oafish buffoon most people thought he was by virtue of his size. That would come later but for now, they all appreciated and respected what the others were and there would be no point in playing pretend.

"Only two of you came?" Skharr asked, sat on the bed with a soft grunt, and motioned for his two guests to take the chairs in the room. "I thought the emperor was never meant to leave his palace without a retinue that some would call a small army."

"This time, a little subtlety was needed," Elric answered.

"Although it is likely that the emperor was recognized and word of his visit here will spread."

"And how did you learn of my presence in the city?"

"Unfortunately," Tryam interjected before the guard commander could answer, "this time, it was not any of my doing but yours."

The barbarian studied the two men carefully before he drew a deep breath. "How? I've not done any fighting since I arrived here. Would your spies not have alerted you that a barbarian was causing trouble that way?"

"Would you like to answer that one?" The emperor looked at his lord commander, who sighed.

"Our spies alerted us to your presence." The man leaned forward and watched Skharr carefully. "A murder occurred late last night and a man of your...uh, unique description was specifically mentioned as being the murderer."

The barbarian shook his head immediately. "I killed no one—last night, at least."

Tryam nodded. "We agreed that it was unlikely but since it was a diplomat from the Sareenans, it did merit at least a moment's consideration."

"I've never met the man."

"Woman," Elric clarified.

"It is rare for me to kill an unknown woman." Skharr growled and shook his head. "Bed them? Certainly, but not kill them."

His two visitors exchanged a glance before the commander nodded. "In this room with no ears listening, we can agree that all signs point to trickery and deceit. It's likely someone is attempting to make it seem as though you are responsible. But without other witnesses…"

He shrugged and his voice trailed off, and both men looked at the barbarian.

The giant rubbed his temples and Tryam noticed an unusual pallor to his skin, visible now that he was in the sunlight.

"I can barely remember last night. What day is it?"

"From what we can tell, you have been missing for the past two days and nights." Elric pulled a sheaf of notes from his pouch and examined them. "While it is unlikely that you are the killer we are searching for, the fact that no one can account for your whereabouts for the last day and a half at least bodes poorly for you."

A flash of recognition crossed the barbarian's face as he considered what was being said.

"Sareenans have a longstanding issue with DeathEaters," Skharr stated slowly. "And they are looking for any reason to start a war with the empire. If this were an official visit, there would be talk of preferential treatment and the assumption that the attack was sanctioned by the emperor himself. Which explains why there are only four of you."

The emperor waited for him to assume that it was only him and Elric, but it seemed the barbarian had heard the other two guards who waited at the base of the steps.

He stood, took his dagger from his belt, and sheathed it properly.

"Is this an attempt to capture me, then? Peacefully?"

"In a manner of speaking," Tryam said. "If I can convince you to be captured quietly and without incident, there is a path to be followed."

Something about that caught Skharr's attention, although not in the way the young man had expected. He didn't think his friend would be easy to convince on the matter, but it at least had his attention.

"A what?"

"A path," he explained. "There is a way that all this trouble can be avoided but you will have to trust me to help us all emerge from this without starting a war."

"Does it mean I will have a chance that does not involve a fat, pompous judge deciding my fate?"

"It means you will have the opportunity to die with your sword in hand if nothing else." Elric was interrupted by Tryam, who hammered his elbow into the lord commander's ribs.

Still, Skharr smiled and appeared to need no more convincing. "Well, that's all I needed to know."

It wasn't the answer the emperor had expected. "You'll do it?"

"I was not aware that I had much of a choice. At least not without decimating your army and making a show of turning you into an enemy."

"Or at least kill Elric and me and escape through the window."

Tryam could see that the guard commander was disturbed by the suggestion. He snaked his hand toward his sword as if waiting for the barbarian to make the attempt. Neither man believed that the man stood much of a chance against Skharr but if he sacrificed himself, it would give the emperor the opportunity to escape.

That was how the lord commander thought. Tryam had begun to think of it as a rather depressing way to live.

"Let's not tell the barbarian of his second option," Elric muttered.

"Your emperor has the right of it," the warrior answered with a soft chuckle. "He knows I have already considered and dropped the idea. His grasp of executioner's humor is something that came during his trials to ascend the throne."

The guard commander finally managed to force a smile to his lips. "At least dying at the hand of a barbarian will not befall us this day."

"This day," Skharr agreed and pushed to his feet. "I'll carry my bags, but I have a feeling that Elric should carry my weapons."

Tryam nodded and gestured for the man to take the sword and dagger that were surrendered freely as they began to move down the steps to where the other two guards waited. He motioned them back when one produced manacles.

"Let it be known that the barbarian surrendered of his own

accord," he stated loudly and ignored the look of shock on the faces of those in the inn's common room as they collected their breakfast and discovered that the emperor was present. "The Barbarian of Theros is still to be trusted. Fuck those who would see him dead."

"If they are women and attractive, I would welcome it," Skharr replied and earned a laugh from the group that watched the performance as they stepped out to where the horses waited for them.

CHAPTER TWO

As places of incarceration went, Skharr knew there were certainly worse places for an accused murderer to be housed. The nice bed and the soft, expensive rugs were the kinds not generally found in the average dungeon.

He scowled as he ran his fingers over the rug. He was familiar with many things in the world, but rugs did not fall among them. Still, he could guess that they were expensive enough to set this dungeon apart as extraordinary, and he knew it was not that the emperor regularly housed his criminals in such luxury.

His inspection of his cell was interrupted by a knock on the door. He decided he was curious enough to find out what would happen if he simply didn't answer when another knock followed quickly.

Soon enough, the door was unlocked from the outside and Elric stepped in, his hand on his weapon like he expected some kind of attack.

"Why didn't you answer the door?" the lord commander asked, took another step inside, and inspected the surroundings.

"Curiosity," he answered simply and raised an eyebrow.

Elric did not appear to be amused in the least, but he did

motion a few servants in. They brought a small table, a platter of food, and a jug of something cold enough that beads of condensation had begun to trail downward.

"Is this how the emperor treats all who are accused of murder?" Skharr asked and raised his eyebrow again.

"There are certain benefits to having a personal acquaintance with the emperor," the man explained. "Certain lords and ladies expect such treatment when they are suspected of a variety of crimes from murder to treason. This particular dungeon cell has been furnished accordingly. It abides by the letter of the law if not quite the spirit of it. The emperor will come to speak to you shortly, and he wanted to make sure you were at your best given that we deprived you of your morning meal."

"And a few more meals before that." The barbarian turned his attention to the repast—sausage, bacon, and eggs, all fried, and a few thick slabs of bread with soft cheese and butter on the side.

He was famished and attacked the pile of food as well as the tall jug of what tasted like apple juice. It wasn't his drink of choice but he wouldn't make anything of it. All he could be was thankful that it had been provided at all since he had expected to be locked in a dank cell far from the sun.

Besides, he had a feeling this would be the last time he could eat this much and this freely in a while, and he had finished the food and most of the juice before footsteps approached his cell. He was surprised that Elric had left the door open, but the lord commander's hand remained on his weapon, ready to draw it at a moment's notice if it was needed.

More than a few feet ascended the steps, one pair considerably slower than the others. Skharr was not surprised that the young emperor had joined them, having taken a moment to change out of the common robes he'd worn to avoid scrutiny on the streets of his city.

This time, he was dressed in all the finery of his office. Rich silks in purples and reds mingled with gold, and all led the eye to the light silver crown he wore. While not the one used for cere-monies, it was still indicative of his position at the top of the empire.

He appeared to be waiting for the woman who arrived behind him—an older woman by the look of her with thin gray curls bound severely in a bun behind her head. She was lean and a handful of scars on her hands and neck indicated that while she was slowed by arthritic pains now, it had not always been so. Her robes were rich as well, although a light-blue, and a pince-nez dangled by a golden chain connected to a brooch of a silver eagle attached to her chest.

She had been helped up the steps by a young man, and two more followed. One carried a small desk and a chair for the woman to sit on, and the other a thick pile of documents. Both were out of breath from having to carry it all up the steps, but neither flagged at any point. The one with the table positioned it and the chair for the woman to sit, which she did immediately.

"Skharr," Tryam said while the woman perused the papers spread in front of her. "I trust the accommodations are to your liking?"

"If every criminal were so housed, I would think there would be far more crime in your empire," he answered, used a napkin to clean his lips and his beard, and looked pointedly at the woman. She ignored him as she donned her pince-nez and focused intently on the papers in front of her.

"Skharr DeathEater, might I introduce the Lady Morana Wysell, Chief Imperial Archivist and Keeper of Records. Lady Wysell, Skharr DeathEater, the Barbarian of Theros."

"Charmed, I'm sure," the old woman muttered in a posh tone without so much as looking up from her papers. "Quite a predicament this DeathEater has found himself in. A surprise this certainly is not."

He opened his mouth to contest the woman's apparent disdain for his people but for once, he listened to his inner caution. It could not be said of him that he was able to stay out of trouble, no matter how hard he tried, but perhaps this was a situation in which he should wait and see what happened.

Besides, it looked more like she was stating facts instead of using the opportunity to voice her prejudices. Perhaps she had a great deal of experience with DeathEaters or had enough records to show her that his kin were not the type to avoid trouble if they ever encountered it.

"She is the one who told me I could bring three warriors with me when I attempted my trial," Tryam explained. "The one you were there for. It's odd how it seemed to have slipped the mind of the folk who presented me with it. But I suppose you were all I needed, after all. But water under the bridge and all that. She also directed me to a way to beat the predicament you are in. You will have to run the...the Path of the Gods."

Skharr's eyes narrowed. It sounded somewhat melodramatic, but everything involving the gods had a touch of that. As far as he was concerned, it was practically a requirement.

"The...what?" He shook his head. "Is that the Ruin of the Souls?"

"Some call it that," the archivist replied without shifting her gaze from her papers. "The other names are the Last Chance of the Damned, the Fate of the Cursed, and the Damnation of the Pitiful."

"And here I thought you would coat the situation with sugar for my benefit," the barbarian muttered, and Elric hastily concealed a grin.

That did make the woman look up and she raised an eyebrow at him.

Before she could say anything, Tryam took a step forward.

"Enough with the dismal names, yes?" He turned to Wysell. "We wouldn't want the barbarian to slit his wrists before we begin, now would we?"

"Of course, Your Grace." She cleared her throat before she

chose a paper and inspected the warrior closely, her eyes comically large behind the lenses. "There are seven tests, purportedly constructed by each god. If a person can pass, the gods have decided they have earned the right to life, regardless of what the worldly laws have decided."

"And what if their judgment is not considered good enough?" Skharr asked. At this point, there was no point in explaining his own experience with the gods, personal though it was. The chances were there was already some document for it too.

"The gods are meant to stand for their respective test," she explained. "Each god to defend their decision."

Given that Janus had used the spirits of dead warriors to eliminate the underworld council in Verenvan, he didn't want to chance an argument.

"You are allowed to bring one companion with you," she continued, still reading from the paper. "Should you fail, it will result in their death. However, should they die, it would not necessarily result in your failure."

"It seems specific enough," he responded roughly and pushed to his feet. "I won't have any friends of mine dying on my account, not for this. If I die, I'll do so alone."

"That is your prerogative," the woman stated and put the paper down.

"It's still not a good decision," Tryam insisted. "I'll go find you some help."

CHAPTER THREE

"Nothing but the odd barfight. It happens all over the continent every day of the week. There's no need to go into it now, is there?" The quarter-orc shifted in the saddle and tried to ignore the fact that his rear end had gone utterly numb.

"Are you joking?" Salis looked up from the path and scowled at Grakoor. "Nothing but an odd barfight? We were heroes, mate —conquerors. Don't take that away by trying to play it down when others are listening. We...saved a woman, a barmaid who was being threatened by a couple of traveling toughs. We taught them a lesson, we did."

"But there weren't no barmaid."

"Well, they don't have to know that. When folk see us bruised and battered like this, they'll assume the elf-dwarf mongrel and the quarter-orc are the type to stir the locals up and get into fights. You need to be on top of those stories and make sure the narrative comes from you. It won't be like anyone will question it and if we make the story a good one, there might be a couple of drinks and even a decent meal in it for us. You need to work on your storytelling abilities."

Grakoor nodded, although his friend didn't expect him to put much effort into it. Like his orc kin, he wasn't entirely comfortable speaking in the common tongue, which meant his storytelling would have to involve considerable reenacting. This was never a bad thing, especially if he had someone to partner with.

That was her job.

"We got a camp ahead," he muttered.

"Just because there's smoke in the air doesn't mean there's a camp. Remember the last time you thought that and led us directly into a small brushfire? And we had to stay to help the locals put it out before it spread to their barley fields."

"They paid us for it."

"That's not the point." It emerged a little sharper than Salis intended and she bit her lip.

If the truth be told, it had been fairly easy work and the pay had been good. Helping folk and getting paid for it was always a good way to make coin and they'd added dried meat and oats to make sure the two were properly compensated.

"What is the point?" Grakoor sighed as if he regretted asking the question.

"The point is, how do you know that this is a camp and not another fire?"

"Folk don't burn their koffe. I smell koffe."

He made a good point there, and Salis tilted her head as they continued down the road to where Grakoor's suspicions were confirmed. A small campfire had been built next to a stream a short distance from the road, and all the accouterments of a camp were spread around it. A shorter female carefully stirred and inspected the contents of the pot she had over the flames.

And it did smell of koffe. Her mouth was already watering at the aroma.

The woman did not immediately hear their approach but when she did, she snaked her hand to the seax she carried at her hip, her eyes wide, and appeared to be ready for a fight.

Salis raised her hands and brought her mount to a halt. "Fear not. We are simple travelers like you. If you want us to continue on our way, we will, but if you have a mind for company, we would be happy to share ours."

Her gaze lingered on their weapons but after a moment, she finally relaxed onto the tree trunk she had used as a seat. "Feel free to share my fire."

"If you have a mind to share your koffe as well, we would be willing to part with some food in exchange."

She nodded as the two approached the campfire but watched them carefully as they dismounted and relieved their horses of the saddlebags. It seemed like good manners to leave their weapons behind as they joined the woman's campfire, and Grakoor began to add root vegetables, dried meat, and oats to their pot before he poured water in and positioned it over the fire.

After a long moment in which she watched their preparations in silence, their new companion poured herself some of the steaming hot koffe and indicated for them to present their cups.

The brew was a little older, which made it more bitter than when it was fresh, but it was still delicious. The three savored the hot drink for a while with no conversation. The comfortable silence was soon underpinned by the happy bubbling from the stew Grakoor was preparing.

"Have you been on the road long?" the woman asked finally.

"We are never off it for long," Salis answered with a smile. "I am Salis, and this is my comrade Grakoor. We enjoy the appeal of the open road as often as we can, and there is enough coin for those of our inclination to make. It's made better by a handful of our past endeavors."

"Ah, yes," the woman muttered and sipped her koffe. "I thought I recognized the names. I had a friend of a friend who knew of Abirat. It was through him that I was introduced to this particular beverage, although it is growing more difficult to find.

Merchants are loathe to travel the roads from their groves in the south."

"Unfortunate, but true," Grakoor muttered and stirred their stew a few times before he pulled it from the fire to let it cool.

"My friend learned of it through one of his traveling companions—and yours from the stories that are told of your travels. Do you know the barbarian known as Skharr?"

"It's hard to forget the man," Salis admitted with a chuckle. "You traveled with him?"

The smaller woman nodded. "He is...difficult to forget and I've listened for news of him as I go. It's difficult to separate fact from fantasy, but what I heard of him last was that he was arrested in the Imperial City and accused of murder."

"It is hard to imagine a place where Skharr doesn't find himself in some kind of trouble," Grakoor grumbled and began to serve the stew for the three of them as their new companion set her bowl out to partake as well. Three equal portions and some waybread were handed out and the three began to eat their evening meal. "Although knowing the man, I would say there was probably a good reason to kill them."

"Whatever the reason, Skharr has appealed to the highest law of the land and committed to taking the Seven Tests to prove his innocence. They say he is searching for companions to take the tests with him."

Salis and Grakoor shared a glance, and she had a feeling she knew what was going through the mind of the quarter-orc. There weren't many people in the world they would go out of their way to help. It was usually a matter of stumbling on those who needed it, acting, and hoping there was some remuneration in it for them.

But Skharr was one of them, oddly enough. They did owe the barbarian as it turned out.

"I suppose we need to travel to the Imperial City as quickly as possible." Salis scratched her jaw.

"Truly?" the woman asked. "You would do that for him?"

"He would have done the same for us," Grakoor answered simply. "He has done the same for us. Besides, there might be some coin in working with Skharr again."

The woman nodded slowly, her hands cradled around her koffe. "Interesting."

In that moment, as she placed her cup down, something in the world changed around them. Salis drew a deep breath, blinked, and tried to shift the sudden fuzz that appeared on her eyes. Once it cleared, she bounded immediately on her feet and reached for the sword that was still with the rest of their saddlebags.

The question of how it happened was somewhat irrelevant as both she and Grakoor realized they needed to find out what had happened.

They were no longer in the camp they had been in seconds before. The small stream was gone, as was the thicket they had traveled through. These were replaced by a mostly open road with farms spread as far as the eye could see and wheat starting to turn golden in the fields.

A small stream nearby and their campfire provided the only similarity. Their companion was gone, but the bowl of food and the pot with cooling coffee inside were still there.

"What...trickster madness is this?" Grakoor found his feet, his fists clenched and ready to swing, but there was nothing for them to swing at.

Even worse, Salis recognized the single peak they could see in the distance and the walls that rose about a day's ride away from where they stood.

"It must have been a god's work of some kind," she muttered and picked her cup of koffe up, which was amazingly still warm.

"How do you know?"

"Because we are a day's ride from the Imperial City. It can't have been a coincidence that the bitch talked to us about Skharr and then dropped us less than a day away from where the bastard is locked up." Salis glowered at her cup.

"A…a god then."

"Do you know of any other beings who could bring us here in the blink of an eye? And our horses as well?"

Neither beast looked particularly perturbed by the change in scenery, which was an oddity all its own but something to think about another time.

"Why did you call her a bitch?" Grakoor fixed her with a genuinely curious gaze.

"Because she transported us without our consent or knowledge. No matter that it was where we intended to go in the first place. It's rude to do so without at least asking us."

"No, I mean how do you know that it was a woman? The gods are known to be able to shift between one or the other without too much trouble."

"Is that seriously what you have in mind at the moment?" She grasped at something to which she could direct her irritation.

"It's something to consider, at least. If you're going to insult the gods, you might as well do it right."

Salis shook her head and sat on the log that was also still there.

"Which one do you suppose would be this determined to ensure that Skharr is properly supported on the path?" Grakoor asked and perched next to her as the sun began to set. "Theros is the obvious choice, of course, but I've never known him to transform into a woman. Usually, it's an old man with a donkey."

"It might be him, but I would imagine more than a few of the gods, high lords and not, want to see that Skharr remains alive and well."

"Do any names come to mind?"

"Not really." Impatience slid onto her face. "Is this the best way to spend our time?"

"We can't travel with the sun setting now, anyway. Skharr will be in as much trouble tomorrow as he is today. We might as well rest and discuss what type of trouble we've gotten ourselves into."

Salis sighed and took another sip from her cup. "Whichever god it was, they could have provided decent koffe."

"You know that if Skharr finds out about you doing this, he won't be happy," Elric muttered and folded his arms.

Tryam sipped his chilled wine before he turned his attention to his lord commander. "I'd rather him be cross and alive than the alternative. Besides, the idea is that he never finds out at all."

"You're making the mistake that so many others have, Your Grace."

He only ever called the young ruler Your Grace when he was upset about something and wanted it to be as clear as possible that he wasn't being disrespectful.

"And what mistake might that be?" he asked and tried to not sound annoyed. He wasn't, but when people thought he was, they tended to immediately bow and scrape.

"Underestimating Skharr, Your Grace, and especially his intellect. He's not the fool he pretends to be, and if he realizes we are influencing his friends and comrades to help him, even I wouldn't be able to imagine what he might do. He might choose to end it all with his own life, or he might choose to break out and die that way. If we're lucky."

"I suppose you think it is best to simply let him run the Seven Trials on his own? As far as we know, those who would be willing to help our barbarian are spread across the godsbe-dammed continent. I doubt we will even have sufficient numbers for the task as it is." The young emperor sounded a little discouraged.

"We'll find a way. Even if we have to delay the process to wait for them."

"It might come to that."

CHAPTER FOUR

With the sun setting, the tavern was full. It was one of the more popular establishments in the town and seemed almost to have grown beyond its capacity overnight. Men who worked in the lumber yard came in with the coin they'd been paid for a week's labor and those from the quarry did the same. For a few days, the town would be awash in drunken workers who were determined to pour all their coin into the hands of the purveyors of vice in the settlement before they were transported to the yard and quarry again.

His fingers toyed with the rim of his mug and he wondered if it was time for him to order a little more. There was the question as to whether the barmaid would be able to hear him if he did, but if he ordered one now, there would be a chance that it would arrive by the time his was empty. He did not want to tolerate any part of this evening with an empty cup.

"Right, then!" A melodious voice from the corner of the room carried through the crowd around him. "A little more music to lighten the soul. What would my adoring audience like to hear of this night?"

He strummed his lute and started a light, jaunty tune as the patrons of the tavern began to shout the names of different mythical heroes whose tales were sung across the continent, but one name seemed to have gained significantly more popularity.

"Skharr DeathEater!"

"Aye! Sing us the tales of Skharr the DeathEater!"

"It's not a fucking title, it's a name."

"It can be both. He's a DeathEater, isn't he?"

"Aye, but it's his name, not his title. It's Skharr DeathEater!"

"It can be fucking both, you dumb shit!"

Opinions were interestingly divided on the matter and he couldn't help a smile as the patrons seemed to grow increasingly hostile to the point where it was likely that the whole room would erupt in a skirmish.

"It don't matter. I can't be singing about him anymore," the bard answered with a laugh, quieted the crowd, and prevented the imminent violence from erupting. "The DeathEater has been captured and put behind bars. An assassin, they call him now, and I'm likely to follow him into prison if any of the guard were to hear me singing about that blaggard. You'll have to choose someone else, I fear."

"Oy, we don't give a shit about whatever political reason why folk have arrested him. He's still a damn hero and will be treated as such."

"A hero wouldn't be in prison for murder now, would he?"

The one who spoke wore a Janus amulet around her neck, as did the others at her table who very firmly agreed with what she had said.

"Who gives a shit why that child of an emperor decided to toss the DeathEater behind bars?"

"And even if he did kill someone, they was likely deserving of it. Plenty of folk in the Imperial City need some killing. He was probably killing a murderer but as it turns out, it was the son of some powerful lord who wants to see him hanged for it." The

Theros camp seemed determined not to take any insult to their hero barbarian lightly.

"Listen to yourself. You would say that about anyone the fucking buffoon trod on, simply to hold onto your belief that he's some sort of hero."

The room erupted in an argument again, and it was clear who were loyal to Janus and those who weren't by how the lines in the room were divided.

"You might want to sing about the downfall of the Barbarian of Theros," one of them shouted. "Show how terrible the old man's taste is when it comes to his fucking followers!"

"Or you'll want to sing about how the followers of Janus would be willing to see an innocent man condemned to die because they're insufferable idiots who need such idiocy to make them feel better about themselves."

There were too many drunk folk who were used to working with their bodies for the peace to be maintained for long. It was difficult to tell who said what when all those present in the room began to shout. The bard looked rather pleased with the confusion he'd wrought, although he continued to strum his lute like he was thinking up new stories.

He would have to find an alternative or two for his repertoire. Given how popular Skharr was, he was a favorite topic for a song —although there was a fair amount said about a certain princess who performed feats in the east. Still, if they couldn't sing about Skharr, it made sense that they would need to find something new to replace him.

Few tales of heroics were shared these days, which meant little to choose from, and bards hated having to come up with their own material. They would have to make their heroes up since there weren't many to be found in the world.

Despite wishing for another drink, he didn't want to be in the room when it turned into a battle. He pulled his cloak a little lower over his head to hide his features from the torchlight and danger poised in every patron around the room, drained his mug to the last, and stood. The drink had already been paid for when he arrived but even if it hadn't, with the fight that was about to erupt, he doubted the tavern owner would realize that one or two drinks had not been paid for.

One item of interest that did require attention was the musician, of course. He slid his hand inside his cloak and a small smile touched his lips as he withdrew a gold coin and dropped it into the bard's cup.

"Very generous of you, good sir."

The figure made no attempt to answer but a smile touched his lips as he turned, strode out, and closed the door behind him as the first punch was thrown.

"Brighten up, Elric. You look like you've been summoned to your own execution." While Tryam stoically maintained his gracious expression—reserved for this type of public occasion—his tone betrayed the smirk he should have worn instead.

"That is what it feels like, Your Grace. I do believe this is the first time I've been summoned to one of these…banquets."

"It's a celebration. I assume you've been to a few of those before." The young emperor knew he shouldn't tease his lord commander too much but honestly, he couldn't resist and especially because he knew the man couldn't retaliate.

"Aye, Your Grace, but those tended to involve a few more horns of mead, shouting, singing, and fighting and a great deal less…stringed instruments and…" The guard commander scowled as he studied what was presented to him by one of the servers on a silver platter. "What is that?"

"There are a few names for it, but I do believe it is the liver of a goose that was force-fed corn until it died."

"How...appetizing." Elric's expression slid into polite horror before he managed to school it to simply polite.

"Indeed. If the truth be told, these...events could do with more drinking and fighting." Tryam tugged at the collar that was arranged so close to his throat that it was what he imagined a hangman's noose felt like to those about to die.

"If you feel so, Your Grace, why do you attend?"

"Because it's the birthday of my...third cousin, twice removed. He came all this way from Trezalin to celebrate it with me." The emperor sipped his watered wine. "How could I decline? Besides, my advisors tell me these social events are the proper means to be introduced to a variety of the young, eligible women in my domain. They encourage a marriage that would strengthen my position and especially when a variety of diplomatic parties are in the city. They think I should find myself a young lady from Yorunn to strengthen our alliances there."

Elric chuckled. "And yet you are here, speaking to me. You have the future of your empire to attend to, Your Grace."

"I've been at it from the moment I arrived and was introduced to the eligible young ladies of the land, all of whom I had to hold polite conversation with. I needed a little time. It would be boorish of me to be drunk for those conversations, would it not, my friend?"

"It would. Although I think it would make these conversations at least a little more tolerable."

"In that case, they would have to be drunk as well." Tryam grinned and hid it quickly behind his goblet.

"It would make it tolerable for them too. You could issue some order and tell everyone to raise their cups in toasts often enough to ensure that all your guests are good and drunk before the first course is served."

"I don't suppose you have any suggestions as to what we might find ourselves drinking toasts to."

"Any number of military victories—and the birthday of your

cousin, of course." Elric looked longingly at a tray of drinks and wished for a single brief moment that the lord commander of the Emperor's Elites could indulge his need to drink himself silly.

"Third cousin."

"Whatever. You'll find a reason to drink. Unless, of course, you would rather not."

Tryam narrowed his eyes and gestured for the musicians to move a little closer to them to ensure that no one could overhear what was said. The Sareenan diplomatic corps were present for the feast, one of the few signs that they were at least willing to take a step in friendship now that the purported assassin of one of their own was imprisoned and awaiting execution.

"And what reason might I have to remain sober on this night?" He was all business now, the joking young man tucked within the serious ruler.

"The same reason you wanted me here. You made a decision that you are not sure about, and drinking would only serve to cloud your judgment. Some might even say cloud it further."

The emperor leaned a little closer and kept his voice low. "Would you care to expound on that statement, Lord Commander?"

"I saw the names you wished me to pass on to your Eagles. The names of those you wish to be here should Skharr need them."

"A fair number there were too. Is there anything in particular about them you wish to discuss with me?"

Elric drew a breath before he continued carefully. "I suppose you have your reasons for sending summonses to your sisters—"

"Half-sisters."

"Aye, half, but I should tell you it is not advisable. There is a reason, after all, why your father determined that they would not return to the Imperial City after their mother was sent away."

"I don't care. In this case, it is important for my family to be present." The young man's face hardened a little, a faint mirror to the determination Elric had so often seen in his royal father.

"Family is a word that represents strength for all those who do not wear the imperial crown. For you...it represents division. Those who would see you cast from your throne would find their position strengthened if they could find someone to replace you."

"No matter." Tryam sipped his drink casually. "I need family. And I need them now."

"Of course, Your Grace."

"Now, if you'll excuse me." He waved to one of the servers, determined to issue orders to fill every guest's goblet. "I have a few toasts to announce."

CHAPTER FIVE

"Seven bloody trials. You'd think a DeathEater would be grinning at the opportunity—especially that DeathEater." The old dwarf stretched to ease the stiffness in his joints. He'd spent long days on the road and less time resting than usual. Some news needed to be shared with interested parties sooner rather than later.

Throk Anvilforged nodded. "How did you find out about it?"

"Folk are being told. It seems the emperor wanted to let the bastard go free, but the one who was killed was a diplomat of some kind. If he is released, war would break out. He realized he couldn't do that and justify it to his people, so he went in hisself and collected the barbarian in person."

"Why would he do that?" The master smith gestured for more ale.

"I think it's because the barbarian was responsible for putting him on the throne. He told him to call for the trials so he could be tried properly and still have a chance of life."

"No, why did the emperor go himself? Why not send a...well, a fucking army to collect the giant?"

The old dwarf shrugged and drained his tankard as the next

round arrived. "I suppose he thought Skharr would fight. In that case, the guards would have been honor-bound to kill him."

Throk leaned back and grinned. "How many do you think Skharr could have killed before he was overwhelmed?"

"Knowing the man...I would say the streets would run red for a week. At least a dozen. Me cousin—who was at the tavern when he was arrested—says the barbarian could have put at least twenty to grass before succumbing to his wounds."

"Your cousin was there?"

"Aye. Having his brekkie like a regular bloke when the emperor says the barbarian will go quietly, and his lord commander is holding Skharr's weapons. He says he does not believe he is the assassin but will make a show of it for peace."

Throk ran his fingers through his neatly combed beard before he shook his head. "Even if Skharr did kill someone, he had a damn good reason for it. I know the DeathEaters well enough to know that although they might present themselves as savages to the world, they are not the type who would walk about the world killing anyone with a foul breath. No, indeed. I've seen Skharr fight often enough and I can tell any who ask that he knows how to rein himself in. A beating, yes, but kill?"

The other dwarf shrugged. "I suppose the emperor thinks the same but he has committed to the trials. It's one way to beat the executioner's ax, I suppose. Although it don't mean he won't die, mind, but he'll die with his sword in hand, make no mistake."

"Aye." Throk stood. "But he won't stand alone. I might not be able to fight alongside him, but I'll get the word to someone who would be willing and able."

"What about armor? It would benefit him and you if he were to enter the trials in the very best armor ever Anvilforged."

"Aye, but time is against us. Even if we keep the forges burning day and night until the armor is completed it will never reach the Imperial City in time." The smith looked disappointed, as well he might.

He frowned as if considering how it might be accomplished, then turned to a young dwarf seated at the next table.

"Cornin?"

"Yes?"

"Bring me my messenger stone. I'll send word to others who should know that Skharr has need of their aid. Knowing the pride of the barbarian, he will not like it, but he can swallow his pride and complain about it once he's survived." It wasn't Anvil-forged armor, but a stout body to fight at his side might be almost as good.

"He what?" Brahgen fixed his mother with an affronted stare that seemed to make no impact on her at all. She showed no remorse whatsoever.

"Your uncle—the message was sent for you but I managed to read it somehow."

The young dwarf narrowed his eyes. He knew for a fact that his mother was trying to coddle him into the young boy she remembered so fondly. It was a daily struggle to remind her of the fact that while he was still young for a dwarf, he was more than capable of handling his own business.

Even so, she had a habit of looking through any communications directed to him as part of her efforts to control his life. He loved the old woman dearly but there were limits.

They kept telling him he needed to be married if he wanted to get out of her home, and all that was well on the way with the planning already in motion for a marvelous feast to celebrate it. Still, Brahgen knew his need to see more of the world would be difficult to resist. He wouldn't be quite the warrior Skharr was but in the end, that didn't matter much. His skills were different. He was a better thief than most and there was abundant work for that around the continent.

"I wasn't...I didn't mean to shout at you." He wasn't quite sure why he felt the need to apologize to her. She had invaded his privacy after all.

"But you did."

"No, I was shouting at the message. I'd have shouted at Uncle Throk if he'd had the stones to deliver the message to me personally, but he didn't." He shook his head.

His mother sighed and tucked the message stone into her pockets. "You won't go off to find this Skharr, then?"

"I don't know what I'll do. I certainly won't make any decisions this late at night, will I?"

"I should hope not." Her affronted tone was sufficient to assure him that he'd managed to divert her somewhat.

"So I'll get to sleep and decide what I'll do in the morning."

"Well, be sure to tell me if you're out and traveling again." A sly expression slid onto her face. "I'll have all your clothes washed and packed and all the food ready for your journey."

It was an innocuous enough request but he knew better. She would abscond with his clothes for about a week, saying she was washing them, and then take another week to prepare the food.

A hovering parent, she was. Maybe he should have a word with his dad to make sure she didn't hover too closely. Still, that would have to wait until tomorrow. Brahgen moved to his bedside table, took a small candle from one of the drawers, and used a small flint and steel to light it.

He had his place of prayer to Ahverna, of course, but she wasn't like the other gods who required constant prayer and adoration. Almost anywhere would do.

The candle was lit and he closed his eyes and let his mind go blank for a moment. It wasn't the easiest task for a mind like his, but one he'd gotten the hang of it. To sit with none of his thoughts traveling through like galloping horses quite peaceful.

The young dwarf hadn't expected much to come of it—

nothing ever did—but a sense of vertigo hit his stomach and made him feel like he was floating, flying, and falling all at the same time. It was warning enough that something was happening.

His eyes were open but also not. It felt like he was dreaming but he couldn't remember any dream feeling quite this real. He looked at his hands, moved them up and down slowly, and noticed a hint of a blur like the soft lights around him made it difficult to see exactly what he was looking at.

"What in the blazes—"

"Now is that honestly the way to greet a goddess?"

He looked up and his eyes widened when he realized he wasn't alone in the room. Or the dream, whatever the hell it all was.

A slim woman with long black hair, dark eyes, and pale skin stood across from him, wearing leathers with a dagger at her hip. It appeared that she was ready for battle, but the fact that her hair wasn't done in a braid or bun or something of the like meant she didn't mean to fight him there and now.

While that was about all he could see of her, it was all he needed to know. Ahverna's appearance was not well-known to all, but he was more than familiar with it, although he had never seen her face-to-face before this moment.

"I'm...sorry... I didn't know—" He wished his tongue was as nimble as his purse-stealing fingers.

She smirked and shook her head. "You have no need to apologize, Brahgen. I know you were seeking me and it is rather interesting to find that you don't expect me to answer your supplications. In fairness, I generally do not, but I try to listen when being spoken to. Now, how can I help?"

"It's Skharr. DeathEater. You know, the barbarian who helped me during my travels from Verenvan?"

"Aye, I seem to recall him. What kind of trouble is he in this time?"

"The Seven Trials." He frowned in thought for a moment. "Or...or the Path of the Gods, I think, is the proper term for it."

She shook her head and leaned forward. "You will have to tell me the whole story from the beginning."

"I don't know the whole story. As my uncle tells it, the barbarian was accused of killing someone important in the Imperial City, and the emperor is his friend but had to arrest him anyway. He made the appeal to go through the trials instead of execution."

Brahgen sighed and raised his gaze to meet hers. "That is all I have been told, but I know Skharr. He would not have killed someone outright. He is no assassin, for one thing, and for another, too many people want him dead but do not want to perform the act themselves. It has to be one of those people trying to drive a wedge between Skharr and his friend so he will be executed. It must be some kind of plot against the bastard."

"And...why are you supplicating me on his behalf?"

"I owe him my life. Well, I did save his life a time or two. The point is that he is my friend and while I have commitments of my own to tend to, I would like to think that he would want to do the same for me if I asked it of him. I am set to be married in a week or so, but we would not be betrothed at all if not for the barbarian, and I... Well, I don't know what to do."

Ahverna's gaze lowered and she studied the ground for a moment before she focused on the dwarf. "Caring is what matters. Skharr's caring for my worshipper is what allowed me to help him help you and your caring allows me to do more than I could before. Now, one of my main priests—"

"Priest?" Brahgen interrupted. "But...I'm no priest."

"Did you think that the priest of the patron goddess of thieves would have a long beard and wear rich white robes and a gilded headdress?" She raised an eyebrow as she approached him and placed a hand on his shoulder. "To my mind, a dwarf priest of Ahverna looks a great deal like you do."

She made a good point. Then again, while he did have the beard, he did think that a priest of any worth would wear rich white robes and a headdress of some kind, but all things considered, she probably knew more about it than he did. The patron goddess of thieves would likely want something considerably more subtle to represent her.

"Well, I...I'm honored. I think." He drew a sharp breath and hoped he hadn't offended her in his bemusement. "Honored is the appropriate response, yes?"

"I like to think so." She chuckled softly in reply to his question. "And now carry my blessing and my promise to do what I can for your friend the barbarian."

Her hand lifted from his shoulder and Brahgen blinked when he realized he was staring at the wall across from him. He tried to decide if he was dreaming or not but his shoulder was a little tender. There was no reason for it to be and when he decided this was not a dream, he approached the mirror in his room and pulled his shirt down to reveal his shoulder.

For a moment, all he could see was a red mark, but as it began to darken, he discerned a clear handprint imprinted on his skin. Almost, he thought in surprise, like someone had placed their hand in paint and touched his shoulder.

It was her mark positioned exactly where she had touched him. He was sure of that although he had no idea what it could possibly mean.

He chose to believe it was a good sign and pulled his shirt up again.

Edge's Rest was one of the few beacons of civilization in this corner of the world, and a paladin would generally raise issues with the business being performed in the region. Almost any vice the mind could imagine was for sale, all driven by the coin paid to the killers who called themselves mercenaries and were ready to slit throats, rob, or intimidate in the name of profit.

A certain freedom could be enjoyed there, but expectations had to be contained. It was not a place for those who were weak of heart and with an idea of the world that involved honor, respect, and glory.

Which was why she was there, Cassandra reminded herself. She knew the world better than most and she could still do some good to help the innocent without causing trouble or falling foul of others with nefarious intent.

Having something of a name in the area did help. The local bandits and sellswords tended to avoid folk who were under the protection of the Barbarian Princess and the Drakehunter twins. Although it wasn't always both, but for folk who made their living preying on the weak, a good fight would see their numbers drop and there would be little for them to do after that.

It made an interesting reality, but one that was all too familiar in this region. Perhaps it would help to change things and usher a little more civilization in. Of course, that would bring lords, kings, and emperors and with them, war and the mess that had devastated the region in the first place.

Perhaps, in the long run, she was doing more damage than good, but she had learned better than to judge the world by trying to see the larger painting.

"You've got that face again." The barbarian twins sounded as alike as they looked, so she had no idea which of the two had spoken.

Cassandra looked up as they approached her with mugs of mead in hand.

"What face?" she asked.

"The face that usually results in us heading off to fight in battles that make us plan for what we might encounter in the afterlife." Bandir grinned to take the sting out of the comment.

"Oh. That face."

"Aye." Tandir folded his arms. "The last time we saw it, we fought an army on our own while you went off to ensure that a gorgon did not change us to stone while our backs were turned."

"Yes, I do recall that. It all turned out well enough in the end, didn't it?"

"Well yes, but—"

His brother cleared his throat. "We're not saying we wouldn't like to continue fighting alongside you, mind."

"Aye, but…eventually, we'll encounter an impossible task that will live up to the name. Knowing that, you can understand a little dread from our side."

Cassandra laughed and sipped her ale.

"So what's got your brow furrowed?"

"Word from the Imperial City," she answered and shook her head.

"It had to travel rather far to reach you, I guess." Tandir smirked, knowing it was the kind of bland comment that would prompt her to share more details.

His brother was a little more forthright. "What word, then?"

"Skharr. He's been clapped in irons. It seems he's murdered someone."

"Murdered more than one someone, between us." Bandir grinned, his expression approving.

"But this time, they'll punish him for it." The former paladin sighed. "He was destined for the executioner's ax but he chose instead to take a series of trials. They are the kind that could mean losing his life anyway, although I suppose he prefers them to an execution."

"You're off to help him, then." The way Tandir said it made it more of a statement than a question.

She nodded. "I would ask you to come with me, but—"

"Someone's got to keep an eye on this place in your absence. Besides, Langven needs help to hold the line in these parts."

"And you'll make a fair amount of coin with the work too."

The twins grinned and nodded. "When are you off, then?" Bandir, ever practical, drank lustily and set his cup aside.

"As soon as I finish my drink."

"You cannot simply walk through the temple as though nothing has changed. You renounced the order and are no longer a paladin!" The high priest's agitation was such that he seemed to not notice that he'd followed her into her former quarters.

"Yes, you keep saying that." Cassandra shook her head. "This is the fifth time now by my count. It's as though you think repeating it will have some bearing on what I plan to do."

"Taking up your armor again—"

"I need armor and I haven't the coin to buy more." She cut him off impatiently. "I might as well use what is mine."

"You gave it up when you became—"

She pulled her shoulder pauldrons on and turned to the man. "I still hold to my vow. I still follow the same god, as does the man who needs my help. I'm sure Theros will not mind if I use the armor he granted me as his servant."

He scowled, unable to think of any good argument against her logic although he still appeared to want to argue with her. She had no notion as to why. It wasn't like they used the armor for anything else. It would not fit any other paladin and she doubted that it could even be refitted since Theros had given it to her.

This provided another reason why he had no real grounds to argue with her. It was her armor, whether she was a paladin or not.

"You expect us to let this...this robbery happen without reprisals?" the high priest demanded as she tucked her helm under her arm.

"Yes." Cassandra growled in annoyance and strode to the door, the old man close behind. "But if you must, you can hold a full trial when I return. It is not theft, you see, but a loan. I will return the armor if I survive."

"And if you do not?"

"Well then, holding a trial would be an utter and complete waste of time, wouldn't you agree?"

The high priest had no answer to that either, and his brow furrowed and he tried to decide if he could counter what certainly felt like a challenge. Many thought they could define what a paladin had to do based on lines that had been read from books written by the wise men of old. In the face of reality, however, it somehow all fell short of what was needed.

"Will you try to stop me?" she asked as they approached the gates where a handful of the guards had already rested their hands on their weapons.

"Would it matter?" For the first time, he seemed to have lost a little of his indignant bluster.

"I'll try to not kill them if that's what you're worried about, but you should avoid calling for their aid. They would not thank you for their injuries. I must do this."

"I...understand," he replied in a tone that contradicted this. "But do you truly think the barbarian would want to put his friends in danger in this manner?"

"Knowing Skharr, probably not. But he knows me too and I don't care. If he doesn't like that I intend to help him, he can go fuck himself." She fixed him with a determined expression that made it very clear that she would not be denied.

After a moment's thought, he motioned for the guards to return to their stations and she heaved a soft sigh of relief as they passed through the doors of the temple and descended the steps.

Cassandra narrowed her eyes when he gasped and she paused to see what he was looking at.

An old man stood at the base of the steps. He took an apple from his pocket and fed it to a small donkey that followed him with no need for a lead. Strider approached them as well and there was an apple in it for him too.

From the high priest's reaction, it was obvious that he knew who the old man was, but there was no sign that any of the others knew. They would certainly not have ignored the old man if they did.

"I believe he'll have more to say to you than I," the man beside her muttered, bowed his head gently, and rushed up the steps as quickly as his tired old legs could carry him.

Cassandra descended resolutely and studied the old man while he patted Strider on the nose.

"I assume this might not be the day for you to show all these people that you do occasionally visit your houses of worship?" she asked and ran a hand along Strider's neck.

"Aye," Theros answered. "Although these temples have more in mind than my vanity and have done for many years now."

"Of course. You might want to show them who you truly are, then?"

"Do you think my ego so fragile that I would need the adoration of the crowds so badly?"

She raised an eyebrow and the god laughed.

"It is best to not answer that, I suppose. But maybe this once a public display of my capabilities should suffice to keep folk on their toes."

The former paladin smirked and remained silent as he scratched his donkey's nose and prompted a soft bray of affection from the beast. In the blink of an eye, it was transformed into a warhorse, seventeen hands tall, at least, and complete with full battle armor that glistened in silver and gold.

Theros had another appearance as well when she turned to him. Gone was the old man and a warrior had taken his place. He was almost as tall as Skharr, with broad shoulders and armor of the same color as the horse's, although he had no helm. His beard was thick and brown, and his similar-colored hair rolled over his shoulders in thick, lustrous curls.

His transformation went unnoticed at first, but a gasp and a shriek here and there indicated that his presence had begun to draw attention.

Less than a minute passed before the whole courtyard in front of the temple had come to a halt and gaped at the presence of the god before them.

"Come, my paladin," Theros rumbled and his voice carried so that all could hear it. "We have work to do."

Perhaps his ego did need a boost, although Cassandra wasn't about to condemn the god for it. She grasped Strider's reins and in that moment, the world faded away from them.

CHAPTER SIX

"We couldn't ever commit to a change like that." The undercity merchant's indignation was underpinned by a thread of outrage.

"The costs are prohibitive enough, but we would have to face much worse along the line if the guards believe we'll move our supply line to the docks." The second man hastened to add his protest. "They might decide that since they cannot extort us for the merchandise coming in through the gates, they'll have to find another way to make their coin and start disrupting our houses of vice."

Micah sighed as loudly and as dramatically as she could, mainly to stop the men from arguing in her presence. All three of them turned to her, their eyes wide, and they looked a little afraid of her open display of annoyance.

"The costs will not be prohibitive, for one thing," she stated. "The ships have already been acquired, and we expect a decrease in the shipments being attacked or lost to elements out of our control. The second consideration is that the guards know better than to cross me. If they want more coin, they will have to earn it like everyone else. And lastly, calling them the houses of vice might serve to ease your wretched conscience—although why you should have one is beyond me—but it is inaccurate and I despise inaccuracies. Call them what they are—whorehouses."

"Of course, Madame Ferat." The man bowed his head. "But do you believe that the Verenvan guards wouldn't find a way to cause trouble for us if we were to keep them from the coin they believe they are owed?"

"I would imagine there are a few who might take offense and they would have to be reminded that they still have their place. And they would have to earn their keep. A few might rot in the bogs before too long, yes, but the rest would fall into line quickly." She kept her tone deliberately cold and ruthless.

The third merchant leaned back in his seat, his expression cynical. "I wish I could share your...optimism."

"And I do not care if you share it or not. It is already done. Your work is to ensure that everything is altered to streamline the delivery of our merchandise, understood?"

All three opened their mouths to protest but before they could, they were interrupted by a soft cough from the door. Denir stood there, one hand tucked behind his back while he held a tray with a few goblets on it in the other.

"Pardon my interruption, Madame."

"You did not interrupt. These men were just leaving." She smiled slightly at the old retainer.

"But Madame—" The whorehouse overseer's shrill protest jarred her nerves and she cut him off.

"Just...leaving," she stated emphatically. "Their business here is finished and they have responsibilities elsewhere. If you wouldn't mind showing them out?"

"Of course, Madame Ferat." Denir nodded. "However, I must inform you of a particularly interesting visitor who has arrived at the door. I did not say you would see him, but he insisted that the message he carried be presented to you in person if at all possible."

Micah raised an eyebrow and motioned for the men in the room to leave. They knew the way out themselves and also knew better than to try to delay. Guards were stationed across the villa and if they managed to evade those, they were all too aware that she didn't mind dealing with intruders herself when it took her fancy.

They closed the door behind them and left her alone in the room with Denir.

"Well, there is no need to keep me in suspense, my friend."

He glanced at the door and waited until he was sure that none had lingered to eavesdrop on what was being discussed.

"Two members of the Eagle Corps have been sent by the emperor, Madame. They come bearing a most urgent message... for the emperor's sisters."

Now that was curious. While she made no attempt to conceal her heritage, she had no ambitions to ascend to the throne. Hers was a dangerous position. Even more dangerous was that of a pretender to the throne. She knew it was much safer to work from the shadows, and not only because one had a considerably better chance to achieve something from those shadows.

It still didn't explain why Tryam now tried to contact her.

Micah nodded, pushed from her chair, and followed Denir to the lower levels, where the two Eagles had already been provided with refreshments. She might have thought they would stand tall and proud, but from their travel-worn clothes and the exhausted expressions on their faces, they appeared to have journeyed without stopping through the night and day.

The Eagle Corps was rather impressive in this particular regard. Travel time was reduced to a minimum as the men were able to sleep in their saddles, pushed their horses to great speeds, and replaced them with others that waited for them in outposts. They needed only a moment to transfer whatever saddlebags they carried to the next horse before they continued.

In some cases, transferring their saddlebags was not even

necessary and they could simply jump from one horse to the next without needing to stop.

They partook eagerly of the refreshments, although they stood immediately and cleaned their faces with napkins the moment she appeared in the chamber with them.

"Madame Ferat," the apparent leader stated and bowed his head gently in deference. "We come bearing news from—"

She smiled graciously. "From my younger brother, yes. I hope he is well? You'll have to extend my compliments for his ability to take over the empire so quickly and with such efficiency."

"He would ask you to deliver such compliments to him in person, Madame. The emperor has requested your presence and that of your sister if you could direct us to her."

Micah's eyes narrowed and her fingers clenched around the dagger she carried. The Eagles noted her reaction and took a step back. There was only one reason why the ruler would want to see someone who had as much claim to the throne as she did.

"Please understand that the emperor means you no harm. A man he respects has elected to take the Seven Trials and needs the help of those who would want to see him live. In this case, a barbarian by the name of Skharr DeathEater."

"Oh." She approached the table as she tried to think of a suitable response. There had been a time when she had been more than willing to gut the barbarian herself but that had changed, and she was willing to admit a grudging respect for the man. He'd drawn something out in her that she had not seen in years, and it was not necessarily a bad thing. "Have you met the man, then?"

"Madame?" The officer looked confused.

"Skharr. You've met him?"

"In passing, Madame."

"What did you make of him?" It surprised her that she was genuinely interested in what he thought of the barbarian who had been such a thorn in her side.

The two men exchanged a glance but it was clear that they had no intention to avoid the question.

"A dangerous man," the leader began after a moment. "The fear was that he would resist. Some among the emperor's guard took bets as to how many would be killed before the giant was subdued or killed himself. We were all surprised when he surrendered without so much as a fight. Do...do you know him?"

"Not as well as my sister does, by my estimation. But there was a time when I wanted the bastard dead. It was all business, of course, but he proved a great deal more resourceful than I expected. I eventually helped him and my sister with a task taken up at the behest of the emperor, although I do not believe I ever acknowledged my involvement openly before. Well then, I suppose it's about time I meet my half-brother. You can return to the Imperial City and inform the emperor that I am on my way. I will gather supplies and be on the road today."

"With respect, Madame, we were instructed to escort you to the city immediately. All the necessary supplies have been arranged, as well as a fast horse. You will be given time to arrange your affairs, of course, but we were instructed to not tarry."

Micah should have been offended at being summoned like a dog, but they were pressed for time. She could only imagine how difficult it was to delay an execution with this much scrutiny, and if her brother was seeking all those who could help the barbarian, time was of the essence.

"Very well." She cleared her throat and Denir approached. "I have some letters to send out. Gather what I might need for my travels. I shall need you to see to my business interests in my absence."

"Of course, Madame."

"Undead. Folk who raise the undead. Rapists of all types. Theater productions that aim for drama instead of humor."

After the third day in his cell, Skharr had told himself there weren't many things in the world that he hated more than sitting on his rear end and waiting for something to happen.

He'd lost count of the days he'd spent in the cell. Occasionally, Elric, the emperor, or a handful of others would arrive to break the tedium, but hours had turned into days in which he was expected to remain in his luxurious cell. Even the time when he was allowed to stretch his legs out in the courtyards under constant supervision began to lose its allure once it was clear that he would not be allowed any weapons to train with. Exercise was all well and good, but he had no interest or skill in the sports that were played by the guards with padded cloth balls.

It was interesting to watch, however, and a few of the men showed remarkable skill in getting the ball past the defenders and into the fishnet held up by a steel rectangle. They could carry and catch the ball with their hands but could not move more than five paces before they had to pass the ball to one of their comrades, which could only be done by drop-kicking it.

But even that started to lose its appeal, especially since the invitation for him to play resulted in many protests that he was a little too rough in a sport that required as little contact as possible.

And so, on what felt like the anniversary of his imprisonment but could only have been about a week, he was left with nothing else but to list what exactly he hated more than the boredom of his imprisonment.

It was a short list. Skharr shook his head, dropped onto his bed, and stared at the ceiling. The evening meal had been delicious and it made him wonder who prepared all the food. More importantly, maybe it was time for him to seriously consider the reality that there were still folk who wanted him dead in the world. This meant that the people who made the food were those who could end up poisoning it, thus making the emperor's choices that much easier.

"The godsbedammed isolation is making me fall into paranoia," he muttered and pushed from the bed again.

He would surely go mad. It was only a matter of time until it happened, but it would undoubtedly happen. All he had to think about was how difficult it would be to break through the bars and go on a rampage that would end with him dead.

It would be better than sitting there for another night.

Maybe a night of passion was what he needed. The barbarian had no interest in finding out if Tryam had begun to arrange a harem for himself like his father had, but asking for a whore felt like it would be an imposition, especially since he was a prisoner.

Still, it could not hurt to ask.

Skharr approached the door and tried to determine whether the guards stood outside the cell or were in the small living area below.

There was not much point in remaining near the door, but a few of them said they were stationed there to ensure that he did not take his own life. They even checked through the window with the bars in it from time to time.

He reversed the position now and peered out of the window to determine if any were in his immediate vicinity he could speak to. The flickering torchlight revealed no shadows seated or standing near the door.

"Godsbedammed fucking useless idiots. What's the point of being a guard if you don't guard?" He shook his head and stretched through the bars for the little bell that had been installed so he could call for his jailers. He'd never used it before, but he knew the room had been made with lords and ladies in mind—the types who had numerous demands for those who were guarding them.

His thick arm was difficult to maneuver through the hole, and before he could accomplish this, his heart jumped to his throat.

The door pushed open without so much as a sign of the locks that should have been in place.

"Odd."

He could think of no other word for it and winced when the door groaned as it swung open slowly. For a moment, he waited for the expected rush to ensure that the barbarian was not trying to escape. The door should have been locked, after all, and he'd heard the padlock click into place when his supper was delivered.

Had they merely not done a good job of it? Skharr inspected the lock and realized that the key was inside and the lock had been opened. Maybe they'd neglected to lock it, thinking that he would not break out.

Tryam would want to know about the laxness from his guards, however. Skharr didn't want to seem ungrateful, of course, but what would happen if they had to guard someone who was a genuine menace?

He shook his head and stepped out of the room. Although he was dressed in nothing but his trousers, he liked to think he was still a threat or could be if he wanted to. He stepped close to the little bell, tugged the rope a few times, and heard the ringing echo through the staircase that led to his cell.

His effort brought no response and he frowned and listened into the silence. He heard no sounds of heavy boots climbing the steps, no shouting, and no drawing of swords. Even with his cell door closed, he could generally hear them downstairs if they were too raucous, which meant something was wrong.

The barbarian felt a little naked without any weapons and mostly unclothed as he was. Nevertheless, he descended the steps cautiously and jerked every time one of the torches flickered and made the shadows appear to be something a little more threatening.

Nothing emerged to hinder him, however. His bare feet made little noise on the flagstones, and the door into the living area below was open as well. He could hear the fire crackle happily in the fireplace, which meant someone had recently added wood to it. Still, he could distinguish no sign of any movement aside from the blaze.

After a moment's consideration, he pushed the door open slowly and his blood ran cold when he finally heard the sound of humans in the other room.

He felt rather silly when it turned out to be someone snoring. It was a relief as well as it reassured him that at least no one had been killed. His mind had jumped to the conclusion that this was all perhaps a dream, but he doubted that even he would dream this.

All five guards in the living area were accounted for. They sat around the fire in the comfortable chairs provided and were fast asleep.

Skharr approached one of them, leaned back a little, and wondered if waking a sleeping guard was the best thing to do.

Eventually, he realized he had no other choice and nudged one of the men in the shoulder.

When he received no response, he narrowed his eyes and stepped forward to nudge him again. He couldn't for the life of him remember the guard's name, but it was the one with bright red hair and no beard. His second attempt to wake him failed as well and he grasped him by the shoulder and shook him vigorously.

A grunt and a snort brought some hope but in the next moment, the snoring continued.

"You godsbedammed lazy bastards." The warrior growled, moved to the next man, and shook his shoulder as well with a similar lack of response. He hauled the third one out of his chair and shook him as well before he dropped him into his seat.

Three of them all but comatose was enough to tell him that this was no ordinary sleep. No human slept this deeply. He knew of a couple of dwarves who slept like the literal dead and only woke when they determined it was time to do so. Usually, they lived under the mountains, as they were more comfortable under the earth than over it, as a rule.

Most, but not all. Skharr knew at least one dwarf who enjoyed life out in the open.

"Bloody hell, what will they say if they find you all like this and I'm standing over you?"

"There's a simple answer to that," said a whispered voice. "Do not be here when they are discovered."

He whipped toward the stairs leading to the living area. That entrance had no door on it, although there were a few more locks and keys between where he stood and the open courtyards of the palace.

Footsteps approached—not wearing boots and very light. Skharr imagined some kind of soft sealskin, although that in itself did not explain the lightness of the steps nor how they seemed to need to take the steps one at a time.

Something or someone light and small was ascending—a woman by the sound of the voice, even if it was whispered.

He narrowed his eyes and noticed that his guards had weapons strapped to their hips. If the new arrival proved to be a threat, he was ready to draw them.

CHAPTER SEVEN

The footsteps continued up the steps and Skharr finally saw a shadow in the torchlight above whoever approached. Above them seemed appropriate as the new arrival was short—a woman, given the shape, although about half his size. Thick brown curls showed even before he could see her properly.

He should have recognized the voice, even if it was whispered, and he allowed himself to relax somewhat when he recognized Leahlu as she turned to approach him once the steps had been conquered. It explained why she had taken them one at a time. Perhaps he had misremembered, but the halfling was even smaller than he'd thought she was.

"What did you do to them?" His scowl seemed to have little effect.

"Is that honestly the question you want to ask?" She raised a brow but ruined it with a smirk.

"I am already accused of one murder. I'll not add to the list without need."

She shook her head and her curls bounced as she moved to the nearest guard. "It was merely a trace of something to make them sleep until the morning without waking. They will be more rested than they've been in years. In the meantime, the whole palace could fall and they would still be dreaming."

"If that is the case, why did you whisper on the way up?"

"You can't deny me a little fun, now can you?" She grinned. "Besides, I've no idea how many of the bastards are in this part of the palace, and these places have a way of making a voice carry."

"Is that why you're here?" Skharr watched her warily as she approached him. "To give my jailers a good night's sleep?"

"As long as it allows me to get you out of here," she answered with a cheeky grin and punched his thigh playfully. "I know your skull is the thickest on the continent but it cannot be this dense."

"What are you talking about?" He knew but he wanted to hear it directly from her. It would be easier to counter that way.

The halfling rolled her eyes. "I'm breaking you out of this shite situation. I thought I would be blessed with the gratitude of the Barbarian of Theros, but I am instead bombarded with endless questions."

His eyes narrowed again and she tilted her head in a challenge. He could tell that she'd expected him to jump at the opportunity to run off and break free of the bonds that held him. But there was a reason why he hadn't attempted a jailbreak before.

"I can't leave." The blunt statement almost spoke itself.

She frowned at him. "Did one of the emperor's mages spell you into remaining? Because I have something for that as well."

"What? No, of course not."

"That is precisely what someone who had been spelled would say." She folded her arms and tapped a small foot on the stone.

"It is also what one might say if one had his reasons to do so."

"And what reasons might those be?" Leahlu took a few steps away so she didn't have to crane her neck to look at him.

"I am held here by my word that I will see this false murder accusation through to the end. If I leave, I will all but put Tryam on trial and allow those who hate his efforts to undermine his decisions. No, I'll not do that. I'll ensure that whoever is trying to kill me by turning the emperor against me will fail."

"As opposed to killing you by way of...what are they called again?" Her sarcasm was sharp but good-natured.

"The Seven Trials," Skharr answered and gestured for her to join him as he began to retrace the steps to his cell. "If I die, it will be with my sword in hand and going through the Seven Tests. Not by killing soldiers who have been manipulated into taking my sword through their chest."

"I doubt that will happen."

"Precisely." He darted her a smug glance.

"No, I don't mean it that way." She shook her head as they entered the cell. "Well, yes, you'd kill a couple, but you'd be more likely to run into a gauntlet of crossbowmen, all of whom would be more than willing to stick you with more holes than a pincushion."

"Oh. I suppose you're right about that." He scratched his reddish beard. "It would be a considerably less heroic means of reaching the afterlife."

"You are sure, then?" Leahlu closed the door behind her as he moved to one of the chairs in the room and sat. "You are determined to ensure that I broke into the imperial palace for no good reason?"

"I would not go that far." He took the jug of wine that had been sent with his evening meal, filled the two goblets beside it, and handed her one. "I have been bored to madness while locked in this fucking gilded cage. Besides, it does make my heart glad to see you alive and well. Am I to believe that many cocks have been crushed by your mighty punches on the path between our last meeting and this one?"

The halfling smirked, sipped the wine, and looked impressed by the quality. "Only those that deserved it, mind you. Are these the accommodations all the emperor's prisoners can expect? I might want be accused of murder one of these days."

"Unless you find yourself someone highly esteemed by the emperor or the local gentry, I would advise against it. The dungeons on the other side of the city and closer to the walls are far less…accommodating."

"You might be surprised by how highly I am esteemed by the local gentry." She sounded almost teasing and he narrowed his eyes at her.

"Is that so?"

Leahlu grinned and cocked an eyebrow before she drained her goblet in one swallow. She placed it on the table, moved to where he was seated, and climbed nimbly to straddle his lap, although she needed to push herself up a little to finally press her lips to his. He could taste the wine on her tongue for a moment.

It was an interesting sensation, and he waited for her to pull back with a soft gasp and lick her lips.

"I've been meaning to do that for a while," she whispered and ran her fingers over his beard.

"What stopped you from doing it the last time?"

"I realized the paladin was enjoying your attention and she did not seem the type to share, no matter how bountiful the meat."

She grasped his hands and slid them over her curvaceous hips to cup her breasts. Despite the halfling's size, they were still well-formed and firm to the touch.

"Am I allowed to assume that your boredom here is matched by a great deal of loneliness?" Her voice was low, and he felt her hot breath on the skin of his neck before she kissed it—tenderly at first, but he winced when he felt her teeth.

Skharr tilted his head to give her easier access, took full liberty of what she was offering, and let his hands explore. "You might say so. I intended to ask the guards outside if there was any precedent for allowing the esteemed prisoners the chance to talk to their horse or the company of a whore or three to alleviate boredom and loneliness. They certainly have not been offered, although the thought likely did not occur to the boy's mind."

"Ah, the innocence of youth," she whispered against his neck and ran her hands over his chest. "In that case, I suppose you have no objection to allowing me to relieve you of both ailments that currently assail you?"

He stopped himself and lowered his hands to stop hers from moving any lower to where she would find an immediate reaction to her touch already waiting.

"As curious as I am, I would not want to injure you," he explained. "I do not mean to brag, but I fear I might split you in half."

A pout touched her full lips as she settled on his lap and took a moment to grind her hips gently over him. "I am curious as well. I have wondered as to the size of your...dragon, and my going bet is that it is the size of my arm. Even so..."

Her voice trailed off as his eyebrows raised when he felt her growing against him. He tried not to jump and fling her off when the woman on his lap transformed and grew almost a foot and a half in the blink of an eye. Thick brown curls were replaced by long, silky black hair. Cold blue eyes took the place of the warm brown ones, and pale skin replaced ruddy and tanned.

Her grin was the same as she wiggled into his lap again and pressed against his growing arousal still tucked inside his trousers.

"I think you'll find I'm more than woman enough to suit you," she whispered and traced her nails down his bare skin to leave angry red trails.

"Ahverna..." he answered and wondered if his eyes were bulging from their sockets. "You?"

"Yes. Me."

She bit her bottom lip and moved a hand to trace down her neck and lower. Her clothing vanished the farther her fingers went. By the time they fumbled at his trousers, she was completely naked. She raised the hand to bring his to her breasts again, leaned into his touch, and moaned softly as she pressed herself closer to him.

Skharr cleared his throat, still trying to come to terms with what happened. "You are—"

"In need of your cock. Yes."

"But you were—were you Leahlu the whole time or..." His tongue couldn't seem to shape the words as easily as it should.

She smiled, his cock in her hands now, and she stroked him slowly. "Yes, the whole time. And as I said, I wanted you then but I had no intention to anger the paladin."

"She isn't—"

"There is no need to speak of another woman until later," she whispered and breathed him in slowly. "It would be a shame to not take a little pleasure even when things on this path look...difficult."

"Path?" He stilled for a moment.

Ahverna placed a finger over his lips but quickly replaced it with her lips. She still tasted of the wine too.

"Did I say path?" Her voice was breathy and her strokes moved faster as she adjusted herself and guided him between her thighs. "I meant to say, 'fuck me, now.' I might not be allowed to do this again."

He saw no reason to contest the point any further.

"No," Skharr's voice was low. "I do not know how she made this happen but she is a goddess and has told me I have five minutes before I am back in my cell." He snatched an apple from a bucket outside Horse's stall. "Here. I have no idea if this is a dream or this is real. But, either way, eat up my friend."

Truly, Skharr believed this was a dream. While it wasn't outside of the realm of a goddess to accomplish unbelievable acts it was easier to believe she created a dream that was real for both man and horse.

The slobber from Horse taking the apple seemed real enough.

He sat on a stool. "It was the first time I've had any kind of visit from a goddess while in prison."

Horse regarded him solemnly.

"No." He shook his head. "I won't do this again simply to see if she would appear. Besides, you can't throw any accusations at me. I tried to give you a future with all the mares you could satisfy. Now, you end up here with me."

The barbarian sighed and stood to pat the heavily muscled shoulders of his friend. "Which brings me to the point of this talk. If something happens to me and Tryam allows you a choice...well, go back to Sera. She will take good care of you brother."

Horse turned, nudged him, and pushed him a little.

"No." Skharr put an arm over his neck. "I won't make it easy for anyone to separate us. But so far, no one has passed the trials so we have to be realistic."

The stallion neighed.

Skharr took another two apples from the bucket. "Fine. Two more and that is enough. The boys who take care of you might be accused of stealing if too many are missing."

A couple of minutes later, a guard walked through the stables and confirmed that every stall was empty before he continued on his rounds.

The room was opulent, but the meeting hadn't started and Micah's attention was more on the man in front of her than the intricacies of the beautiful carvings around her.

"Would you like to take a seat?" The young ruler had been nothing but gracious.

Everything about this seemed wrong, but Micah was surprised to realize that the feeling in her gut that usually warned her of imminent danger was not present. She merely felt uncomfortable. In the presence of her younger half-brother, the emperor, she did not quite feel herself.

She had always felt comfortable as the largest fish in the pond known as Verenvan and with nothing much to fear even from the count who ruled over the city, but she was swimming in dangerous waters in the Imperial City.

Tryam was younger than she thought he would be. He was barely out of his teen years and while he had the build of a warrior—she was told that he had been a champion of the arena as a teenager, which did require some skill—his face looked like that of a boy who was too interested in what was happening under a woman's gown to care much about the running of an empire. There wasn't even a sign of a beard showing on his chin.

But this was one of the most powerful men on the continent and by all accounts, he was rather competent in the role.

Micah did as was suggested, sat opposite him, and studied him over his desk.

It was a private meeting and although she had been relieved of all her weapons, guards were everywhere. Three of them stood in hidden slots, ready to fire at her with crossbows if she so much as twitched the wrong way.

"I was surprised by your invitation," she said finally and looked around warily.

"You've been away from the Imperial City for many years now," he noted. "How does it feel to be back?"

"I was very young when my mother was sent away, along with my sister and myself. A few memories remain, but I recall it being…" She looked around the room a bit and out a window. "Bigger somehow."

"You were smaller at the time, I suppose."

She turned to him as she smiled. "Yes, that must be it."

"And what about me? You've scrutinized me from the moment you saw me."

So he had noticed, despite her effort to do it unobtrusively. He also didn't seem afraid to challenge her outright on it. She chose her words with care. "First impressions are still being made."

Tryam chuckled and sipped from his goblet. "A diplomatic answer but I suppose you must have those in great supply, given the company you keep. From what I am told, you have most of Verenvan under your thumb, although you remain in the shadows. I am learning that the shadows are where all the work is done."

That drew a genuine smirk from her. "You've had folk watching me?"

"Well...it is a matter of great interest to my spymaster to know where all the potential heirs to the throne are and what occupies their time. You and Sera are amongst the most...occupied, I've learned."

"Is that why you called me here, Your Grace?"

He shook his head. "No. Your interest in and knowledge of Skharr DeathEater affected my decision the most—at first. I've come to trust the barbarian's judgment of character. If he chose to work with you even after you made an attempt on his life, he must have seen something. If he hadn't, he would have simply killed you. He is rather predictable that way."

"True enough," Micah admitted. "Although I would venture to say that my connection to my sister was what stayed Skharr's hand."

"I suppose so." Tryam studied his goblet intently. "Or the fact that Skharr trusts Sera's opinion enough that she would have done it herself, sister or no."

She was willing to concede that she had thought the same thing on more than one occasion.

"I trust my sister's judgment of character over almost all

others, even my own," she stated firmly and leaned forward. "And I'll admit that Skharr has a keen eye into the minds of others, which is why he seems to enjoy playing the fool when he can manage it. Through it, he can force others to expose themselves to a mind they think is dim. He did help you rise to power, did he not?"

The emperor nodded slowly. "I would be dead if not for him, and I owe the man a great deal."

"Is that why you are helping him?" It sounded all well and good and she was sure that was part of it, but as the emperor, there must be more and she needed to know what that was.

"It's one reason, I suppose. There is also the fact that it is well-known that I trust the barbarian a great deal. If he were to be executed, it would be a blow to my credibility as well."

"I think your credibility might survive. The peaceful transition alone was enough for your people to trust you."

He sighed, his expression almost a grimace for a moment. "It was not...quite so peaceful."

"Open any scroll on the histories of the various kingdoms and empires in the past, and you'll find that yours was more peaceful than most. No wars, genocides, pogroms, or other atrocities were committed. A few dead matter little to those tilling the fields and plying their trades."

"I cannot claim credit for that either."

His need for honesty seemed oddly appealing. "You miss my point. It is the foulest myth for people to think that good leaders need to do all the work of leading and governing on their own. The finest leaders find those who can help them the most. They enable these people and ensure that they are in a position to do what they do best. Delegating work is the greatest skill an emperor can have."

Tryam leaned forward. "You're flattering me."

"Maybe a little. Then again, can an older sister not tell her younger brother how proud she is of him?"

"I was never on the best of terms with most of my other siblings. I blame our father for that, personally. But you knew that already, yes?"

"Naturally," she answered with no attempt at false modesty.

"Your skill in spy craft is practically legend in Verenvan. Once all this business with Skharr is finished, I would like to know if you are interested in discussing a more formal arrangement between us for the future."

The suggestion was certainly intriguing. She wasn't sure what he meant by it, but she leaned forward, immediately interested. It was what she wanted, in a nutshell, but she was wary of any offers from him—and all offers that seemed a little too good to be true.

Finally, she nodded. "That is an interesting idea to be discussed at length later. For the moment, I think we should save a foolish barbarian with an arguably powerful mind for reading the intentions of the folk around him."

Tryam smiled and raised his goblet, and she did the same.

"I'll drink to that." He took a long sip from his cup and placed it on the desk. "Now, let us discuss the trial, what I would like you to see, and what I would like you to study a little deeper."

CHAPTER EIGHT

Numerous complaints emerged over the Skharr matter. The Sareenans began to grow restless at how trials were delayed, even though the entire process was done legally. Instructions to the judges in the city were to delay the process as much as possible. Tryam was not as knowledgeable as he thought he was, given how many details allowed them to slow it to a crawl.

Then again, maybe it was best that he didn't know how it was all done. That way, when there were official complaints instead of rumblings, he would be able to honestly say he was doing all he could to ensure that justice was served.

He was far from the only one who wanted the barbarian alive for as long as possible. The man had become something of a folk hero over the past few years. Demonstrations had been held by the common folk outside his palace to see the prisoner released, no matter what the political ramifications.

More than a few had demanded he be released purely on the principle that it would annoy the Sareenans. Thankfully, these were in the minority, mostly those military men who had lost friends and comrades in the various border skirmishes before the tenuous peace accords had been reached.

As much as the emperor wanted to simply get the whole process started so the escalation wouldn't get worse, considerable work still had to be done. Messages needed to be sent and certain people needed to make an appearance.

They would make the most of it. Tryam had learned long before that folk would make their own decisions about him regardless of what he did. All he could control was whether he could live with his decisions. As it stood, he tried to avoid an all-out war that would result in the deaths of thousands, avoid the warrior's death—or at least give him the opportunity to save his life—and generally keep the peace.

Of all the problems he could have anticipated, the one that had never occurred to him was that of the horse named Horse. He'd addressed the name with Skharr before and there was no changing it. He hadn't been quite sure of the horse's intelligence and understanding of the situation until he was told, when he woke in the morning, that the beast had fought the guards who had been sent to move him to the stables in the palace.

He'd managed to laugh it off when he saw the report from the men who survived the battle. Among broken ribs and bruised feet, two of them had chunks bitten out of them and another had managed to circle the beast and have his knee kicked in.

"We might be better served putting the horse through the trials in Skharr's stead," Elric commented as the two descended the steps and approached the stables. "If I might ask...why are you going there yourself? I do not think Skharr would appreciate having to find himself another horse in his time of need, but we will kill it if it attempts to attack you."

"You will do no such thing, and such action will not even be necessary. He has been through a great deal with Horse, and having his companion with him in the trials to come might prove to be instrumental."

The lord commander did not look like he completely supported the emperor's opinion, but he knew better than to openly disagree with the younger man as they stepped into the stables. Those tending to the horses inside immediately stopped what they were doing to offer the emperor a bow before they returned their work. They put a little more effort into it than they had before, even if they were all somewhat reluctant to work this early in the morning.

Those ordered to guard Horse were still in position. Although the men who had been seriously injured had been sent off to be tended to by physicians, those who remained still showed the signs of having been in a melee with a horse. Each man had a few bruises and cuts to show for it.

"I told you to take apples to assuage the beast," Tryam muttered and gestured for them to open the stable door.

"Yes," one of the guards answered. "Yes, you did. I can see why the barbarian refuses to ride it. A foul-tempered cretin if there ever was one."

The emperor fixed him with a hard look. "I've seen Horse be more than placid in the presence of folk he trusts. You thought a DeathEater's horse would merely follow you because you had hold of the reins. Well, you forgot the kind of respect the barbarians treat their horses with. How did you get it to follow you, anyway?"

"After a struggle, it—"

"He." Tryam held the man's bewildered gaze for a moment.

"He...stopped fighting and followed us out, although he did make the whole walk miserable by antagonizing and biting at our horses any time we pulled the reins."

"I would guess that one of you mentioned that you were taking him to Skharr and he finally complied."

The guards exchanged a look and it wasn't difficult to realize what was on their minds. While no one would openly disagree with him, they didn't quite believe that a horse could understand what they had said.

"Believe me, I had the same look when I first met him, but the evidence is difficult to ignore." He stepped into the stable.

The emperor wondered if they had the wrong horse when his gaze first settled on the beast. He remembered Horse being older with a slower step but more than capable of following Skharr on his long journeys across the continent provided that he did not need to carry the barbarian's weight.

This animal looked at least five years younger. There was a sheen to the stallion's coat that had not been there before, but the white star on his forehead was identical to the one he remembered. Whatever the barbarian had done over the past year or so since the two had parted had certainly agreed with Horse.

Or maybe there was some type of magic involved. He remembered Skharr mentioning that he wanted the beast to carry an amulet that would allow him a little more power and stamina for their coming travels. It seemed that whatever had been done had worked true wonders.

Horse appeared to recognize the young emperor and he snorted and walked lazily to where he stood next to the door.

"It's been a long time, my friend," Tryam said and extended his hand for the stallion to sniff before he petted his nose. "You look well. I almost did not recognize you."

He felt like he was going mad, speaking to a horse the way he was, but he gestured to Elric. The guard commander brought him the bucket of apples that had been specifically acquired for Horse as the stallion turned his attention to the bag of hay hanging in the corner of his stable. The smell of apples brought him back almost immediately, and he sniffed and snorted before he took a bite from one of the topmost fruits.

"I do apologize for how you were brought here. I probably should have done it myself, but you'll understand that a person in my position can no longer move freely about the city." The emperor chuckled. "Well...I hope you can understand. Maybe horses don't have much of a concept for how politics are carried out."

The stallion made no attempt to reply, his face still buried in the bucket while Tryam patted his neck.

"I did tell them to bring apples and to talk things through with you, but some folk have difficulty understanding how intelligent a horse can be. All I can hope is that the story of your valiant efforts to defend yourself will spread through the palace, which will mean that all who encounter you from this point forward will know to speak softly and bribe you with apples to avoid being crushed."

That did get a response from the horse, who snorted and tossed his mane. He couldn't help a grin when the guards outside stiffened at the sound.

"Although I suppose I have your quick thinking to thank for not forcing me to use more potions to heal broken legs, ribs, and chunks bitten out of the men. They will not thank you for it, of course.

"Micah Ferat is here as well, and I assume her sister is not far behind, which means you will find a few more familiar faces in the coming days." Tryam sighed. "Skharr is in a fix, and I'll be willing to admit that I played a part in it, albeit unknowingly. He will need the help of his friends, and that does include you as well, whether you like it or not. He will fight through a handful of challenges, and I am told he needs speed to survive one of them—the seventh, I think. Frankly, you might be the only option we have for that. And I know he will hate it, but I suppose you don't care about that either. Either way, I intend that you get at least a little time to talk to him."

The stallion showed no sign that he was listening, although the young ruler did find that the ability to simply talk and hear the sound of his voice on matters was beneficial. Perhaps he would have to find a horse of his own to speak to from time to time.

It seemed there might be something in speaking to Horse. Elric knew better than to think the beasts could understand the tongues of sentient species, but he had been in the cavalry long enough to know that horses responded well when their riders spoke to them.

Of course, it was not necessarily because they understood but because the human let the beast know where its rider was at all times. They were skittish creatures as a rule, with a tendency to jump, kick, and bite anything that startled them.

Still, speaking to the stallion as though it could understand what he was saying did feel like going too far. The guard commander shook his head. Either way, the emperor was not in any danger of being attacked by the creature. He did not need to continue listening to what he knew was a pointless endeavor.

"You're going to leave the emperor in there with...the beast?"

He looked at one of the guards who had dared to voice a mild protest. They would rush in to help if needed, but he could see they would have preferred for him to do so instead.

"The emperor traveled with the beast, as you call him." He studied the men closely. "I'm sure you all heard the tale. It was spread across the land with astounding haste. Skharr traveled with the emperor, and the horse with them, so the two are acquainted."

"A beast like that might turn on anything that moves, acquainted or no." The man remained unconvinced.

The comment drew a smile. "Have any of you spent any time in the cavalry? Among the Eagles, perhaps?"

The group all exchanged a look.

"Infantrymen, the lot of you, yes?"

They nodded slowly.

"Then listen well." Elric cleared his throat to ensure that they all paid attention to him when he spoke. "Horses are intelligent beasts in their own right. Not as intelligent as humans, but I would put them on equal footing with your average goblin and more intelligent than most trolls. That one is a war mount. It has seen war and skirmishes, is loyal to its master, and will openly resist being stolen. You were foolish to think that a trained and experienced beast would simply follow you, and when you grew more aggressive, so did he. And you forgot that you were dealing with a beast many times your weight and size."

The men looked away and avoided his gaze like they felt they were being chastised. And maybe they were. They might have been considered worthy to be elevated from the ranks of the foot soldiers in the emperor's army to rank among his palace guard, but they needed to prove themselves better still if they wished to survive.

When it came to the safety of the emperor, Elric would chastise, beat, and even kill to ensure there were no weak links.

"Back to your posts," he ordered, and the men straightened at his tone. "I'll send men to relieve you shortly."

He moved out of the stables and his gaze scanned the shadows that still clung to the palace. The sun had barely begun to crest the horizon and was still out of view to any who were behind the walls. He grasped at the sword on his hip a little tighter as the faint hint of a chill shivered up his spine. A foul taste entered his mouth as he studied the shadows a little closer.

The lord commander nodded gently before he turned sharply on his heel and strode to the palace. Hopefully, those in the kitchens would already have food ready.

One of the shadows continued to move as Elric walked away. The naked eye could not discern it, but it continued to shift and shimmer through the darkness and edged ever closer to the stables.

Torches were still lit, but the shadow showed no fear of them, slid beyond the touch of their light, and then shimmered again when the light faded. It stopped when the guards approached. Occasionally, it paused and looked around as if it thought something was there. Movement was caught in the corners of its eyes, but when it stood and watched a little longer, it knew it must be mad. Nothing was there and it chuckled and shook its head as they continued.

Reassured, the shadow continued to move, approached the stables, and hugged the stone walls, ushered on by the approaching sunlight.

The palace was cleverly designed through magic and sharp masonry that allowed the sun to shine in despite the walls built around it. It had been constructed by minds that knew all too well what dangers were posed by the darkness and ensured that there would be few places for the shadow to hide.

In the next moment, it froze although no guards were present. None could have approached them without them hearing and hiding.

Despite this, a sharp blade pressed against the skin of its throat. A single tug or even a deep breath would cause it to draw blood.

"The emperor's guards may not be able to see you, but my eyes are not so easily deceived." The blade pressed a little closer. "Please, do give me a reason to cut your throat."

CHAPTER NINE

The sound of the lock and bolt being drawn sounded like it came from miles away—almost like an echo through tunnels.

Perversely, the noise became more insistent, which made it more difficult to ignore. Skharr sighed, rubbed his eyes, and rolled to try to escape the creak of the door opening.

It was too late, however, and he growled softly in protest. No matter how or why, he was awake. The one day when he had hoped to sleep in well past the rising of the sun, someone wanted to see him.

He turned and scowled in concentration as all he could see in the cell were a few shadows. Eventually, a figure emerged, then the details. One man was inside, and a familiar one at that.

"I don't suppose you're here to take me to the first of these fucking trials?" Skharr asked, pushed from his bed, and shoved his blanket aside as he felt for his trousers. He hadn't bothered to put them on again and there was no shame in nudity, not to his mind.

"I suppose it would be too much to ask for you to be dressed?" Elric turned to give him some privacy.

The barbarian raised an eyebrow, finally located his trousers, and pulled them on quickly. "I did not know I would be visited, and I am only allowed out of my cell once the sun has been up for a few hours."

"Of course. I...suppose I owe you an apology for intruding, but it could not wait." The guard commander paused, tilted his head, and sniffed. "Did you have a woman here?"

"And here I thought you were the lord commander of the Emperor's Elite Guard. Wouldn't you know if a woman had been allowed into my cell?"

"I...I suppose. But I can't ever be too sure with you, though, can I?"

"I have been meaning to ask." He waited until he had the man's attention. "Assuming this imprisonment is to continue, of course. I cannot be sure, but my assumption is that a few lords imprisoned here were allowed a little tension relief before they were sent to be beheaded."

"I'll see what I can do. For the moment, you'll need to be dressed, shaved, and about as presentable as we can make you on such short notice. Your case will be brought before a judge when the sun reaches its highest point in the sky. The hearing will be where the charge of murder will be officially stated and when you will claim your right to take the Seven Trials."

Skharr scowled and yanked his shirt on.

"Shaved?"

"Aye, shaved. Your beard is in desperate need of a trim." Elric almost sounded like he was addressing one of his men.

"Why should I wait for a hearing to be charged?"

The lord commander sighed. "You should. It will buy you more time—all of us more time."

"Time for what?"

"The emperor and Micah have been—"

"Wait—Micah Ferat?" Skharr couldn't help the disbelief in his tone.

"The very same."

"What is she doing here?"

Elric shook his head as if the question was unnecessary. "She has been helping the emperor to find whoever is truly guilty of the crime you have been accused of."

The barbarian raised an eyebrow. He hadn't expected Micah to care that much about what he was doing, but any help would be appreciated at this juncture.

He paused and sniffed the air as well. Ahverna had left no trace of her presence, not that he expected there to be.

"Well, at least I know my death will be avenged if it comes to that."

"Of that you can be assured, Master DeathEater," Elric replied and made sure the prisoner was fully dressed before he turned to face him. "Of course, the plan is for you to be alive and well enough to avenge yourself if you have a mind to do so."

"Aye. That I do." Skharr grinned and tied his hair back with a strap of leather. "I have to say, I like this plan most of all. So, I am to sit around while folk talk about what a shit barbarian I am, and then request the Seven Trials as early as I can because it shows…"

"That you do not believe you will have a fair trial. And be sure to explain it as such. You will not be allowed to speak at first. There will be a song and dance as the lawyers and judge follow their proper procedure. Then the charges will be presented and witnesses will speak. It's all merely a necessary performance since this is for the judge to decide whether you will be brought to trial or not. The decision is already made, and you will be summoned to make your statement of the events. You will state that it is all a machination, a scheme, and an assassination of both your character and body through the courts."

The barbarian nodded. "I know how it all works. As amazing as it might seem, this is not the first time I've been tried for murder."

"Really?"

"I've killed more than my fair share of folk. Do you honestly imagine that no one tried to kill me in return?"

"Well...I suppose that makes sense. Come along, we'll see you to a barber's razor."

His beard was not all the barber took to. Skharr didn't think it wise to push the man who handled a blade so skillfully, no matter how small it was. His hair was attacked as well and bound into a braid that was carefully arranged on the back of his head.

He was willing to admit that he was more presentable now than he had been for years, especially given the stiff, formal attire he'd been fitted with. He shifted in his new clothes and tried to find a way to make them comfortable.

It was, he told himself, an exercise in futility. He would be uncomfortable, especially since his hands were manacled as he was led into the courtroom.

Not the emperor's court, he realized, but a smaller room. It seemed almost like a house of worship with the pews positioned for folk to study. At the far side of the room was a pulpit where a judge was already seated. The older man was gaunt and with long, greasy gray hair and thick stubble on his chin that he scratched.

The lawyers were dressed in long black robes and watched the barbarian as he was led to the dock below the judge's pulpit.

Almost a hundred people had crammed into the pews to watch and all studied every step he took until the guards manacled him to the dock, let him take his seat, and turned to face those gathered for the trial. In that moment, Skharr realized that the guards were not there to stop him from escaping but rather to protect him from the crowd.

Most appeared to be members of the gentry, but the pale skin

—almost translucent—of some and their straight golden hair told him the Sareenans were present. They displayed barely contained rage at seeing him still alive.

People talked, muttered, and discussed the situation, and others arrived until the pews were full and the newcomers had to stand at the back of the room. The prisoner looked around and tried to decide what they were waiting for.

Finally, it became clear. The midday sun reached its peak and struck something glass or maybe a jewel at the peak of the roof and gleamed into the center of the room, where a round, marble table was suddenly illuminated and glowed red. In that moment, the guards shut the doors to indicate that the court was in session.

The judge struck his table with a hammer. "This court will come to order!"

His voice boomed through the room and immediately silenced all those inside the chamber. Every gaze fixed on him.

"We are assembled here this day to pass judgment on the barbarian known as Skharr the DeathEater."

"Just…DeathEater," Skharr muttered.

"Silence!"

He leaned back in his seat, stinging from the rebuke.

"The charges presented for the barbarian are as follows—murder, most heinous and vile. How does the accused plead?"

Skharr raised an eyebrow and looked at the old man. "Does it fucking matter?"

He realized that a handful of scribes sat in the room to take notes and one was writing his words as they were spoken.

"How does the accused plead?" the judge insisted.

"Innocent." He growled and rolled his eyes.

The official gestured impatiently and one of the men in stiff black robes approached the red marble table. Although the sun began to move away from the gemstone in the ceiling, the table continued to glow a deep, ominous red. The man who'd moved forward had the same pale skin and gold hair, although his was done in a braid. Skharr was under the impression that the Sareenans only bound their hair for battle.

Perhaps they considered this to be exactly that.

"The barbarian known as Skharr DeathEater did knowingly and in full control of his actions murder Pawella Unsari, Diplomat to the Kingdom of Sareena and personal friend to Prince Woraj, Heir to the Throne. Witnesses saw him murder the honored diplomat and leave her body in the street like so much refuse."

There certainly was rage buried barely under the surface as he placed a few papers on the table.

The judge cleared his throat as one of the aides collected the papers and brought them to his pulpit.

"And who will speak on behalf of the accused?"

Skharr looked up at the official's question. He'd not lied to Elric and he had been accused of murder and even brought before a court before. A couple of trials had even taken place, but he'd never been offered the possibility of being represented.

Before he could answer, the doors to the chamber were opened. It was enough of a surprise that the guards stepped forward to try to stop the new arrival from entering, but the judge raised his hand and motioned them back.

The barbarian narrowed his eyes when he recognized the face and for a moment, he couldn't understand why Sera had come to help him.

But as she approached, he noticed something harder about her features and realized this was her sister. There was a familial resemblance, though, and he couldn't help a soft chuckle as he shook his head.

"I was held up, unfortunately, but I will represent the accused," she stated and held a few sheaves of paper up for the judge to see when the guards allowed her to pass. "I will speak for the accused."

She placed the document on the red table as she circled it to approach the dock Skharr was bound to.

"I apologize for my tardiness," Micah whispered and leaned close to him. "Do you trust me?"

"Never."

"Well, you'll have to now." Her tart reply was delivered with an undertone of humor.

"I can live with that."

"You had better."

She winked before she returned to the table where the Sareenan lawyer waited for her. He looked a little more furious and a great deal more confused.

They would not find much common ground, but Skharr had no idea what she was up to and the chances were he would not be told. Perhaps his confusion was part of the plan.

The judge cleared his throat. "State your name for the record."

"Dame Micah Ferat of Verenvan," she answered immediately. "The accused was identified by witnesses who had never seen the barbarian before and knew him only by reputation. The witness states, and I quote, 'a barbarian of enormous size and possessing bright red hair.' Anyone who might have heard of any number of the barbarian's tales would know that description of the man."

"I object to this line of questioning, your honor!" the Sareenan lawyer roared.

"The objection is sustained." The judge rapped his gavel on the desk. "The reliability of the witness will be established during the trial itself. For the moment, we will determine whether a trial is required. Restrain your questions to the matter at hand."

"We have more than one witness," the Sareenan continued, "all of whom have sworn to the matter. The barbarian was seen committing the murder. Furthermore, none can verify the barbarian's whereabouts immediately prior, during, or after the murder was said to have occurred."

The judge nodded and looked at the papers that likely contained what the witnesses swore was the truth.

"Unless the accused can produce witnesses who can make a statement as to his whereabouts during the time in question, the trial will be declared valid."

All was going according to plan. The question remained, however, as to whose plan it was. Whoever had killed the diplomat was likely who had poisoned his drink and had left him helpless in his room. The timing was a little too convenient.

The judge stood from his seat at the pulpit. "The trial has now begun. If the accused wishes, he may make a statement on his behalf or he may have his representative make that statement for him."

He sat again and every gaze turned to Skharr, who pushed slowly from his seat and tugged the uncomfortable clothes he wore. The speech had repeated relentlessly in his head from the moment he knew he would have to make it—short, simple, and designed to deliver his message as curtly and clearly as possible.

The warrior cleared his throat before he spoke. "We all know how this will end. Decision's made. I will not sit and be accused, murdered in reputation and through executioner."

He sat again and he could see Micah grinning. Although he was not sure why, he had pretended to be the idiot again. Perhaps it was about time for folk to see something different, but he was far from being in the mood.

"As the DeathEater said, he has no intention to have his character assassinated, and he would not see the imperial justice system made a mockery of by doing the work of assassins," Micah explained. "Skharr DeathEater will take the sole path left to him and claim the Seven Trials."

Those words triggered a reaction from all those in the room, including the Sareenans. Their surprise and rapid conversation between themselves indicated—to Skharr, at least—that they were not the guilty parties and genuinely believed that the only DeathEater in the city was the one who committed the murder.

Even the judge appeared confused by the declaration and leaned forward. "Dame Micah Ferat, would you explain the process of the Seven Trials for the record?"

"Of course, your honor. The Seven Trials—or the Seven Tests —are conducted by the gods to determine the worth of a man's life. These trials are dangerous and will take place over the course of fourteen days. There will be one day of rest, after which the first trial will begin. Should the accused survive, he will be granted another day of rest before the next trial begins, and so it will continue until the accused is dead or until all trials are completed."

The Sareenans appeared more than familiar with the concept of the trials and made no attempt to protest his decision.

Skharr studied them closely, as well as the judge, and waited for any sign that they might have engineered this from the beginning. This had been his assumption until now, but he was no longer so sure.

"Does the accuser agree to these terms?" the judge asked and turned his gaze to the Sareenan lawyer.

"We find these terms acceptable, your honor," the man agreed almost immediately. "Let his fate be decided by the gods. Their justice will more than suffice. If they find he is not guilty of murder, neither will we."

It didn't look like what they wanted but he could see why they agreed. They must know that while his chances of survival were slim, they were better than his chances of surviving the headsman's ax.

"Very well." The judge thunked his gavel on the desk. "It is decided. Who will be chosen to support the barbarian for his first trial?"

He opened his mouth to state that he would not commit the lives of anyone to save his when another door was opened. Two people were escorted into the chamber, and he recognized them immediately. Grakoor was difficult to miss with his broad shoulders and distended jaw, indicative of his orcish ancestry.

"Salis and Grakoor will join the barbarian for his first trial," Salis stated. She also stood out in almost any crowd. Dwarves and Elves rarely mingled, and the resulting offspring was fairly unique at barely five feet tall with the thick brown curls dwarves were known for. Beneath her hair, her ears were pointed and there was an odd fluidity to her movements that indicated her elven heritage.

He hadn't seen either of them since their little scuffle with the cult that had attempted to raise their god. As such, the question remained as to how the fuck they had come so quickly and why.

The Sareenan looked confused for a moment but shook his head as the two approached the dock. "The trials only allow for the presence of one companion for each trial. He cannot bring both of them. Or all three, if you consider the size of the..."

"Quarter-orc," Grakoor clarified.

"Whatever it might be. The barbarian can only be accompanied by one."

"What the fuck are you two doing here?" Skharr demanded under his breath.

"Oh, that's nice," Salis answered with a smirk and folded her arms. "We've come to save the bastard's life and that's the kind of thanks we get?"

"In case you missed it," Grakoor added. "We're here to save a barbarian bastard's life. Perchance you met—tall, ugly red hair, no manners?"

"Fuck you."

"See?"

"The plaintiff's objection is sustained," the judge interrupted and cleared his throat. "Skharr the DeathEater, you must choose one companion to accompany you for the first trial."

Micah approached and looked like she intended to gift them with advice.

"Trust the path," she whispered. "You'll need a sharp mind for the first trial."

Skharr nodded. "The quarter-orc will join me."

The look on Micah's face told him she would probably kick him when they were not under the vigilant gaze of the judge, but he matched her stare. He was supposed to trust her at this point, and while he was willing to make the attempt, she needed to trust him as well.

"Shocking," the lawyer muttered. "Two brainless oafs wandering into a trial would appear to be…well, he might have taken the smarter of the two to offset his…obviously lacking condition."

The Sareenan did not expect his mutterings to be heard, but the silence in the courtroom made him turn after he had spoken. Gazes were fixed on him, and he growled something quickly under his breath and pretended to inspect the papers in front of him.

"Well," Micah whispered. "I guess you are not the only one with a lacking condition, eh, Skharr?"

"Silence!" The judge hammered his gavel down again. "It has been decided. Skharr the DeathEater and Grakoor will enter the first trial. May the gods be just. This court is adjourned."

After another tap of his gavel, the man stood and marched away from the pulpit, followed by a small army of aides.

"The DeathEater?" Salis asked and moved a little closer to the dock when most of those gathered to watch began to file out.

"I tried to correct him but he shouted me down," Skharr answered as the guards undid his manacles.

"But how hard did you try to correct him?" Grakoor asked.

"Shut it," Micah snapped. "I told you to trust me, did I not?"

"And I do," he answered and kept his voice low. "I would appreciate it if you returned the favor."

She paused and tilted her head. It looked as though she was trying to determine what he was doing—like she expected him to have some scheme hidden in his inordinately uncomfortable sleeves.

"So," Grakoor commented with a grin that revealed the hint of tusks growing from the lower half of his jaw, "a barbarian and an orc wander into a dungeon. I think I've heard this one before."

───

There was no telling where Theros would take her. Cassandra knew it was the peak of summer in the Imperial City, but the immediate impression that touched her was that it was cold and even possibly icy.

Her armor was meant to protect her body from extreme heat or cold, but there was a limit. She'd learned that in her battle with the dragon and was reminded of it now. With a slight shiver, she looked around as the world materialized to confirm once and for all that they were not in the Imperial City. This raised one very important question.

"Where the fuck are we?" she whispered. They were in the mountains as far as she could tell. Wind whipped around the road they were on and made the cold seem even worse. Even though they were in the middle of summer, the snow line was only a few hundred yards up the mountain from where they stood.

"In the mountains," Theros answered. He had reverted to the form of an old man followed by his faithful donkey.

"Amazingly, I did manage to deduce that for myself. What are we doing in the mountains?"

"Exercising a little patience." He turned to pet the donkey. "Those who are watching are attempting to determine whether they should simply kill me right away."

Cassandra turned to face the old man, her eyes narrowed. "Where are we?"

He paused for a moment like he was choosing his words very carefully. "Merely…a little further north than…most of the continent."

"Fucking hells—you brought me to the Clan?" She shivered as another burst of cold wind whipped through the canyon they were in.

Amusement twinkled in the god's eyes now. "I…might have."

"And I'm—"

"Not dressed appropriately, I agree."

"I'm too cold, even for this," she snapped. "But we'll not discuss this now."

"Why—oh."

Theros shifted his focus to two barbarians who approached them on the road ahead. She hadn't even heard them, and since neither was on horseback, it could be assumed that they had been in the rocks, hidden from view while they decided whether to attack the people who had suddenly appeared.

"That's recognizable," she whispered and stared at them as they made an effort to hurry. "Skharr had an odd habit of appearing without ever showing sign of where he'd been."

"And who are you?" one of the barbarians asked. She realized both were carrying axes, ready to swing into battle if they had a mind for it. They probably also had a few of their people in the rocks above, prepared to skewer her with their famously powerful bows.

"I am Cassandra, and this is…" She turned to where she realized Theros no longer stood. "Was Theros."

"Who?" The two exchanged a glance and narrowed their eyes. "Clan lands."

"Fine," she muttered under her breath. "This is how you're going to hang me up to freeze."

"Who are you speaking to?" the second man demanded.

She turned to the barbarians, who now handled their axes a little more actively in a way that said they were moments from attacking.

"I am Cassandra, the Barbarian Princess. Take me to the chief of the Clan."

"Or what?" the first challenged. They stopped short of being close enough to swing at.

"We have heard of one who calls herself the Barbarian Princess," the other stated. "The tales say she is known to charge into battle naked, so I assume your armor is only for show?"

"I didn't expect to charge into battle," Cassandra answered and took a step forward. "And it was not completely naked—only mostly naked."

The two narrowed their eyes even more, although she could tell their gazes were focused well south of her face.

"All right then." She rolled her neck. "I've needed a good fight for a while so might as well make it now."

CHAPTER TEN

It was all starting to fall into place as planned. Too many people thought they could survive the tower these days, but with a little work and creativity, it would return to being the most feared and terrifying dungeon folk could profit from.

"Making a few changes to your dungeon? I thought you considered it to be of a unique perfection."

Janus roped the magical threads binding the tower together to his belt before he turned to face the intruder. He was in no real danger since the dungeon was closed. As such, very few in the world could reach him, and those who did could never cause him any harm.

Not that they didn't try, but through pawns. No harm could be done to a lord high god by another, at least not directly.

In this case, his visitor wore a familiar face. The brothers tended to drift to and from each other over the centuries, but they were now closer than they had been in years. Theros had abandoned his idiotic portrayal of a poor old man traveling with a donkey and manifested himself in full vitality and power.

"It continues to be, yet I find that inspiration has struck again."

Janus shrugged as though it was a matter of little consequence. "A few new additions to the dungeon should ensure that any who enter will face a few surprises. I've found that too much is known about my tower and so felt a few changes were in order."

"I can see that. Complex spellwork too. One might even think you are designing it with a particular barbarian in mind." Theros smirked, his expression irritatingly smug.

Janus scowled. "I'll admit that Skharr did reveal a handful of flaws."

"In your perfect creation? It cannot be!"

"Shut it before I remove you from here. What in the hells are you doing here anyway?"

Theros adopted a slightly more serious mien. "Coincidentally, it is the very same damned barbarian who has inspired you to do all this work in the first place who brings me here."

"Oh." His brother grunted dismissively. "My debt is paid to the man."

"Actually…"

"What?"

Theros scratched his chin idly. "I thought you went above and beyond in repaying your debt to Skharr."

"Right. Of course I did." Janus shook his head. "I could have sworn he would break his word to me as well, but no. None questioned that my followers cleared that dungeon of the undead. For a barbarian, he is at least honest."

"I'd like to think he's more honest than most humans, never mind barbarians."

"Or dwarves, for that matter."

Both gods snapped toward the third voice. For a moment, it had no source, but as Janus took a step forward, something shifted in the shadows and approached him.

A woman seemed to appear from nothing. It was an interesting trick, how she shed the shadows like they were a cloak, and Theros already recognized her. Few in the world had eyes like that.

"Ahverna," he said with a chuckle. "It is always a pleasant surprise to see you, sister."

Janus didn't share the sentiment but made no mention of it. Instead, his head tilted back and he drew a deep breath of the air.

"Odd," he remarked. "There's something different about you."

Theros looked at him and nodded. "True. You stink...of a god —almost as though you've elevated yourself. And here I thought you were not willing to take on the necessary followers for it given how it would put constraints on how you chose to live among the mortals."

"And the trouble you like to cause both of us," Janus added with a deep scowl.

She smiled and put her hands on her hips. "Perhaps I've matured."

Janus snorted.

"Never you worry," she answered and studied him carefully. "I'm happy to keep a little of the uncivilized about me."

"Your followers are thieves."

"But they aren't assassins." Ahverna's voice was firm and cold, and Janus felt a chill trace up his spine. It was an unfamiliar feeling that brought a smile to his face.

"Why are you here?" Theros asked. "You know how your brother likes to develop his dungeons without interruption."

"Assassins are the reason I am here," she answered.

He nodded. "We come for the same reason, then."

"What are you talking about?" Janus demanded.

"We've come to ask you if you have anything to do with the trap that is closing around Emperor Tryam and Skharr DeathE-ater," his brother explained and folded his arms across his chest. "A keen mind has pitted the two against each other. While they have managed to find a fighting chance, reason suggests that whoever made the attempt will try again."

"I know nothing of this," Janus answered truthfully enough. "I've been committed to this dungeon for the past month or so, preparing it for when the tower is set to reappear. If someone is plotting against your favored barbarian, you may be assured that I am not the cause."

That appeared to satisfy Theros, but Ahverna's expression showed doubt. Not that he cared what she thought—or either of them for that matter.

"That is good enough for me," Theros stated finally with a smile. "I do thank you for being quick to answer."

"What is that supposed to mean?"

"What our brother is saying is that you have a habit of giving folk the runaround," Ahverna explained and rolled her eyes.

"Indeed," Theros agreed. "But you did not this time and for that, you have our thanks."

"It's because I do not enjoy having my work interrupted. Now, if that satisfies the two of you, I will resume it."

He turned but paused when he felt the pressure of a blade at his throat.

"Feeling rather full of ourselves, aren't we?" he asked and shifted his head slowly to Ahverna, who held the dagger. "You think that because you're a fully-fledged god now you can threaten me?"

"As a fully-fledged goddess, there are now certain rules I am not allowed to break. Our brother trusts you, Janus, but you and I will never fully hold the other's confidence, will we?"

"You're a thief and a troublemaker," he answered. "The knife is a nice touch, although you must know that it cannot break my sk—"

Before he could finish his sentence, she twisted her wrist enough to flick the blade and an unfamiliar sensation of pain rippled from where it cut. He raised his hand and tried to tell himself it couldn't be true and was merely a trick on her part.

When he touched his neck, however, his fingers came away wet and stained red with blood.

"I'm not the fool you believe me to be, Janus," she snapped. "I may have been the cause of much trouble for my immortal kin over the years, but I take my responsibilities seriously."

He watched her warily as she moved the dagger away from his throat. The moment the blade was no longer in contact with his skin, the cut healed and left only a few droplets of blood as evidence that it had been there at all.

"I understand your trepidation, my brother," she said as she sheathed the dagger. "But you'd be wise to remember that many of your folk are also thieves. Consider how much they would have to gain with a true thief on their side. One who has prowled the world for centuries, her skills honed and her followers chosen from among the finest."

She turned and waved her hand like she was summoning the shadows. They wrapped around her and in the blink of an eye, Ahverna was gone.

"Well." Theros cleared his throat. "I suppose she makes a strong point."

"What is happening?" Janus hissed his outrage and wiped the blood angrily from his skin. "And where did she find a Knife of Clerostine?"

"I would assume while she prowled the world over those centuries," his brother replied. "Likely when you threatened to track her down and cook her on a spit while you fuck a dozen virgins around her."

"I...that was a joke. A jest. She should know I wouldn't do that!"

He shrugged. "I suppose our sister does not know you quite as well as you might like. Besides, you had lightning in your eyes and your voice had a thunderous quality to it. You were rather peeved at the time, as I recall, but I cannot remember why."

"She pilfered two of my temples for no damn good reason."

His brother smiled mockingly. "Technically, she stole back the stolen treasure a couple of your priests who possessed sticky fingers had acquired."

"Possession is the majority of the law."

"Which means it was hers once she stole it back."

Janus huffed. "What are you, a lawyer?"

"I have been in the past. It was a lifetime I enjoyed."

"Then why did you not represent your barbarian for his trial?"

"Wha...how—" For once, Theros was caught with no ready answer.

"It isn't that difficult to determine. Skharr would find a way that would allow him to die fighting without killing the emperor himself. He elected to take the Seven Trials, which would mean he is tried in court beforehand."

"Well. Aren't you a sharp mind?"

"Ahverna is not the only one who has prowled the world for centuries."

"True enough." Theros shook his head. "Now I suppose I'll have to leave you to your business."

"If you think I'll give you an easy way out, you will be sorely disappointed."

"It never occurred to me. Although I would appreciate it if you did not make my path any more difficult than it already is."

"Are you referring to yourself or your barbarian?"

"Both. You would have the opportunity to murder him during your trial."

Janus chuckled. "That should not be a problem. Although if there were spikes in the ceiling..."

His brother grinned and shook his head. "I will see you around the world, brother of mine."

"Yes, yes..."

Tryam looked up from his desk. His head still ached from the drink he had imbibed the night before. He'd had company with him, but he couldn't remember anything—or not the details, at least.

But there was still work to be done. He'd been drinking far more since he assumed the throne. From what he'd heard, the same had happened to his father and he knew what was happening to him. But that was something to worry about at another time.

The door opened as he sipped the tonic that had been provided when he woke. The alchemist had told him it would work in a few hours, but he felt no effect from it yet. Still, all he could do was drink it and hope it would meet expectations.

He knew who was coming to see him, but something about Skharr made him want to watch. Anyone that large was usually seen as slow-moving and clunky, but the barbarian managed to make every movement fluid and seemed to be barely a moment away from attacking.

Almost like a cat the size of a bear.

The young ruler couldn't help a grin when he noticed that the barbarian's beard and hair had been trimmed. His hair had even been done in a proper braid.

"I see you were tended to by a barber?" Tryam asked and raised an eyebrow as the guards left and the door was closed behind them.

"Shut up." Skharr growled. "A day might come when I'm used to looking gods-fucking-bedammed presentable, but it is not this day."

He laughed softly. "Well, you certainly can't bring yourself to sound presentable. I heard you put on quite a performance for your trial. I think half the empire now believes you are an oafish buffoon."

"They thought that already. I needed to give the people what they expected to hear, or there would have been suspicions raised. I suppose you couldn't attend for fear of anyone thinking you were giving me any preferential treatment."

"I suppose so." He took another sip of his tonic and winced. It was sour and a touch of honey did little to assuage that. "What do you think of the accommodations?" he asked once he was sure his visitor was provided with something to drink.

"A good breakfast was certainly the highlight of my morning. But one day does not feel like adequate preparation for a trial like this."

"It is a battle to the death. I assume you did not have that much time to prepare for your other fights." The boy was not wrong about that.

"I am still not sure why you keep me under guard," Skharr muttered. "I might as well be allowed to train and have my weapons returned to me."

The emperor shrugged and regarded him frankly. "The guards are there for your protection. I hope that keeping guards around you at all times would dissuade any who might want more assurance that you are dead than simply sending you through the trials."

"I suppose you might say it was an absolute success." The barbarian opened his arms mockingly. "I'm still here, aren't I?"

"For now. Your trials begin when the sun reaches its peak." He raised a hand to stop the question he knew was coming. "Yes, I know. The men who built this palace designed most of it around the midday sun. It's one of the many things I've needed to learn about this place."

"So why did you call me here?"

Tryam sighed and looked at the table. "We've been through a great deal together. I only…I wish there was more I could do."

"You already prevented me from being executed as things stand. The way I see it, you've put the political state of your kingdom in peril to keep me safe." Skharr shrugged. "I do appreciate that and I think you would be disappointed in me if I didn't tell you that you were being an idiot."

The barbarian did have a point and he laughed and ran his fingers through his dark hair before he stood and moved around his desk. The warrior pushed to his feet as well and grasped Tryam's outstretched hand firmly.

"Good luck out there," the young emperor said.

"I don't need luck. I have a sword."

The kid had not been joking about the midday sun. Now that he'd mentioned it, he realized that almost everything in the palace revolved around the sun reaching its peak.

It was an interesting design and he had a feeling the magic in the building was drawn from the sun as much as anything else.

The barbarian was once again escorted into the palace's sanctuary, where a fairly large number of people had gathered, trying to catch a glimpse of the barbarian before he set off on his test.

Given how the trial had gone, he'd assumed there would be more to see him off, for better or worse, but maybe the boy had done his part to ensure there were no real crowds for an assassin to hide in.

At least there were no manacles this time.

"Skharr."

He turned to where Grakoor approached, although with no escort. The quarter-orc was fully armored and armed, ready for battle. Skharr's weapons and armor had been returned to him less than an hour before, which gave him precious little time to prepare them and ensure that they were all ready to be used in combat before the fighting started.

"So you are still set on joining me, then?" He had hoped his friend would have seen reason by now.

"To the end of the first trial."

"I still think you and Salis should have remained on your own path but I do appreciate the support."

The quarter-orc grinned slyly. "Of course you do. These folk can't see it but I know you're trembling in your breaches."

"I'm not the one who should be. We will have a day and a night to leave the fucking dungeon. I can leave without you but if I die, so do you. Have you considered all that?"

"No, I'm charging into a dungeon without any knowledge of how to survive." Grakoor nudged him in the shoulder. "I must have learned from the best."

Skharr smirked as they were escorted to a large boulder that looked like it had fallen from the sky to bury itself into the earth in the very center of the path.

A handful of priests were present, belonging to various deities or worshipping a variety of gods. They had already begun their prayers as the group approached.

"What happens next then?" the barbarian asked and double-checked to ensure that he had everything he might need for a dungeon.

The priests didn't reply and the guards fell back.

"Nice place," Grakoor muttered. "I do like the birds."

Skharr looked around. It was practically a thicket in the middle of the palace, although everything had a neat, trimmed look to it, even the stream alongside the path.

"It's too peaceful for me."

"But...the birds." His companion's protest was unexpected.

"You like the birds?"

"I do." The quarter-orc seemed unperturbed about admitting something so unwarrior-like.

"Well...I suppose they are very nice."

The barbarian drew a deep breath, intending to ask one of the praying priests to tell them what would come next, but as he approached the boulder, it began to move.

It cracked loudly down the middle, parted, and opened to

reveal a portal in the center barely large enough for the barbarian to pass through.

"Well, come on then," Skharr muttered. "There's no point in waiting around, not when killing needs to be done."

His companion chuckled and stepped through the portal behind him.

For a moment, it felt like they were stuck in a pool of darkness in the center of the boulder. The barbarian assumed the sun was still reaching its pinnacle.

As the thought occurred to him, the portal flared and the whole world fell away from them.

"I fucking hate portals." Grakoor growled his displeasure.

He could at least agree with the sentiment. It always felt more or less the same. The world dropped and left them hanging for a moment while they were magically transported to the other side of the portal.

It had been explained to him a dozen times, usually simplified by the mages holding the corners of a sheaf of paper together and making a hole through them with a stick. It was like they rehearsed the story.

Even with that, it still didn't make any sense and it made even less when they experienced it. The world tugged him back while it seemed to twist uncomfortably, and too much light immediately made him wince and mutter a curse.

The glare of it made his eyes water as they plummeted to land hard with a thud. He groaned softly as he pushed up, shielded his eyes, and let them adjust.

"I hate the godsbedammed fucking heat," Grakoor protested. "The first dungeon had to be a fucking desert."

"It's not any desert I've ever traveled before," Skharr answered and shook his head.

"Traveled many deserts then, have you?"

"Most." Skharr only now realized how many.

"It makes sense, though. This is a dungeon. The desert can't be real." Grakoor sounded obstinately hopeful.

"Why not?" He regarded his companion with a small grin.

"Well...dungeons are all underground, aren't they?"

"Most are, but it doesn't matter now. We have a day and a night to find a way out of here or there won't be a way out left."

With an air of resignation, the quarter-orc looked around. "Well then, we have to find shelter. The first trial must be to survive what the world can throw at you, seems like."

"Seems like," Skharr agreed, collected his things, and pulled them up and over his shoulder. "Rest during the day and only move at night?"

Grakoor smirked as he shouldered his belongings as well. "Fucking barbarians."

DeathEaters were notorious for their stamina and ability to carry heavy burdens over long distances. They were even able to carry such burdens up the sheer rock faces of the mountains they called home.

Turan could see that the two DeathEaters who walked up the path were the real evidence of that. Their faces were covered in bruises, cuts, and all the signs that they had been in a fight, but they were still able to assemble a travois and had dragged it up the mountain.

It meant they had likely come upon something on their patrol and were bringing it back. He doubted it was a body, but there was still enough weight on it to indicate that it was something important.

If not, it would have been pitched over the side of the mountain and they would have found another way to tell the news.

A few other members of the Clan approached and regarded the two curiously. They all had something to do, and if there was anything that required attention, the scouts who noticed their ascent would have already lit the warning fires.

Most were already moving on, but Turan knew it was his responsibility to see how the men had been so severely wounded.

They finally came to a halt, still with the improvised sled, but took a moment to catch their breath. Each one released an eruption of steam from their lips into the icy air.

"Pavet, Kull, you both look like shit," Turan announced as he approached them. "If I find you've bothered the dragon's nest again, I'll ensure that you're not out on scouting missions until fucking winter."

Neither man spoke and exchanged a glance.

"All right, you can stop. Let me down," a woman's voice demanded from behind them.

Turan approached and his eyes narrowed. He eased his hand to the ax he carried at his hip but fell short of drawing it. The two barbarians were still armed and showed no sign of being captives in any way, but there was always the possibility that their minds were befuddled by some spell or another.

It wasn't entirely likely but not impossible either. They were not the brightest, after all.

Pavet and Kull both did as they were told, set the travois down, and stepped aside. An impressive set of armor was visible on the sled, although it was a little too small for almost anyone in the Clan.

Still, it could be altered by their smiths or failing that, it could be handed to their dwarf allies, likely to be sold. It wasn't the type of armor that allowed for climbing the mountains or any other activity in the inhospitable terrain.

But what caught his attention was the woman who stepped around his clanmates. He was not sure how he had not seen her before, although the two had blocked her briefly from view.

His instincts were keen, which suggested some type of magic, surely.

"Who goes there?" he roared, drew the ax, and held it ready to strike or throw.

Both the DeathEaters' eyes widened and they shook their heads immediately but moved away from the woman. As she approached, it was clear that she wasn't dressed for the cold. More surprising, she appeared to not be touched by it although she wore nothing but mail undergarments, which would only make the cold worse.

That was most certainly some kind of magic, although Turan could appreciate the woman's beauty as he readied himself to strike.

"I am Cassandra," she stated calmly and her hair billowed in the wind as she marched toward him. "The first Barbarian Princess. I am here for the Ax of the DeathEaters. It is noted that you failed to give the one who paid for the ax his due."

He didn't like her smile. It was a little too calm and confident to come from a woman who was sorely overmatched and outnumbered. Those who hadn't been interested in the approach of the two scouts gathered again quickly with their weapons at the ready, and she continued her approach regardless.

Turan shook his head. "He pays lip service to—"

She cut him off coldly. "He fought through dungeons, assassins, and more to earn the gold necessary to pay the finest dwarf weaponsmith to craft the most exquisite ax and allow his Clan the honor of holding it for generations. Your disrespect for the most famous of your people is astounding. I foresee that it will discourage future DeathEaters from attempting to reach such heights."

"What Skharr doesn't know cannot hurt him." Turan smirked. "And he would have to return to here to learn of it, after all."

The self-proclaimed barbarian princess nodded and stopped a few paces away from him. "Where is it?"

"If you believe you'll touch my ax, you must be mad."

Her smile was almost feral. "I've been called worse. Madness is merely another word for the small of mind to describe those who are willing to take risks. Either way, you can keep your weapon but I will take Skharr's ax back."

That was all he needed to hear. Whether this woman was a princess or not, she certainly had the demeanor of royalty—a mighty woman indeed. It was a true pity that he would have to kill her.

"You'll have to pry my ax from my cold, dead fingers." He growled and hefted his weapon—not the one Skharr had sent of course. That one was better used as a symbol than in a skirmish like this.

Besides, his weapon was more than sufficient to send this bitch to whatever awaited her on the other side of death.

There was no need for him to abide by any rules of combat here. DeathEaters didn't believe in them and he would not take this threat to authority lightly.

He took one step and swung his ax. The blade sang in the icy air and she jumped back and evaded his attempt to behead her by mere inches.

"None come to the DeathEaters and make demands!" he roared.

Her smile appeared again, infuriatingly calm and confident.

"Your princess does!" Her voice carried through the camp with unnatural power and in that moment, he felt her power explode from her like a firepowder blast. It hurled him back a step and dislodged the few pockets of snow that remained from the past winter.

The power was immediately directed to the suit of armor that rose as if summoned and drifted closer to fit over her body and make her more than ready for battle. Her power no doubt explained her calm confidence.

She laughed as the helm dropped into place and obscured her entire face except for her eyes. "And prying it from your lifeless fingers is most certainly agreeable."

CHAPTER ELEVEN

"It seems like an odd place for the goddess of nature to make her trial." Grakoor finally broke the silence between them.

Skharr looked at him. "What makes you say that?"

"Well, you would think she would want it to involve a little more...uh, you know, nature. I would imagine a jungle full of insects and poisonous creatures."

"Maybe not." He drew a deep breath and tried to distract himself from the blazing heat. "Jasmine, it is said, is the goddess of all nature, which applies to deserts as much as it does to jungles, I suppose. Besides, there are numerous creatures here that can kill us as easily as a venomous snake."

"Either the sun will kill us while it is up, or the cold will when it is gone." The quarter-orc sounded bluntly accepting.

"The most powerful forces of nature are heat and cold."

"I don't think that's right."

The barbarian wasn't sure either but it had sounded good enough when he'd said it. Perhaps the heat had begun to play tricks on him.

"You might be right. But the lack of any of the monsters we

would find in other dungeons suggests that this might not be a test of fighting prowess."

"What then?" His companion posed the question almost as if they were discussing lunch.

He didn't have an answer to that. A test of endurance seemed the most likely. Still, he had traveled through more than a few deserts and he had come prepared for more than merely a day out in the sun. He couldn't shake the feeling that Jasmine had something else in mind.

It was possible that the portal out was located at a distance that could barely be reached over a day's travel. If so, it gave them nothing to do but survive the heat and the cold so they could travel without stopping.

"I can see a small rock outcropping ahead," Grakoor called from the top of the dune. "We might find something there to shelter in."

Skharr nodded, climbed the dune, and followed his companion to where rocks pushed out of the ground. The shade they cast was minimal but it was better than nothing, especially with the sun only two hours past its highest peak in the sky.

"These are very odd rocks," Grakoor muttered when they reached them and he ran his hands over the surface.

The quarter-orc was right about that. They were soft and prone to crumbling. Bits and pieces dislodged from the surface when his hand touched it.

Still, the foundations seemed solid enough, and it wasn't long before they found a small canyon leading deeper into the formation. Barely twenty paces into that was a small tunnel that was thankfully cool and gave them some respite from the heat and the elements.

"I don't like this," Grakoor said as they stepped into the shadows. "Something is not right about how this formation was made."

"What do you mean?" The barbarian narrowed his eyes and

looked around. "It seems like it was formed by water rising to the surface on the few days a year when rain does fall here."

"It would harden the sand a little but it would not create caves like this," his companion disagreed and chuckled when he saw Skharr's confused expression. "I have traveled many deserts myself, barbarian."

"Right." He scratched his beard and looked away. It seemed silly that he tried to explain what deserts were like to an orc. Even more impressive was that Grakoor hadn't corrected his erroneous assumption already. "How do you think this cave was formed then?"

"It might have been some type of creature. My grandfather spoke of his people having trouble with sand wyrms in the deserts. They would bury themselves deep in the ground, find pools of water, and allow that to sustain them, then would come up every few months to find any creatures or plants for them to consume."

"How would they find creatures or plants without being destroyed by the sun?" He wondered how much of the tale was fact and how much pure myth.

"Some would swim through the sand like a fish through water. Others would find a way to draw the water up from their wells during their months underground. The area would grow a little and flourish before they emerged to devour anything that had been drawn to them."

Skharr settled into a crouch and studied the cave. "Is this one of the latter?"

"It might be. I've never seen them myself. Folk say the sand wyrms have been extinct for many years."

The barbarian sat, drew his sword from its sheath, and rested it across his lap. "It could also be that a god managed to drag one into a little dungeon like this. What else did your grandfather say about the wyrms? Are they some type of dragon?"

His companion thought for a moment. "No. I think it would

be more accurate to describe them as closer to a mixture of worms and snakes, although not one or the other."

"How would we kill the creature if it appeared?"

Grakoor narrowed his eyes. "I would have thought you would know how to kill almost anything you encounter. You have a way of improvising when you attack something."

"That's true enough, but it does not mean I don't appreciate what tips I can find. Forewarned is forearmed, as they say."

A moment of silence told him the quarter-orc seated across from him was deep in thought, trying to remember anything he might have learned.

There would be no point in pressing him. What he'd been told as a boy was likely deeply steeped in myth and storytelling and would be difficult to remember at the best of times.

"There was the tale of an orcish hero…his name does not come to mind, but he was famous for killing one of the sand wyrms. He used a goat to draw it out of its cave and stabbed it from behind with a spear. I seem to recall that the scales on its body are meant to defend it from attacks from the front but are open to any that can catch it from behind. But don't you think we should move on and find another place to rest if these are the dangers we will face here?"

He shook his head. "We would die if we remained in the sun much longer—the mightiest monster of them all, I suppose. We can remain here for a few hours until the heat is a little more bearable."

"And if the creature realizes we are here?" Again, Grakoor's tone was perfectly calm and reasonable.

Skharr drew a deep breath and sensed something stale and unpleasant in the cool air around them. "I suppose the choice is yours. You know more about it than I."

The quarter-orc watched him carefully before he retrieved his war hammer, balanced it across his lap, and shook his head.

"You're right about the sun being a greater danger to us but I still think that this is a bad idea."

"Noted."

Neither of them was likely to sleep. The barbarian had bad memories of trying to sleep in a dungeon, and it looked like his companion would not. That was the kind of reaction one had when seated in the nest of the source of so many childhood nightmares.

"Why did you choose me?"

He snapped his head up, widened his eyes at Grakoor's question, and realized that he had nodded off. "What?"

"Salis might have been a better choice for you to bring into this type of dungeon. She has a sharper mind, and...well, she reads a great deal. I'm always telling her to stop carrying books around but she does anyway. She would know about the sand wyrms, I'm sure of it."

It was a good question. "It was an impulsive decision but I stand by it. I wasn't making deep plans in the moment."

Grakoor chuckled and leaned his head back against the wall. "Well, I do appreciate the…"

His voice trailed off and Skharr leaned closer when he saw his companion's sudden look of panic.

"Something's shaking the ground." The quarter-orc pushed into a crouch.

He couldn't feel anything but he was willing to trust his comrade.

"Get out—get out now." Skharr pushed from the ground, his sword already in hand as he began to feel the earth shaking too. It wasn't enough that it felt like an earthquake, but rather that something large was moving closer to them.

He looked around and noticed there were ribs all along the inside of the tunnel. The way they encircled the whole of the tunnel so perfectly told him two things. The creature likely used the scales Grakoor had described to help it move through the tunnel.

And worse, the creature was large enough to fill the tunnel in its entirety.

The quarter-orc was already in motion and bounded to the lip of the tunnel, and Skharr realized he had fallen behind. His companion was fast and he was out of sight before the barbarian emerged from the cave. The ground shook in earnest, and the confined space suddenly smelled of rot and decay.

He didn't dare look back but pushed himself into a leap. Never mind that his legs were still a little stiff from having been seated until only a few moments ago. Something grasped the rocks behind him and moved alarmingly fast to close rapidly on him.

There was no telling if the creature was woken by their being in its trap or if it had simply waited for prey. Perhaps this was the time when it woke from its hibernation to find if anything had stumbled into their lair.

Something tangled with the back of his legs, and Skharr suddenly lost his balance. He fell heavily and his head hammered against the hard-packed earth. His teeth cut into the inside of his mouth as he turned when the same tendrils began to pull him back by the leg that had been caught.

"Grakoor, where the godsbedammed crotch-licking fuck are you?"

The breath rushed from his lungs when he saw his attacker. Whatever it was still jutted from inside the cave. The whole creature was covered in ribbed scales that protected it from anything that might have attacked from the front, but they were also what found purchase to allow it to move so smoothly.

While the monster looked like a snake to some degree, it was somehow otherworldly as well. There were no eyes in the front and no way for it to see where he was. Its mouth was essentially its face and this opened in a triangle to reveal thousands of razor-sharp fangs ready to grab him. The tendrils emerged from the mouth and seemed to act like they were eyes for the creature that had none. Tiny little fingers emitted a stench made even more powerful by the close confines of the cave.

Skharr had never seen anything like it and he would have preferred not to, but he managed to shut the fear into the back of his mind. The terror was not gone, but the reflex in him said that his body was reacting even though his mind was bound by fear.

His sword whipped to slash at the tendrils that dragged him toward the mouth. They were severed smoothly and he felt a rumble of pain from the monster. It was a little too close for comfort, and more of the tendrils now slid out while the flapping triple jaw reached for him.

"Fuck, fuck, fuck." The barbarian hissed, scrambled to his feet, and jumped back to avoid the hungry maw. The teeth missed him and they gouged a chunk from the wall as it passed by. "You stinking, maggot-infested, overgrown godsbedammed slimy troll dick."

Something hot rushed through him and he bounded forward and swiped his sword through the scales protecting the creature. It wasn't his best strike but the magic in the blade still cut straight through, opened a shallow wound, and forced another roar of pain from the creature as the flap mouth opened again. Its wild, unfocused reaction hurled him through the entrance.

That was fortuitous, as it turned out, as it had pushed him away from what appeared to be dozens of tendrils the thickness of reeds. They groped for him and tried to find where he was as the creature continued to move into the canyon in search of him.

With any luck, Grakoor was already long gone, too far away for any harm to come to him, but Skharr knew he needed to survive. His companion would die if he did not, and he would not let anything like that happen.

He could see the opening at the end of the canyon in front of him when something flew out from the creature that pursued him like it was spitting. He could see what looked like the same rocks and dirt that made up the rockface around him. It caught on the wall and landed in front of him to block his path. He couldn't even climb it since it continued to roll like a landslide.

He was well and truly trapped.

"Son of Janus' poxy goblin-spawned whore." Skharr snarled and came to a halt ahead of the substance, which steamed in the air like it was boiling. He could feel the heat coming from it and knew there was no way out, not unless he suddenly learned how to climb walls.

If the monster intended to kill him, however, he would kill it too. There were no two ways about it. His armor could stop the worst of the teeth and his sword could carve the creature open from the inside.

A flicker of shadow obfuscated the sun for only a moment before Grakoor leapt from the canyon wall, shouted an unintelligible warcry, and drove his sword between the scales. He pushed it deep inside while the wyrm tried to whip him off.

The quarter-orc refused to be dislodged. His sword was buried in the creature's neck—or as close to a neck as it had—and he drew his hammer and used it to pound the sword into it as it writhed and twisted.

The barbarian took a step back but something closed around his boot. He turned and realized that whatever the monster had spat out now sought to trap him.

It was still warm and he could feel his boots start to sink into the sand.

When he looked at the wyrm, the monster was no longer bucking or resisting, although Grakoor continued to hack at it as if to make sure. "I killed a fucking wyrm!"

That was good to know, although it sounded like he was celebrating.

The quarter-orc jumped down, yanked his weapons from the creature, and looked at him.

"I killed a sand wyrm!" he shouted again and gestured with both weapons to the dead creature. "Did you not fucking see that?"

"I did. What your grandfather could not do, I guess?"

"Well...yes. Why are you not more excited about it? Have you killed too many dragons to make killing a sand wyrm impressive?"

"No, it was damned impressive but somewhat less impressive from the perspective of the fucking goat."

"The what?"

Skharr rolled his eyes. "The story of how the goat was used as bait so the young hero could kill the sand wyrm."

"Ah. Yes, I do suppose that you...were the bait in this case. Not intentionally, of course. Right." Grakoor nodded and his gaze swept the canyon they were still in. "We should probably leave now. You never know if these creatures travel in packs."

"And that would be a wonderful idea but there will be a problem with it."

"What problem?"

He pointed to his feet and the sand that had begun to creep around his ankles and climb higher as he tried to pull himself out.

His companion narrowed his eyes and studied the phenomenon carefully. "Ah, the creature creates quicksand as a way to capture its prey. It's rather interesting and I would imagine it consumes the sand while digging it out."

"Can we save the godsbedammed nature lesson for later? I am...well, being sucked into the sand like a goblin's cock into a horny swamp rat."

"No, you're not. Throw me your weapons and your pack."

The barbarian complied before he looked down and again tried to free his feet from the damn sand. "And, yes...yes, I fucking well am."

"Yes, you are, but it is not difficult to pry yourself free."

"I am trying and I cannot."

"It'll be easy."

"Why don't you get your godsbedammed boots stuck in the sand and try to get out?"

Grakoor approached, careful not to let it touch him as it began to alter the sand ahead of them. "It should be easy enough. There's no magic to it, not as far as I can tell, at least. Honestly, there's nothing to be worried about."

That was not much comfort, and Skharr cleared the dryness from his throat but the lump remained. Few things in the world terrified him, but dying by being smothered to death was certainly not the way he wanted to die.

He drew a deep breath and tried to calm himself.

"First of all, you need to remain calm." How in all the hells could the quarter-orc manage to sound so fucking unbothered?

Nothing came to mind for him to say in response to that, and all he could do was nod slowly.

"You'll likely lose the boots so try to kick them off as best you can. And stop moving. It'll only make you sink faster."

Everything he had heard seemed like it wouldn't work, but he took control, pushed the fear into the back of his mind, and did as he was told. He wasn't sure how he was supposed to remove his boots without moving and sinking more. His heartbeat raced and thudded in his chest, but he continued to look at his companion. He had no choice but to trust him to save his life.

Grakoor continued to study the sand intently. "Take the weight off your body. Move yourself to the side and lie down as best you can."

"Lie—"

"Lie down as best you can and lean forward toward me."

The barbarian nodded, reclined slowly, and leaned forward. In that moment, it felt like the substance began to push him out of it.

It held onto his boots, however, and he managed to wiggle

himself free of them in his new position. Grakoor leaned forward as well, grasped his hand, and pulled him free.

The situation was worsened by the fact that he could not yank himself loose, which was his instinctive response. Despite this, it was happening slowly on its own.

After a few tugs from the quarter-orc, he shifted away from his boots and was dragged slowly over the surface of the quicksand. His companion's hold remained steadfast and he didn't stop pulling until the ground felt a little firmer under him.

Skharr gasped for breath and pushed suddenly to his bare feet. He couldn't stop himself from brushing the rest of the sand off with a kind of desperate reflex to protect himself.

"Stupid fucking sand-gobbing, useless, snot-for-brains, ass-fucking…"

Finally, the sensation of being swallowed by sand faded. Grakoor studied him closely until they both settled on the ground, their backs to the wall of the canyon with the corpse of the wyrm on one side and the quicksand on the other.

"Thank…thank you." The dryness would never leave his throat, he was sure of it, but he needed a moment to catch his breath—a moment, that was all.

The sun had begun to set and a chill crept into the air.

"I don't think I've ever seen you like that." The quarter-orc sounded bemused.

"Like what?"

"You seemed…I don't know…"

Skharr nodded. "Afraid. Being smothered to death is…not a pleasant death."

"You're the type who prefers to die with your sword in hand and a pile of bodies all around you instead of being crushed by an immeasurable force with no one but your own company as you die." His companion nodded. "It's a rather common fear."

"Then why were you so surprised by my fear of it?"

"It is common among mortals, but something about you seems...immortal."

"I'm sorry to disappoint you." He couldn't help the sarcasm.

His companion laughed at that and stood slowly. "I am not disappointed. It is good to know that you are human, even with all the legends about you. It gives the rest of us mortals hope that we can aspire to similar heights."

He extended a hand and Skharr took it and accepted the help onto his feet.

"Where do we go now?"

The barbarian opened his mouth to answer but tilted his head as he looked at the dead corpse of the wyrm. Something glowed in the mouth. A portal began to open, flared with power, and flashed to catch their attention.

"Is that...the portal?" Grakoor asked in disbelief.

"It would seem so."

"I thought we had to survive three trials." The quarter-orc almost sounded cheated.

"The sun, the wyrm, and the quicksand. I would call that three trials. I wouldn't have survived any of them if not for you. Come on."

Skharr motioned for his companion to join him. He didn't want to take any chances with the quarter-orc somehow dying because he went through first or last. They would go through together.

The world shifted again and fell away as they were drawn to the other side. He felt like the air was sucked from his lungs as they were dropped to earth. The flagstones were cool against his bare feet and the world was still dark to his eyes, but torches were all around. The priests were still gathered around the boulder in prayer but jumped up as they came through the gateway.

Micah waited there too and looked like she had just had her

evening meal. She wiped her mouth as they hesitated and looked around.

"You two are a little early," she said and narrowed her eyes. "What happened to your boots?"

Skharr looked at his feet. "They were required as payment for my survival."

"One of the trials was for you to surrender your boots?" She frowned in disbelief.

"In a manner of speaking," Grakoor answered. "We could use some water if you could arrange it."

She gestured to one of the servants and they immediately rushed closer with water they already had waiting.

"Once you are sufficiently refreshed, you will both be shown to your quarters," Micah said, shook her head, and smiled. "I am glad to see you both survived the ordeal."

CHAPTER TWELVE

I t appeared that the test did not agree with Skharr. She had seen it from the moment he came through the portal. Something was unsettled about him and she wanted to know what had so disconcerted the giant barbarian. She'd seen him in various situations and she'd never seen him so much as a little rattled.

As much as she wanted to explore the mind of the man, it was her job to see that he survived the next trial. From what she had been told, it would be a location with the type of trickery and traps she would be the most useful in.

"I swear to every god who is listening, this makes us beyond even," Micah muttered. She owed her sister a great deal, and now that she was offering herself up to save Skharr, it would mean that Sera had to forgive her.

Of course, she was also looking into who was trying to kill him too, but that was more of a favor to her half-brother and an introduction to her network of spies so he would see precisely how impressive it was.

If she could prove herself there, it would open the door for her and Tryam to work together more often. It was the kind of family connection she had always wanted with Sera and perhaps it was something that could now be shared between the three of them.

Someone knocked on the door but she didn't look up from the scroll on the table in front of her.

"Come!"

The door opened slowly and creaked gently as a young guard stepped inside. He was handsome in the way she generally liked her men, with a strong jaw and a cleft chin. Maybe once he was a little older, she would consider breaking her standing rule of not letting pleasure interfere with business.

"Skharr DeathEater for you, milady."

She finally looked up to where the barbarian stood in the doorway. The giant of a man filled the entire aperture and stood just shy of needing to duck his head to step inside.

"Thank you, that will be all," she said and motioned for the guard to take his leave. "And shut the door behind you."

"Milady."

She could tell that Skharr had not expected to find her there, but he kept his mouth shut until they were alone.

"They told me I would be speaking to someone who was knowledgeable regarding the next trial," he muttered and raised an eyebrow.

"You expected the archivist?"

"Yes, as a matter of fact."

She smiled. "Well, I have studied the matter and the archivist was busy with other matters. Given that we will head into that particular trial together, I thought it would be best that we prepare ourselves for it together."

"What?"

She had expected the question, but Skharr looked a little more drained than usual. It had been a late arrival for him and Grakoor, and while she knew the barbarian needed his rest, he also had to prepare for the battle that was to come, especially since her life would depend on whether he made it out alive or not.

Perhaps he needed to be reminded of the stakes. "Are you so surprised that I would risk my life for yours?"

"Honestly, your life is the one I would be least inclined to save during the trial, so I am rather pleased that you have chosen to come with me."

She narrowed her eyes and wondered if he truly was that cold-hearted. In all honesty, it would earn him a little more of her respect than he already had, but she caught a twinkle in his eye. "You're joking."

"Of course. Do you think I would do that to your sister?"

It was odd how she felt a little disappointed. They were not friends but he had a reputation for having a soft heart under that mountain of muscle he called a body. It did warm her heart, but a part of her had hoped it was all an act—or at least a part of himself that he needed to keep in control for fear that his more violent nature would take hold.

From what she learned of his past, it was very clear that it was a nature he needed to keep on a very short leash, especially while he was at sea.

"Of course not." She kept her tone controlled and unconcerned. After all, she wasn't surprised by his response.

"I owe her a great deal. And you too now."

"Most of what I'm doing here is for my brother's benefit," she answered. "You'll understand that, of course."

"And risking your life in the trial for me?" He sounded curious.

"I'm doing that for my sister."

"Well, I still appreciate it, no matter what the reason."

That forced a smile from her. Something plain and honest was a rarity in her life.

"Can I ask you something?"

"I cannot stop a free woman from speech. I also cannot promise to answer."

"How did you know to choose Grakoor? It would appear that all the accounts of that particular trial tell differing tales, but you brought a quarter-orc with you for a trial in the desert. It seems like a stroke of good fortune."

He shook his head as if to indicate that it mattered little. "If you're looking for a scheme I'd hatched in my mind, you might want to remember that I knew nothing of Salis or Grakoor joining me in the trial until they stepped into the room. I made a spur-of-the-moment decision based on instinct, nothing more."

"Nothing more?" It seemed far too simplistic.

"I seem to disappoint everyone with the fact that I am a mere human." Although he laughed, she sensed an impatience behind the words.

"Not disappoint." Oddly, she wanted to reassure him. "I think it has more to do with seeing the man behind all the legends. A few have looked behind those curtains, but the rest of us have had to make do with stories."

"It was never my intent." It was less a protest than a simple statement of fact.

Micah raised a brow in a teasing challenge. "Not that you ever tried to stop your legend from growing."

"Why would I?" Skharr shrugged. "I need coin to live, and folk are willing to pay more for it."

She could understand that and she was all too aware that he had a living to make. All things considered, however, perhaps all this would help his reputation, although it would be the kind of tale that tied him to the emperor for good, at least in the eyes of the local populace. If he traveled beyond the borders of the empire, he would have to be careful of those who wanted to inflict personal injury on the emperor through him.

"How is Sera?" His question startled her.

Micah realized she'd not spoken and let the silence last a little longer than intended.

"I...am having difficulty finding her," she admitted. "She is supposed to be traveling, but none of my messages have been answered, and she has not been among the caravan she was meant to be with. My guess is she is coming here to see how she can help you."

"My hope is she comes too late." There was no doubt that he meant it.

"You still think there will be a chance that you do this alone? From what Grakoor said, you would have died if it had not been for him."

Skharr nodded. "Aye, and he could have died on my account."

"Wouldn't you be willing to die for any one of your friends?" The retort came quickly and she had no desire to stop it.

"Of course, but—"

"And you think they wouldn't do the same for you? You would deny them the opportunity to do the same for you?"

The barbarian had no answer to that. Frankly, there was no answer to that. She had no idea how the taciturn giant had inspired such loyalty in so many people, but it was an element she would be sure to study about him if he survived.

Finally, he sighed and shook his head. "Are you sure your sister is coming here?"

"It is not my place to tell you."

"Whose place is it?" He sounded impatient, as if the politics and schemes were too much.

She studied him carefully and watched the wheels spinning in his mind. He worked through it almost immediately.

"Tryam is playing the puppet master."

Micah smirked. "Well done. I can see how he won the throne —aside from having you there to crush the skulls of his detractors."

"He has skill with the blade."

"I've heard. And I hear that he trains every morning at the crack of dawn too, at least when he hasn't been drunk the night before."

"Drinking regularly." He looked impressed. "The boy has become a man."

———

The barbarian was quicker on his feet than anticipated. He was older, with streaks of gray already showing in a thick black beard, but he moved like a boy hoping to peek under a woman's skirts. Even worse, he displayed the experience that neither of the youngsters she'd dealt with possessed. He watched and waited, trying to drive her into the smaller patches of ice while he used his longer arms to keep her attacks at bay.

In truth, it had become an enjoyable fight.

She ducked under one of his harder swings, dropped to her knees, and slid over the ice he had tried to force her onto. Her motion fast and deft, she slashed her blade to tap him on the back before she stood.

It wasn't enough to penetrate his clothes and she needed to move away as his ax dropped toward her neck again.

Cassandra laughed and twirled her blade smoothly over her fingers as he slipped a little on the ice.

Surprisingly, the barbarian grinned and lifted his ax over his shoulder for a powerful swing. As she raised her blade to block it, his whole body twisted almost unnaturally and the weapon arced from the other side instead. She was barely able to angle her blade to block the worst of the blow, but it dislodged the sword from her hands.

His weapon still hammered into her shoulder pauldron with a loud clang.

Instead of trying to recover her blade, she hooked her arm

around the ax's haft and dragged the chieftain closer to pound her head into his, drag the weapon from his hands, and fling it aside.

He grunted as his nose broke from the impact with her helm, and she leaned her head into his fist as he raised it to try to punch her away. He had gloves on, but it still forced his hand back, although it snapped the strap of the helm and the piece of armor clattered at her feet.

It was a stunning blow for her, and both took a step back and attempted to recover.

"You are quite a warrior." He growled, cradled his injured hand, and ignored his nose for the moment. "It is shocking to think that Skharr calls you friend."

Cassandra laughed again and rolled her neck. "Skharr would match and best me in combat, whereas all you have accomplished is to wind me a little."

"You have seen the barbarian fight, then?"

"He helped me to kill a mad dragon. I don't suppose you ever managed to do the same?"

She watched him look around at the others. While she understood that dragons held an important place in their culture, something like awe was visible in their faces.

It didn't matter that it was an older dragon bound to a place where it could not put its full talents to use. Killing it was still a feat. Hells, she wasn't sure she even believed it herself half the time.

He rushed forward again, and the barbarian princess sidestepped his wild swing. When his knee came up to hammer into her gut, she dropped her elbow to stop it and pushed him back. Off-balance, he fell but regained his feet before she could press her advantage.

"We also fought an elder god together, one summoned from the depths." She couldn't resist taunting him a little. "He attacked the beast with only a sword, smote it in its heart, sent it back to where it could never be summoned from again, and came away from it covered in the god's black blood."

The chieftain nodded and swung a hard punch with his injured hand. Cassandra pressed forward, drove her fist into his gut, and followed it by stamping on his instep. The man stumbled back again.

As she took a step forward, he raised his hand.

"Enough!" he cried to the laughter of the rest of the Clan. "Enough. You have made your point."

"For myself or for Skharr?"

"Both." He straightened and used his sleeve to wipe the blood running from his nose.

She fixed him with a bold expression and drove her point home, her tone as sharp as her sword. "You understand that the DeathEaters might never have another as great as him, yes?"

"It is true that we knew little of Skharr's achievements." A few of the younger lads rushed to him and began to tend to his wounds as the chieftain sat on a nearby boulder. "Or at least the truth of them. The few tales we know to be true are from long ago, and perhaps it is not for me to judge that a man cannot change."

"What do you mean?"

"No warrior—no DeathEater—can accomplish as much as you claim without being mighty indeed. We judge a fighter by their deeds, yes, but also by those who fight alongside them, those who willingly join them in the shield wall. Skharr has not always walked with those like you, paladin."

She narrowed her eyes as she picked her sword up and sheathed it smoothly.

The chieftain saw her look and chuckled, although it made the blood start flowing from his nose again. "You believe we are ignorant up here in the frozen mountains? Even we have heard of the powerful Cassandra, Paladin of Theros, who also claims to be Cassandra, the Barbarian Princess. We might not appear intelligent or speak with long, unpronounceable words, but we are not completely ignorant of the world around us."

One of the boys who had been sent away returned with a bundle in his hands. She could immediately make out the dwarvish markings on the leather, which told her exactly what was carried to the chieftain.

He took it, rested it across his lap, and with what could only be called reverence in his eyes as he undid the wraps, revealed the ax she had asked for. It was a beautiful piece and the steel glinted blue in the torchlight around them.

"Here is the Ax of…" He paused, looked at her, and smiled. "The Ax of Skharr of the Clan, the Mighty Barbarian of Theros!"

He was no longer speaking to her but to the rest of the Clan, and they immediately cheered as he raised the weapon high to ensure that all could see its magnificence.

"Who will run with me to bring it to him?" the chieftain roared.

Cassandra's eyebrows raised when she realized what was happening and the Clan bellowed a response.

"What?" the man asked and turned to her again.

"Nothing. I was not sure what to do with two DeathEaters, given that I found myself in trouble the last time. How many are we discussing here?"

"We?"

A crack of thunder interrupted their discussion, and it was quickly followed by a flash of lightning. The fact that one came before the other was enough to indicate that something was amiss, and she turned to see the old man with his donkey again.

"It would appear my paladin has the DeathEaters good and riled up," Theros said as he approached them.

"Your paladin?" the chieftain asked and scratched his beard.

The god smiled at the giant of a man. "Is it fair to guess that all your kin are that large, Turan, or is there a special bloodline among DeathEaters that results in this?"

The chieftain concluded that he was in the presence of a god but showed no sign of being impressed. This was the notorious lack of trust the barbarian clans had for the gods, she assumed, although he made no attempt to remove the old man from the Clan's lands as she expected he would.

"Size isn't everything," Turan answered cryptically and let his gaze drift to the rest of his people.

"I think the honor guard for the ax should be limited," Theros suggested. "Perhaps...six barbarians?"

Cassandra cleared her throat loudly as she retrieved her helm from where it had fallen.

"Right." The god shook his head like he'd forgotten about her. "Six DeathEaters and your Barbarian Princess."

The warriors laughed loudly when he spoke and she could tell that they had all put the pieces together for themselves as well.

"We'll play the biggest joke on the other clans," Turan stated with a deep chuckle. "And we will support our most famous warrior. Gather your weapons! We will be the honor guard for the Barbarian Princess and the Ax of Shkarr DeathEater."

At his order, the others rushed to gather their weapons. She looked at Theros, who had a similarly confused look on his face.

"You could learn everything there is to know about barbarians in a week," the god muttered under his breath. "But after a hundred years, they still surprise you."

It was clear that Turan chose the warriors who would come based on skill and experience, and it wasn't long before those who would join them were selected from those who clamored to be included. The whole Clan would go if they could, but Theros was right to limit their numbers. Having them all march into the Imperial City would cause a panic.

"Thank you," Cassandra whispered when it was only her and Theros.

"For what, my dear?"

"What you do for Skharr, you do for me."

He chuckled as she wrapped him in a tight embrace. "You threaten to warm an old god's heart."

CHAPTER THIRTEEN

He did not expect that Micah would be willing to risk her life for him. He had no idea why she even offered in the first place. That she had aspirations in the Imperial City was obvious enough, but he didn't know where helping to keep a barbarian alive played into those. It was unsettling to think about.

But if there was anyone in the world he didn't mind heading into one of these trials with, it was her. They would both have to fight for their lives, and in the kind of fight that required the abilities the scrolls said were required, she was the one he wanted beside him, oddly enough.

Even so, he did not expect her to be there. He was sure she would send someone else. Micah was never one to stand her ground and fight her own battles. That was always left to the pawns.

And yet there she was. Skharr scowled and tried to determine if it was a body double standing in for her beside the guards who had followed him. Even though he was no longer a prisoner—at least not while he was running the trial gauntlet—Tryam still insisted that they accompany him everywhere apart from his room where a little privacy was required.

"Skharr," Micah muttered as he approached. "You're late."

She was hidden under a heavy cloak in an effort to conceal her identity from those who were watching, but there was no mistaking her iron gaze and the sneer that seemed to be permanently etched onto her features.

He had no intention to allow her to set the expectations of the trial. "The sun does not reach its peak for another two hours. How in the blazes could I possibly be late?"

The first trial had taken more out of him than he had expected, and he knew he could stand to have a little more sleep. It was how his life had seemed to go for as long as he could remember. There were times where there was so little to do that he was bored out of his mind and had all the time to sleep he could ever want. Now, when the time came that demanded his all, it was like his body needed all the rest he could give it and wanted more.

It was one of the first signs that he was growing older. There was no gray in his beard yet but it would come around in a year or so. Skharr had never expected to live long enough to complain about growing old.

"You're later than I'd like," Micah whispered after she'd considered it for a moment. "If we are late, it is back to the courtroom and the headsman's ax for you. I will not have it, so we will be fucking early. Come."

Sera might have been a captain but her sister had everything needed to be a commander if she wanted it. Complaining was merely another way to ensure that he knew nothing would ever be good enough, which meant he would always want to put his finest effort forward in an attempt to finally impress her.

He'd seen it with the commanders who led armies, and it was generally a good way to lead, provided the vinegar was tempered with honey from time to time.

They were not moving toward the same sanctuary where the first trial had been held. From what he could tell, the path they had taken led away from the palace altogether and they moved close to the edge of the city as well.

A handful of citizens followed them, trying to find out where they were going. Enough of them knew sufficient details about the trials to know where they were going. From what Skharr had seen of the map, they were climbing one of the small hills beyond the walls of the palace, although there was a path they needed to follow.

A small forest grew in the area, sealed off from the public and only used by the emperor and those in his inner circle when they wanted to hunt. It was a massive waste, but the roads were maintained and magic stopped the forest from encroaching on the rest of the palace grounds around it.

The crowd continued to follow them until they reached a small iron gate. Their guard stopped there and turned to ensure that only two passed through the gate and no one managed to sneak in behind them. Skharr wondered what happened if one were to accidentally follow them into the trial, but it was probably for the best that he simply left the speculation unexplored.

Once they were out of sight of the crowd, Micah turned to check that they were alone before she removed her cloak and let it drop carelessly onto the ground.

She wore battle leathers beneath, but not of a kind Skharr had ever seen. Something about them seemed to pull in the shadows around her like they worked actively to hide the wearer. Her hair was done in a braid, and she also had a mask that could cover the lower half of her face at a moment's notice.

The shadows did not cover her fully, though. Skharr stepped behind her and tilted his head as she crouched to adjust her boots.

"What are you looking at?" she snapped.

He realized he had been staring and turned away quickly.

"Well?" It seemed she wasn't prepared to simply let it slide.

"Your ass, of course."

Micah straightened and narrowed her eyes as she looked over her shoulder.

"Really?"

He managed to restrain a grin. "Even a blind man would appreciate the view you are presenting."

"Well, this view would appreciate it if your appreciation was directed elsewhere. Maybe at the ass of a woman whose sister would not kill her for saying the wrong thing about you." She turned fully to face him. "Although the appreciation is…well, appreciated, even if my sister would slit my throat in a jealous rage."

"Why is she jealous?" It made no sense to him and he wondered if the woman was joking.

She approached him and rapped her knuckles quickly on his forehead.

He pulled away quickly. "Oy! What the fuck was that for?"

"I needed to make sure there was something other than rocks in there."

"I am a barbarian, Micah, as you have plainly explained on multiple occasions. Hells, you even tried to kill me."

"A great amount of good that did me." She rolled her eyes and directed his gaze to a small cave in the hill they were approaching. "Shall we?"

"I would say ladies should go first, but we both know you are no lady."

"You know my father was the old emperor, right?"

He delivered his retort with an edge of mockery. "If blood made ladies, every last noblewoman in this city would be the pinnacle of purity and integrity. You are the one with all the spies. Is that what is happening in this place?"

She grinned at him. "But you still want me to move ahead of you."

"You're the expert in dealing with traps and the like. You are the one whose skills are honed in that particular direction, which means you should move ahead."

"And it is not because you want to see more of my ass?"

"I did not dress you in leathers," Skharr countered. "I did not even ask you to join me."

Micah opened her mouth but snapped it shut quickly and turned to the tunnel entrance with no sign of a retort. She might have had one but in the end, he was right about one thing at least. Her skills were honed to deal with the traps they would likely face inside the dungeon.

The barbarian had no idea how the gods had managed to sink so many of their dungeons into the Imperial City, but it must have been when it was first built. It was probably their magic running through the walls and the palace, which meant they could wander in and out as they pleased. It was an interesting thought and it explained how Ahverna had managed to sneak in without so much as a single eye detecting her.

They had not gone more than fifteen paces into the tunnel before his companion raised a hand to stop him in his tracks. Her keen gaze searched through the darkness. While a little light still seeped in, he almost couldn't see her anymore—like the leathers had drawn the blackness around them to her and made it easier to simply not see her at all.

After a moment's thought, she turned, withdrew something from a pouch, and tossed it at one of the nearby sconces.

The torch flared with a flash and a splutter of thick gray smoke, and the area ahead of them illuminated immediately. Skharr didn't see it at first, but the slight indentations on the ground indicated that something awaited them that would be triggered if they stepped on it as they approached.

"I suppose this is the part where you begin to regret ever choosing to join me in this," he muttered as she crouched near one of the indentations.

"As a matter of fact, that started three or four days ago," she answered. "The moment I decided I was the woman for the job."

"I suppose there is still time and opportunity for you to leave me at this point." The barbarian turned to where the entrance of the tunnel was still visible. "I am sure no one would blame you."

"If that is what you think, your brains truly are made of stone." Her voice seemed to almost trail off like her mouth spoke while her mind was otherwise occupied. She pressed one of the indentations and something hissed past them to bury itself in the wall opposite—a dart, by the looks of it, and dripping with something he knew he did not want to be embedded in his body.

"It's as I thought," she whispered. "We follow the indentations marked with the names of the gods but avoid the ones with the names of the demigods. From the smell, those darts are laced with crawler mucus."

Skharr studied the indentations carefully. There were markings but they made little sense to him.

"And...how do I know..."

Micah smirked and shook her head. "Follow my footsteps."

She took a step forward, balanced carefully on one foot, and hopped lightly to the next one. From the number of indentations she skipped, it appeared the demigods greatly outnumbered the gods in this arrangement.

"Follow in your footsteps," he mumbled and drew a deep breath to calm his nerves before he leaned into the first step. "Would I could shove that crawler-lubricated godsbedammed dart up a deified fucking asshole right now."

The crowd was still assembled outside the gate, trying to catch a glimpse of the barbarian and his mysterious companion. Dozens made attempts to guess who had gone in with him, but no one had caught a glimpse of their face.

Meanwhile, the guards remained stalwart in their positions and allowed none to pass through the gates. While the crowd remained almost too insistent on the matter, they would not risk the emperor's ire by interrupting the trial of his esteemed pet.

Remaining with the crowd was probably for the best. The guards had their work cut out for them to keep the group contained and could not afford to focus on any particular person. The hooded figure would need to find another way to step away from them but for the moment, it was more than content to wait and see how the whole situation would play out.

Besides, it seemed they were all too willing to sit and wait until the adventurers returned. According to the rumors, the first trial was finished in half the time allotted to it, and each trial was meant to last one day and one night at the very most.

A handful of them were bards looking for the next ballad to sing, and a few others were historians who scribbled their notes or dictated them to aides.

The rest were all curious onlookers, hoping to catch another glimpse of the famed barbarian. For the moment, the hooded figure remained with them. They were less likely to notice if the number of their group increased or decreased as necessity dictated, and even if they did, their eyes were not trained to detect the oddities of the creature before them.

It was an interesting balancing act and one the hooded figure was more than content to play. Watching and waiting for the two to emerge again would take some time and it was best to establish who would be a problem and who would be a blessing when it happened.

CHAPTER FOURTEEN

"In another life, with decades of training, you might have been a dancer." Micah's expression was one of undisguised amusement.

"Not in this one, though."

"No."

Skharr grinned at her and glanced at the trap they had evaded. "I think I might have liked to be a dancer. I could have been in plays and performed elegant pirouettes."

Her chuckle and the way she rolled her eyes in mock horror made him smile. "As interesting an image as you paint, it would be more likely that you would play the part of trees or rocks in those plays."

"Even in another life?" He injected a plaintively hopeful tone into the question.

"Even so."

Dancing would have been a more peaceful living, he supposed, although his people had little need for entertainment—or at least the kind that had little to do with battle. From a young age, all their lives revolved around becoming finer fighters and activities ranged from their ability to climb the icy mountains, play fighting, and other such means to pass the time in the Clan between skirmishes and battles.

Still, there were many times he'd wondered how his life would have turned out if he'd had a different childhood. There were many fantasies, but he determined that he would most likely make his living in a profession that allowed him to use his physical attributes. A woodsman, perhaps, spending his time chopping trees and selling the wood to see houses built or fires fed.

Then again, the chances were that he would have been sent to battle for some king or lord anyway.

"You have something on your mind." He wasn't sure if Micah asked the question out of curiosity or concern.

"I'm considering how my life would have turned out if I were an ordinary commoner."

"You would likely be dead on some battlefield."

He laughed, unperturbed by the brutally blunt answer. "That is what I thought."

She grinned as they continued through the tunnel.

"What would you do if you weren't what you are?" Skharr asked. "Do you have any ideas of what you might have wanted to be?"

Micah shook her head. "I feel as though I am fulfilling all I ever wanted to be. Well, when I was a girl, I wanted to be a princess again, but I know now that is not my destiny. Besides, being a princess is not quite all a little girl might imagine it is—fewer mighty heroes climbing towers and more pressure for you to marry someone you don't know or much like for alliances and the like. Although the number of dragons encountered is surprisingly simi—"

Her voice cut off when something triggered inside the cavern. A soft hiss was the only warning as she took a few steps ahead of Skharr. A tile in the wall moved and a spear launched, aimed directly at her thigh.

The barbarian didn't realize he had moved, but his hands closed around the spear's haft, grasped it, and stopped the projectile from following through on the thrust.

The tip had barely managed to pierce her leathers, but she inched away from it to allow him to release the contraption and let it drive forward to where it was supposed to go. It was a little slower now, which suggested that catching it had caused some damage to the mechanism inside.

"There is no venom on that one," Skharr muttered.

"It serves me right for being distracted." Micah growled her annoyance and checked to make sure the weapon had not reached the skin under her armor. "It must be said, however. That was a fine catch."

He shrugged. "My childhood involved play where javelins or arrows were launched at others and they had to catch them and launch them back. Those old reflexes kicked in."

"And I will forever be grateful."

The barbarian smirked, but his expression faded after a few moments. "It's odd, though."

"What?" She was instantly alert.

"The darts were laced with crawler mucus and the trap aimed for your leg instead of your chest."

She tilted her head and quickly realized what he was talking about. "Crawler mucus does not kill, only paralyze. And the trap was meant to incapacitate but not kill."

"Odd, is it not?"

Her mind worked quickly as it always did. "All it means is that we are not yet in the actual dungeon. The traps were likely set so no one could wander in by accident. It would scare off those it wounds but still give them a chance to turn back should they wish to."

There was little else to say about it. They had managed to survive the warnings but he would be willing to wager solid coin that it would grow more difficult once they reached the trial.

Sure enough, as they came around another bend, another portal awaited them and crackled and roiled with energy. Skharr paused as he approached it and narrowed his eyes.

"You do not like portals." His companion sounded amused.

He turned to Micah, who grinned at him.

"Grakoor talks too much."

Her grin widened. "Possibly. But even a blind man could see your trepidation."

The barbarian scowled at her. "I've heard the stories of portals losing their power before fully transferring folk to their intended destination, cutting them to pieces, or having them arrive without a hand or a foot. I am not comfortable committing my body to a means of transport I have no power over."

"Is that why you refuse to ride a horse?"

"That is not the point."

She grinned again and he ignored her for the moment and gestured for her to take the lead. If he were to die while going through the portal, it would mean her life as well. He might as well let her ensure there were no dangers ahead.

The thought left him feeling oddly guilty and discomforted. Being at the front of any attack was generally where he wanted to be, but he was out of his element in this. Politics was never his domain, but he had drawn the attention of those who wanted him dead and had the means to make others do their dirty work.

It had begun to tell on his nerves and he didn't like it.

Skharr stepped through the portal behind Micah and the uncomfortable feeling touched him again.

This one did not last quite as long, and his next step brought him to a point that appeared to be as dark as the tunnel they had left behind. His companion had already lit a torch and held it aloft.

"Where do you think we are?" she asked once he had recovered sufficiently.

"Underground."

She paused in mid-step. "Well, you aren't wrong."

They were underground, but the chamber was truly massive. The stalactites hung at least a hundred feet over his head, and from the way the chamber opened before them, it was clear that they were in something like a city that only dwarves could properly build.

But dwarves generally knew how to light their cities and none were present. This was deserted, and he wanted to know why and how. Skharr doubted that a god had built the whole place themselves, but it seemed unlikely that they had emptied a dwarf city as well. Dwarves were not the type to abandon their cities lightly.

Questions followed questions, enough to ponder for years if they wanted to, but it was better to simply find out for themselves.

The barbarian drew a deep breath, steeled his nerves, and ensured that he was the first one to take a step forward. A single path cut through the abandoned city and led to what looked like a pyramid at the very center of it. It was smooth all the way around except for a long flight of stairs leading to the peak.

A portal was visible at the top, suspiciously easy to see from the beginning. Perhaps this was to instill hope in the minds of those in the dungeon, but he felt it was more likely that it was meant as a distraction. It seemed so close but one misstep would lead to death and ruin.

And the worst part was that most of the terrain between where they stood and the pyramid was shrouded in complete darkness aside from what Micah's torch revealed.

She seemed a little dubious about how simple it all seemed, but as they continued, nothing attacked, no weapons were launched, and no poison came from the earth. Everything was going surprisingly well but it was clear that neither of them trusted the easy progress.

"Come along." Skharr growled, pulled his bow out, and strung it smoothly as he walked. "This trial will not complete itself."

"No, indeed," Micah whispered. "I wonder what this place was."

"A city by the looks of it. Dwarves sometimes speak of the lost cities, meaning not that the cities themselves were lost but instead, that they were abandoned for some reason or another and now, they cannot be found. I would surmise this is one of those. It might be that a god found it, liked it, and sealed it so no one could find it aside from those who take their trial. Which god did you say designed it again?"

She shook her head. "I didn't, and the archives do not tell. It is assumed that Phaenos, the God of Death, is behind this one, but while these places might be works of art, it is not as though they were signed."

The barbarian paused, looked around, and studied the handi-work on the pillars holding the ceiling up. Rivulets of water streamed down through the channels in the rock, flowing likely from the snow at the top of whatever mountain they were on. Traces of minerals were left behind and had begun to accumulate from the ceiling all the way down.

When the water reached the ground, it disappeared through the cracks without so much as leaving a puddle behind.

It flowed silently, a sure indication that it was going somewhere.

"Where is the water going?" Micah narrowed her eyes as she watched it.

"I was thinking the same thing."

"Isn't it odd how often we do that?" She voiced the thought before she'd considered it but he seemed to take in the spirit in which it was meant.

He shook his head. "Great minds and all that. We might not always fight for the same things, but our minds work in the same way, nonetheless. They always have."

"And what way is that?"

He looked at her, his expression open and honest. "Survival. We've fought for our lives for so long that we've almost forgotten what it is like to be at peace."

"Is that why you killed the underworld of Verenvan for me?" She had often wondered about that.

"They were trying to kill me. I killed them first…with a little help. The fact that you profited greatly from how everything turned out was a secondary concern."

"I am sure it was…"

Her voice trailed off as they reached what appeared to be a massive bridge. The pillars stopped and he could hear the sound of moving water below.

There was no sign of any railing to tell them where the bridge ended and nothing but a drop he did not dare to try to calculate. He would not even look over the edge.

Micah was the first one to move forward. She tested the stonework for a moment before she stepped onto it, narrowed her eyes, and tried to determine what they were facing.

"Do you think you can send an arrow to the end of the bridge?"

He frowned but nodded. "Yes. But why?"

"We need to look at the other side. I want to make sure nothing is waiting for us there."

Skharr shrugged, took an arrow from his quiver, and wound the far end of the shaft with a strip of cloth he'd dipped in oil for an occasion like this. Once he was sure it was secure, he drew the arrow slowly, let her light the cloth, and ensured that it was burning well before he loosed it.

The arrow streaked across the bridge, clattered on the other side, and released a shower of sparks that illuminated the area for a moment before the oiled cloth burned out. The pillars and the pathway continued, but Skharr thought he caught a glimpse of something else on the ground before the flames went out. It had been nothing more than shadow on shadow, and once the flame went out, he couldn't tell if it had been there at all.

"I suppose we must go on," Micah whispered and motioned for him to accompany her.

He could find no reason to disagree but something stuck to the back of his throat and made him question every step they took.

Only five or six paces over the bridge proved him right. A hint of a crack when she took a step gave her pause and when he joined her, it repeated but much louder this time. Both stopped as the bridge swayed beneath their feet. The movement was slight at first but increased rapidly and he turned to confirm that the surface behind them had suddenly fallen away.

The structure ahead of them had begun to tip upward, ever so slightly at first, but it became more and more uneven as they remained where they were.

There was no going back. It was too far to jump, even if they could arrange a running start.

"Forward!" Skharr shouted and pushed her to start running. "Go!"

Micah bounded forward into a sprint. She was faster than he was and immediately took the lead as the structure continued to tilt upward.

When she reached what appeared to be the center of the bridge, however, she skidded to a halt and motioned for him to do the same.

"What are you doing?" His protest was instinctive.

"Stop—stop now!" There was no mistaking the urgency in her tone.

He complied but his boot slipped on the flagstones a little more than was comfortable and his stomach jolted uncomfortably. The bridge still tilted as if to throw them back the way they'd come, but as he came to a halt, the movement suddenly stopped and the structure began to revert to its original position.

In moments, it was level again, although Skharr could see that like the way they had come, about eight feet of the ground on the other side of the bridge was missing as well.

"It's on a swivel," she whispered. "It will dip any way we go. As long as we are at the center, it will have nowhere to tilt, right?"

She didn't seem too sure about that but the steady surface on which they stood was evidence that she was correct.

"We cannot remain here forever, though," he muttered and looked around for anything that might resolve their current predicament. "Do you think you can make the jump over that gap?"

Her expression dubious, she turned to look at him. "Aye. But I won't be able to make it there before the side tips."

The barbarian shook his head. "You'll make it because I will move in the opposite direction to even the weight out for you."

"What?" Micah turned to look at him. "Have you forgotten that your survival is the point of all this? If you die, I will not leave here either. Do you understand that?"

"Of course." He drew a deep breath. "The problem is that I cannot make that jump. If you can, you'll have the time to secure a rope and throw the end to me, and it would enable me to reach the other side. So I ask again, can you make the jump?"

She looked at the gap and drew a deep breath. "Yes. In my sleep."

That was all he needed to hear. Skharr pulled the rope from his pack and worked it deftly into a knot around the hilt of his dagger before he handed it and the rope to her.

"What am I supposed to do with this?" she asked.

"It's a special dagger and you'll be able to plant it in the rocks with little trouble. When you have done that, throw the rope as well you can so I'll be able to use it to cross."

Micah looked at the chasm and then at him again before she muttered something he couldn't catch.

"I'll bet you wish I had a body like a dancer now," he said with a grin.

She looked at him in disbelief. "How are you enjoying this?"

"Are you not?"

That made her think for a moment before she laughed. "Well...a little. It has been a while since I got my hands dirty. Most of the time, I send folk off to do it for me."

"Heavy hangs the head that does not wear the crown." His smirk drew a smile from her.

"Fuck you."

He waited as she drew a few deep breaths, settled herself, and prepared to race forward as fast as possible to build momentum for the jump ahead.

"Ready?" she asked.

"When you are."

She nodded and another deep breath was all the warning he was given before she surged forward as quickly as her soft leather boots could carry her—which was extremely quickly as it turned out. He immediately began to move back but was heavier than she was, which meant he did not need to move quite as fast as she did to keep the structure level.

Toward the end, Skharr realized he had gone too far and it now tilted toward his side, but it did not appear to hinder her. Micah had not lied when she said she could make the jump in her sleep. She leapt smoothly over the gap from a slightly elevated position, landed on the balls of her feet, and rolled smoothly. A moment later, she was on her feet, planted the dagger into the ground, and uncoiled the rope as he began to move forward.

The barbarian liked to think of himself as fast and most were surprised that someone his size could move as rapidly as he did. His best trait, however, had always been his endurance and how he was able to maintain a solid pace over hours.

The truth was that his speed was not quite what one would describe as overwhelming, and he wished he had a little less weight to him now as he struggled to reach the center of the bridge again.

Micah stood motionless and waited for him, her torch the only light, and he took a moment to gather himself and confirm that the bridge had settled into place again.

In all honesty, he was gathering the courage to make the jump. Once he began to, even a trace of hesitation would mean the bridge would tip too low for him to reach the top.

It would require everything he had. He surged forward suddenly and moved as quickly as he could, then pushed himself even faster when the bridge tipped downward again. Desperation fueled him. He did not know what might wait for him at the bottom and had no desire to find out.

His companion tossed him the length of rope as he came within reach. He grasped it and wound it quickly around his arm as he made the leap.

Skharr had been right—he wouldn't have made it, not even close—but the rope tightened around his arm and he hammered hard into the rock wall ahead. His shoulder twisted under the full weight of his body dragging on it, but his desperation fueled his hold and prevented him from falling.

He did not know why he chose to look down, especially since he knew there would be nothing to see. What little light there was in the chamber reflected in the flowing water almost fifty feet down, or at least appeared to do so while he dangled precariously from the precipice.

This was infinitely worse than going through the portal, he decided. With a growl of effort, he forced as much power as he could into his body to twist up and grasp the rope with his other hand. He knew the knot would hold—it was one of his, after all—but it had been a gamble to trust both rope and dagger with his full weight, even if it was for only a short drop.

He groaned softly and hauled himself up, one hand over the

other. Although he felt the strain, he refused to let his hands slip, even when the rope burned his bare hands.

Fortunately, it wouldn't cause real injury. He knew his time at sea would ensure that all he felt was a little sore.

Moments later, a pair of hands caught him by the collar and helped him up and over the edge.

Micah panted and looked like she had tried to pull him up with the rope given the tears he could see on the leather of her gloves. When that didn't work, she had taken hold of him to help him up instead.

Skharr lay on his back for a minute and caught his breath before he untangled himself from the rope.

"Thank you," he said as he pushed finally into a seated position.

"I was saving my own life as much as yours." Her voice sounded shaky, something she wasn't used to.

"I can still appreciate you doing so."

She smirked, stood quickly, and offered him a hand to help him up as well.

The barbarian rubbed his hands as she collected the torch from where she'd dropped it.

"Where did you get that dagger?" she asked as he yanked it free.

"It was a gift from an elf. And no, I haven't the slightest idea where or how she got her hands on it, but it has proved to be what saved my life a few times."

"She?" Her eyebrow rose.

"She was a child, at least by elf standards, but still likely older than you or I."

"Ah. I see."

Skharr looked into the darkness around them. Something appeared to be between them and the pyramid but the darkness obfuscated everything beyond the faint light of their torch. He wasted no time and retrieved his bow and an arrow. Micah lit it and he fired it into the shadows ahead.

The dim light revealed nothing but flagstones and more of the pillars until the projectile suddenly stopped. For a moment, he couldn't quite make out what the arrow was buried in. It was a pale, bleached white, and as they approached, he noticed that something had begun to glow under it as the meager flame attached to his arrow went out.

"What is that?" She had lowered her voice to almost a whisper.

"It could be something that was killed down here," he suggested as they approached it. "Perhaps it is what drove the folk who lived here away and then died when it was sealed?"

He could hear the hopeful note in his voice as they moved close enough for the torchlight to reach what was indisputably a corpse, the skeletal remains of something massive. The skull was about as large as he was, with teeth the size of a sword's blade and a massive horn that protruded from the tip of the snout.

"It's a dragon," Micah whispered. "Or...what's left of one."

"The bones have been here a while. They are picked clean." Skharr stepped forward and ran his fingers over the horn before he stretched forward to yank his arrow out from where the tip was buried. Despite the power of the bow, it had only penetrated about an inch or so, not enough to reach the other side.

"Why would the bones of a dragon be here?" she continued. "I think you're right—maybe it was what drove the dwarves out of this place. I can't imagine anything else would have more of an impact than a dragon looking for a lair."

It looked like the creature had died in its sleep. There was no sign of any broken bones. The wings—or the bones that remained of them—were tucked and the creature's head rested between its forepaws. All were signs that it might have met a simple end, perhaps even of old age.

The problem with that, of course, was that dragons didn't die in their sleep.

"What's that?" The curiosity in her tone caught his attention.

Skharr turned to where Micah crouched close to the ribs and inspected something beneath. Runes glowed faintly and it seemed that the closer she got with her torch, the brighter they gleamed, although he couldn't be sure.

What was beyond question was that the runes followed the contours of the skeleton, although mostly only the spine, and illuminated the bones as she stepped away. The glow was a sickly green, and the runes were immediately exposed.

"We need to go," she whispered.

"What?" He stared at her in bemusement.

"We must go now unless you know how to fell a bone dragon."

"Bone dra—"

She rolled her eyes and gestured impatiently. "The bones of a dragon raised from the dead with foul magic. These are necromancy runes and more powerful than any I've seen."

"Why are they only lighting up now?"

As she pushed to her feet, she gestured frantically for him to join her. "Fire ignites them and gives them power. We approached to inspect the skeleton and the trap was triggered. We need to run!"

Skharr narrowed his eyes, but when he saw the bone wings twitch, it was easy to reach the conclusion that she was right. Bone dragons were used because the bones were harder than most steel and made it almost impossible to dismember the creature, which was the only way to stop it.

"Skharr—run! Now!"

He needed no further encouragement and spun on his heel to follow her while she held her torch up to light the way forward. For all they knew, they could rush into another trap, but he knew for a fact that if they did not run, they would die.

Micah proved again that she was the faster runner, which made it easy for him to follow. She checked the ground and the pillars ahead repeatedly to ensure that no traps waited for them while they sprinted as fast as they could. Something large and heavy moved behind them far more rapidly than he'd expected. The dragon would not be able to fly, not with nothing but bones for wings, but it could still move faster than they could.

The heavy footsteps made the ground shake, and he pushed himself faster as his companion reached the pyramid and tripped over the first step but still scrambled up on all fours.

His gaze fixed on the pinnacle of the pyramid and the portal that provided their escape. It was almost within reach. They simply had to move beyond the dragon's reach and race to the top.

Skharr bounded up the steps and took them two at a time as he rushed to join her. She reached about the midway point when she turned back to check his progress. He dared not look back, and when he saw the pure horror in her eyes, he knew he didn't want to.

"No!" He growled in protest and desperation lent him the strength to continue his ascent when he heard and felt something hiss below his feet. It wasn't only the monster, he realized, although he could feel it gaining on them as he bolted up the steps. "By the blood-sucking spawn of Janus' hairy butt crack—"

Something roiled and whispered inside the pyramid. Unable to summon the strength to shout, he motioned for Micah to continue running and pushed himself despite the fatigue his body felt.

He could only feel the movement at first. The steps they were climbing had begun to shift upward and turn.

They were closing to seal themselves into the pyramid and what had once been stairs was now as smooth as the rest of the structure. The marble gleamed, too smooth and the angle too steep to climb.

Micah could see it happening and pushed herself to reach the top.

His heart hammered in his chest as the step below him disappeared into the pyramid and the one he stood on began to follow.

Without thought or consideration, Skharr drew his sword and thrust it into the gap ahead of him as it closed. He lost all connection to the marble, but the stones sealed around the blade about three-quarters of the way up and prevented him from sliding down.

The process seemed to increase in speed and Micah screamed as she made one last desperate jump to reach the top.

As skilled and athletic as the woman was, she still fell about three steps short and they closed before her. She scrabbled for purchase and tried to reach the pinnacle, but to no avail. Slowly and cruelly, she began to slide down.

"To me!" the barbarian roared, grasped his sword with both hands, and managed to haul himself up. He used his boots to take some of the pressure off his already sore hands.

She slowed her descent somewhat when she managed to grasp the tiny cracks that were still present in the marble here and there. They were not enough to gain real purchase and she still fell at a dangerous speed when he lunged and grasped her by the forearm. She clamped her hand into a death-grip on him as well, and he grunted as her weight was added to his with only one hand holding the sword that kept them in place.

"Don't let me go!" She gasped, held onto him with both hands now, and let the torch slide away. "Please, don't let me go!"

All Skharr could muster in response was a strained groan as he struggled to keep her in his grasp and pull her slowly to where she could reach the rest of his body. She would have to climb the rest of the way herself. Micah scrabbled to reach his legs and clutched them like they were tree trunks as he grasped his sword with both hands again.

The torch slid the rest of the way and he forced himself to look when it illuminated what waited for them at the bottom.

The monster's jaw opened in an eerily silent roar and its

claws reached for them. Like them, it was unable to climb the pyramid, but that did not stop it from trying. It shuffled back into the shadows, made a running leap, and tried to climb with all four legs while its wings flailed at them.

Fortunately, it fell short. This was a meager comfort, however, since they were stuck and hung above the jaws that would easily crush them when their strength finally failed them.

Micah managed to climb up and although she still held onto him around the shoulders, she spread the weight by resting her boots on the smooth surface as well.

She heaved a ragged breath. "I saw something…something up there. A rune of entry. If I can get there to touch it, the steps will open for us to climb up again."

"Fat…lot of godsbedammed pig-poking good…it'll do for us up there!" Skharr shifted his hold when he felt the sweat and soreness make his grip less firm than he wanted it to be.

"I can get up there, but I'll need to use your dagger for the climb."

He sucked in a deep breath and nodded. "You can reach it—oy! If it's a dragon you're after, try that fucking ugly hell-spawned undead monster down below."

"Sorry," she whispered. "It's…uh…right there."

"Take the damn dagger!"

Barbarians were renowned for their endurance, but he knew better than to think he would last forever.

Micah drew the dagger after a few attempts and she continued to clamber over him, reached the sword, and managed to balance on the flat of the blade. It was a testimony to how it was crafted that all he could feel was the gentlest bow under the weight of two people. She vaulted up and Skharr focused on her while he hoped he would not need to catch her if she fell again but prepared himself to do so if he had to.

Instead, the dagger sank into the marble and created a crack in the surface. She pulled herself up smoothly like she curled against the structure and launched herself up again. Her progress was slow, limited to only a few feet at a time, but she managed to plant the dagger almost effortlessly each time. She showed every sign of being an incredible acrobat.

All the barbarian could do was wait and he grimaced when every muscle in his body protested. No matter what he tried, nothing he could do felt like it would take the pressure from his hands and his strength had begun to wane.

His companion's slow climb felt like an exercise in futility, simply because it seemed to take far too long. It was difficult work since she had to climb and ensure that she didn't push herself away from the pyramid. She knew what she was doing, which brought some reassurance. He had to trust her on that, although if she was wrong, there was no way for him to follow her.

Then again, he had spent most of his childhood finding the oddest and most difficult of places to climb. Perhaps this was the time and the place to make use of those skills, although it would have to be something a little slower and more methodical than what she attempted.

For the moment, however, he would have to trust her with his life while he tried to find a way to make himself a little more comfortable in his position.

It felt like hours but it must have only been minutes before she pushed herself to the top and disappeared from view for a moment, leaving him alone in the murky darkness. Skharr drew a deep breath and calmed himself until he heard something hiss and move inside the pyramid again. With soft thuds, the light from the pinnacle revealed that the steps had begun to appear again in slow sequence from the top—impossibly slowly, he thought desperately.

Honestly, they could not have moved slower if they tried. He knew they would be faster once they were past him and he still had to race to the top so they could move through the portal before the dragon had the opportunity to climb.

The steps released his sword and Skharr managed to prevent himself from plummeting when he drew the blade out. He surged into motion and again took the steps two at a time. The ache in his body would have to wait until he was as far away from the bone dragon as he could be.

Curiously, his companion displayed a surprising lack of fear over what he assumed would be coming behind him.

He stopped once he reached the top and looked back. There was no sign of the monster at the base of the pyramid, even though the torch still burned.

"Where is it?" He shook his head incredulously.

Micah shook her head. "When I touched the rune here, it disappeared. I think it was supposed to be sent away once the trial is finished."

The barbarian squinted at the base of the pyramid, unable to convince himself that the bone dragon was all they had to fear. He couldn't find it in himself to trust anything as they approached the portal. It seemed like the whole structure would snap and attack them if they so much as looked at it the wrong way. They stepped through the gateway and all the familiar, uncomfortable feelings caught them, drew them both within, and transported them to the other side. He grimaced, still aching and in pain as they dropped into what appeared to be the tunnel they had started from.

A brief look confirmed that it was not the same tunnel they entered through. No traps waited for them and the pathway leading them out was very visible.

"That was…an adventure," Micah whispered as they stepped into the cool evening air and the same thicket they had traveled from. "Are all your adventures this…"

"What?"

"Well, we survived by the skins of our teeth. And as I

remember from what Sera told me of your battles with her, it was very much the same. The tales tend to portray you as something of a demigod, never in much danger."

"And let them all continue to think that." Skharr winked as they approached where the crowd was still gathered, waiting for them to return.

She couldn't resist pressing him a little. "Why do you want people to continue to think of you as practically immortal?"

"There is no real benefit when dealing with dungeons, monsters, and the like, but when regular folk stand against me, their minds go to the stories without thinking of what the reality might be. I've found there is a benefit to ensuring that they think the battle is already decided, and it might even prove to save a few lives for those who choose to not stand against me."

"Of course, it might lead to those warriors who wish to prove themselves trying to find you—those who want to make a name for themselves by standing against you."

"True." He sounded utterly unmoved.

"One might say this is precisely what is happening right now."

He turned to look at her, his eyes narrowed. "I have a feeling this is not a mere theory that has come to your mind in this moment."

She drew a deep breath and nodded. "Correct. I will refrain from saying anything until my knowledge is more certain, but suffice it to say that I'll not cease to work to save your life."

"So continuing your work from today." He seemed to have reached a place where he was more comfortable with her involvement.

"We saved each other today, I think. And I would ask that you...take care of my sister."

"I'll always help Sera when and where she might need it." The way he said it left her in no doubt that he meant every word.

Micah chuckled. They were in view of the crowd and a cheer went up from those assembled. Skharr recognized the song that broke out among them. It was the one written about when he and Cassandra had battled the elder god.

"Rocks for brains," his companion whispered as the guards immediately surged forward to create a small gap for them to use to begin their walk to the palace.

Neither of them paid attention to the crowd, and the barbarian consciously tried to avoid eye contact with the people. It was enough that they were the center of everyone's focus, something he could do nothing about. Neither noted the shifting hooded figure who watched them with narrowed eyes as they were escorted to the palace.

The figure did not join the cheering crowd that followed them but instead, faded into the night and used the throng to conceal their presence.

CHAPTER FIFTEEN

Watching the old woman work was like something out of the oddest children's stories. Everything about her—from how she needed help to climb steps to how she sank slowly into her seat—said they would have to wait for her for hours.

The moment she donned her pince-nez and collected her pens, however, little in the world could stop her. Tryam watched her work through the papers that had been collected about the Seven Trials with something a little like fascination, and he could tell that Elric felt the same way.

Few people in the palace were honest about anything with him, but the archivist was one of them. Perhaps it was because she was so old and so vital—and she knew precisely how vital she was—that she cared little about causing offense.

He always assumed that she knew her time among the living was limited and wasting time appeasing a youth less than a fifth her age was not a necessary endeavor. Despite this, she did abide by all the proper traditions required from any who worked and lived in the palace.

"Between you and I, she will probably outlive both of us," the lord commander whispered.

"Don't bother to whisper, boy," the archivist stated. "I can hear you perfectly well no matter what you have to say about me."

"I was only saying—"

"I heard you."

"Right." Elric cleared his throat. "The barbarian appears to be doing rather well with his trials. Most who undertake them do not survive even the first, and he is now two in. Aside from a few scrapes and bruises, he appears to be ready for the third."

"Janus' test," Tryam interjected and scowled at the wall for a moment. "As I recall, Skharr had a few choice words to say about the lord high god and I have a feeling he will find ways to make it more difficult than it needs to be."

"The tests are meant to be a reflection of how just the gods are between themselves," the archivist added. "According to legend, at least. If Janus were to interfere with the results of the test, his commitment to a just result would be questioned. He would lose face among the other gods. Skharr would have to be guilty of a great deal of disrespect for him to attempt to assassinate him in such a manner."

A sharp crack ended the discussion and Tryam turned, his hand on his blade. Elric moved faster, his sword already drawn as he stepped in front of the emperor to stand against anything that appeared between himself and the tear in the air that had opened behind them.

"Oh, now that is interesting," the archivist muttered and finally saw something that caught her attention more than the papers brought for her to examine. "I've never seen a god appear in person for this. It will be the most fun I've had in decades."

The tear vanished and in its place stood a group that seemed to fill the room with their presence. An older man stood at the front, cleared his throat, and looked around like he was not sure he had come to the right place. Next to him was a group of six who could only be described as barbarians with their massive frames, weapons, long hair, and thick beards. All of them seemed as though they were ready for war.

The eighth member of the group, however, caught Tryam's eye, and it was not only because she was dressed in what appeared to be undergarments made from chain mail. As armor went, it was better than being completely naked, but barely.

Elric still grasped his weapon and showed no sign that he would surrender. He seemed more than willing to fight all eight as long as it allowed the emperor time to escape. The archivist stood, however, wandered to the group, and stopped in front of the old man in particular.

"Lord High God Theros, you honor us with your presence," she whispered and bowed as well as her arthritic back would allow.

"Theros?" Elric asked her and his expression made it plain that he did not quite believe what she was saying.

The old woman flashed him a look of scorn. "Have you read the old words? How the lord high god travels the world in this very form? There is no donkey at his side, but I assume it could be brought out if he desired to make himself a little more recognizable to the rest of us."

"My...my apologies." The lord commander sheathed his weapon slowly and lowered his head in respect as well.

Theros smiled and gestured for both him and the archivist to raise their heads.

Tryam, however, remained upright and watched the woman carefully. "And who are you?"

"I am Cassandra," she answered and stepped forward with none of the respect that was generally offered to an emperor. "I am the Barbarian Princess."

A few soft chuckles issued from the barbarians present and the emperor understood that a hidden meaning to what she had said was a matter of some amusement to the group. Barbarians were known to have an odd sense of humor and he chose not to force himself in on the joke when it was not necessary.

"I have heard of you," he admitted and raised an eyebrow. "The Barbarian Princess has begun to make something of a name for herself these days."

The barbarians' laughter ceased and they turned to him as if they wondered how someone like her could have attracted the attention of an emperor.

Cassandra smirked at the group before she focused on the young ruler. "I am also known as Cassandra, Paladin of Theros."

Her gentle nod of respect to the old man was interesting. Tryam decided there was no point in pushing his luck with the god and he bowed in respect before him.

"Rise, my boy." The old man sounding a little amused. "I am getting used to the barbarians and in small groups, the bowing can be annoying."

The Barbarian Princess' expression seemed a little confused, almost like she did not recognize who he was.

Theros noticed. "What?"

She shrugged. "I guess the unruly barbarian has a way to change even the gods."

"Humph." The lord high god grunted softly. "He grows on you like mold."

That made her grin and dimples appeared on her cheeks. "I am sorry I ever doubted you."

"I did give you cause to doubt," he admitted. "But I think we should continue this conversation another time. The emperor is a busy man, after all."

"Of course." She turned to one of the larger barbarians and the only one whose beard and hair showed a trace of gray, which indicated that he was the oldest and the most experienced of the group. He produced a bundle and handed it to her. "Thank you."

She removed the leather wrapping carefully to reveal what

must surely be the most exquisite ax Tryam had ever seen. As bearded axes went, it was a little smaller than most he was familiar with, although the haft was still tall enough that he could use it as a walking stick if he so chose.

The blade was painstakingly engraved with intricate markings of gold and silver plated into the steel, which told of the dwarf handiwork that had gone into its forging, and the blade's bit measured about ten inches from tip to tip. A smooth curl at the bottom of the haft would make it easier to swing with full force behind it.

There was only one pair of hands he could imagine swinging the weapon into the faces of others across the continent. As impressive as it was, it was still a fine weapon forged with the intention to draw blood and break bones. Nothing was even remotely ceremonial about it.

"I believe you need a warrior for Skharr's next trial," she said and held the weapon toward him.

Tryam could see that Elric was not comfortable with anyone handling weapons as close as they were to him. The man was already angry about so many people appearing from nowhere, fully armed and ready for battle. More guards were likely already on the way, but he was more than capable of holding his own if it came down it. Still, he doubted it would be necessary.

"Ah." He grunted with a small smile and patted his lord commander reassuringly on the shoulder. "How did you know?"

She cocked her head in the direction of the god beside her. "I don't suppose we need to do the introductions again, do we?"

"Well, most of your party have not been introduced but yes, I can see how that might prove useful for folk in our particular situation."

The barbarians—who he assumed were DeathEaters given how similar they were to Skharr—shared a round of chuckles again. It seemed this would prove to be the story of a lifetime for most of them, and they were more than happy to play their part in it. He knew for a fact that most of the clans did not offer the gods much in the way of reverence, and DeathEaters even less than most. They preferred to leave magic and those who relied on it out of their lives as much as they could, but they did not dabble in politics either. The entire situation was unusual in that they had been approached by a paladin and appeared to follow her without resistance.

In addition, even more remarkably, they had traveled through a portal created by a god and journeyed with the god, who brought them to the emperor's palace.

"Skharr can only have one with him," Tryam told them and raised an eyebrow.

"That'll be me, then," she asserted with the confidence of someone who knew she could talk through any protests her friend might raise over it. "The DeathEaters are here to ensure that the Ax of Skharr DeathEater is protected while it is out of the hands of the Clan."

The emperor nodded. "I see. Skharr might have mentioned that he was having the weapon made, but he did not tell me he would send it away for another to use. He spent a king's ransom on the making of that. Not an emperor's ransom but that of a lesser king, perhaps. A ruler of two or three cities, at least. Might I hold it?"

She looked at the older barbarian, who nodded after a moment's thought. With a smile, she turned the weapon and handed it to him haft first.

The wood was worked with the same markings—those sacred to the dwarves as he had been told. Reputedly, the runes were intended to protect the weapons from harm and some said it would also help anyone who carried them to have a keener mind and body to wield them. A handful of the mages in the palace had told him there was no such thing, however.

Most human smiths liked to cover their runes and instead, added an impressive sheen to the metal to please those who paid them, but dwarves said it compromised the quality. They left all their runes on display, even those on the haft. These had been worked in silver. The knob was shod in steel as well, and a spike opposite the blade made it a little more useful against heavily armored opponents and evened the weight to make it more balanced.

It was a little heavier than he thought it would be, but so was the first sword placed in his hands. A little work and getting used to it would make the weight of the weapon more comfortable, and in the hands of a warrior like Skharr or the other DeathE-aters, it would be handled easily enough and add to the power they already possessed. Hell, Skharr could probably swing the weapon one-handed while he carried a shield or a sword in the other.

The balance was magnificent and it fitted his hands perfectly. It was strong, powerful, and without a doubt the finest weapon he had ever laid hands on. He felt a little jealous that Skharr would be able to wield it.

"It's a fine weapon," Tryam said and tried to maintain appearances. He was unable to help a hint of disappointment as he handed it to Cassandra. "I assume that none should see that a lord high god made an appearance in the palace. There would be questions—the kind I think none of you would like to answer. It would be best to keep your presence here a secret—or at least as secret as your presence can be."

"We wouldn't want to reveal the surprise," Cassandra answered with a smirk.

"I must ask," the archivist interrupted and stepped forward, her eyes narrowed. "High Lord God Theros, would you not want to speak to your brother on this matter?"

"That will not be necessary. As it happens, my sister Ahverna has already spoken to him and he has given his word that he will not interfere in this process."

"Interesting," the old woman muttered. "Not many know this, but Janus is incapable of going back on his word once given."

"Indeed. And…who exactly might you be, my dear?"

She looked down and Tryam could have sworn that she blushed under the attention of the deity.

"Apologies, Lord High God. I am the Lady Morana Wysell, Chief Imperial Archivist and Keeper of Records, at your eternal service."

"Is that so?" Theros smiled and touched her shoulder gently before he took her hand and raised it to his lips. "I am honored to meet you, my lady."

Morana was flustered and muttered something as she tried to avoid the gazes of all those present. It was the first time he had seen the woman at a loss for words and in all honesty, he was not surprised. He knew he would feel similarly if he were to meet with a god or goddess who addressed him in such a manner so it was no doubt for the best that none had so far.

Maybe he did have ulterior motives, given that Morana had a mind like a steel trap and was likely one of the most knowledge-able people in the empire as it stood now. Or perhaps he had an interest in women of experience and wisdom—although what that interest was remained to be seen.

A full day and a night of rest worked wonders and with the help of a few healing potions, he was well on the way to full recovery from the ordeals he had endured in the second test. The fact that he had not seen or heard any sign of Micah from the moment he was escorted to his cell told him that she required time for rest and recovery herself.

Skharr couldn't blame her for it, but her part in this was done.

As he woke with his hands, arms, and shoulders still aching from what they had been put through the day before, Skharr wondered if it wouldn't have been easier to simply fight the guards and ride out of the city before anyone knew he was wanted for murder. He could find a way to work for himself beyond the empire. It wasn't like it was the first time he had been forced to start his life over.

"It appears they have not found someone ready to stand beside me for this trial," he muttered as he gathered his weapons and supplies again and rolled his shoulders.

The last time he'd felt this battered was during his last siege when he'd climbed the walls to fight ladders and towers as they rolled in. It had been a battle with little to no rest and only grew worse when fewer soldiers were left to man the walls.

Hopefully, in this case, it would be over once the trials were finished and he could take some time to rest before he headed off again. He was not very welcome in the Imperial City, given that his first arrival there since the emperor's coronation was met with an elaborate attempt on his life.

The guards waited for him outside his cell and lowered their heads as he approached. He could only assume it was a sign of respect, and they fell into formation behind him as they wound out of the tower he was housed in and descended to where he could already hear a small crowd that had assembled to see him off. He hoped it would not be something he was met with every time. It was a little distracting, and if those who wanted to ensure that he was killed by their attempt to entangle him in imperial politics were watching, the crowd would allow them to follow his movements without being discovered.

"I guess I will not be burdened with help this time around," Skharr commented to the guards behind him. "I've been preparing to battle Janus my whole life, so I suppose it makes good sense that I should be able to fight in his trial on my own."

"As you say, sir." He wasn't sure which of the men had replied.

And sir? He didn't like the sound of that. Even worse, it sounded like the guards were hiding something from him. While he generally didn't care what folk thought of him or why they thought they needed to conceal anything from him, in this case, he had to stand against those who intended to see him dead. Folk hiding something from him generally meant a good chance of a dagger in his back.

His escort guided him to where the people were assembled at the gate. More guards had been posted there to ensure that no one could push through, although his protection was not the reason for their presence.

The barbarian scowled when he realized that Elric and Tryam awaited him.

A loud roar arose from the group assembled, which made it impossible to hear anything they had to say about their presence until it abated somewhat.

"I know you will not join me, Elric," Skharr stated as he approached them. "You'd never leave your charge's sight, not for me. And I also know you would not have allowed the emperor to take the task on himself."

"Allowed me?" Tryam asked and narrowed his eyes. "I am the emperor. He could not stop me if he tried."

"We both know he could have. He would have reminded you of how your duty is to your people, no matter whose life you might have a mind to save. As emperor, it is your duty to send others to do this type of work."

Elric chuckled. "I hate to say it but the barbarian knows me better than I thought."

"Either way, you are right," Tryam conceded and adjusted his sleeves. "But I could not accept having to learn of your reaction from second-hand accounts. Now, Cassandra, if you would join us?"

Skharr wasn't sure if he'd heard right, but he turned to where he could hear boots approach them from behind.

He knew he should not have been surprised that the former paladin made an appearance, although he wasn't sure which of her personas he would see. He had heard tales of the Barbarian Princess out east and no one else could wear armor like she did.

Although the chain mail undergarments were gone, it was still easy to identify her in the full plate armor she'd worn when she was still a paladin. It gleamed brilliantly in the morning sunlight as she walked forward, her helm tucked under her arm.

She was not alone, he realized a moment later and studied the six men who followed her. From their build, armor, and overall rough appearance, he could tell they were barbarians immediately. That aside, he recognized some faces that he had not seen in years.

He had a great many questions about why Turan stood there with Cassandra, although the first one that came to mind was why he wore the thick silver medallion that denoted him as chieftain of the Clan.

"I haven't come alone," she told him as she stopped in front of him. "I thought you could benefit from seeing some of your kin as well."

"Skharr." Turan greeted him roughly as he stepped closer. "How long has it been?"

"Since the battle of Bashur, when you left and returned to the Clan without so much as a word," he answered. "And I see you've made good of it."

"And you've made good of remaining far away." The warrior paused and extended his hand.

He studied the man for a moment. They matched each other in height, build, and looks well enough that they might have been brothers. Turan was a little older than he was, and he had been there to show him the way through the world. His disappearance when he'd needed him was still a sore point, although it appeared it was not the same for Turan.

Still, a long time had passed and he accepted the greeting and grasped the DeathEater chieftain by the forearm.

Turan grinned. "You sent us a mighty gift but we judge that the Ax of Skharr DeathEater must be bloodied by the only man worthy to do so—he who sent it. We are here as the guard of the ax during its travels between the Clan and yourself, brother. Besides, the Barbarian Princess made a sound case for us to accompany her on her travels."

"She tends to do that," Skharr answered and shifted his gaze to the weapon in question, which he assumed was what they had hidden in the thick leather pouch engraved with dwarven markings.

The chieftain turned, withdrew the weapon from the leather wrappings, and hefted it smoothly before handing it to him.

It had hurt him to send the weapon to the Clan but it had been owed. Still, when he saw it now and how it glinted in the sunlight as it was handed to him, his heart twinged possessively. The feeling intensified when he held it in his hands and felt the perfect weight and balance to it, and he knew this was what it felt like to fall in love.

Perhaps it was a bad thing for him to feel this way about a weapon, but he was long past feeling any shame over his love of weapons.

The barbarians chuckled when they saw his expression, having likely felt the same way when they saw the ax.

"May you find someone who looks at you the way he looks at his ax," Turan said to his warriors as he grinned and patted Skharr on the shoulder.

He finally managed to tear his gaze away from the weapon and looked at Cassandra, who laughed with the other barbarians. The people outside had begun to grow a little restless as they could not hear what was being done or said. He wasn't sure why they were interested in what he was doing since he was under-taking the trials instead of being executed. Perhaps there was some kind of context. Bards might have been singing about it and folk wanted to see it for themselves.

Or perhaps folk in the Imperial City merely lacked anything else to do with their lives. It was the talk in the extremities of the empire that those closer to the center lived off what was being drawn from everyone else. He had seen no evidence of that himself but it would explain why so many people studied his comings and goings instead of working for themselves.

He turned to Turan and took the man's extended hand again. "I did not think the DeathEaters would come to my aid. I thought that once the ax was delivered, the Clan would no longer want anything to do with me."

"All of us have had doubts about the Clan at some point or another during our travels," the chieftain answered. "I have too. But your family will always be there for you if you are in need." The warrior leaned a little closer to speak into his ear. "You have mighty friends across the continent as well. They, more than the ax, tell the truth of who you have become. We are all proud to be DeathEaters, Skharr, and you make the Clan's name leave all others in the dirt and dust."

"I believe I should explain that statement."

Skharr turned as another made his presence known. It appeared that Cassandra had traveled with a fucking retinue, but this member appeared to have waited for a particular time to make an appearance. It meant it could be only one person, even if the voice was a little unfamiliar given how he'd heard it before.

Theros looked like the warrior he never wanted anyone to see unless he made a point of the display. It seemed to be precisely what the god had in mind. He stood over ten feet tall in full plate armor that looked suspiciously similar to Cassandra's with a spear in his hand.

"You do like to make an entrance," Skharr commented. "I suppose she roped you into helping me as well."

"It would be poor form to see you be blessed with the help of those who respect you and not count myself among them," Theros answered and his voice boomed loudly enough that those present realized who they were watching and immediately dropped to their knees in reverence.

"I know you'll not face these trials at my side," he replied with a small smirk.

"No, but Throk did suggest that a blessing be placed on the blade and you did not wish to bother me with it." He took the weapon from his hands. "I would be a poor god to not bless the Ax of the Barbarian of Theros."

"True enough." Perhaps it was the presence of the other DeathEaters, but he was a little less polite to the god than he usually was, although it was not saying a great deal as such.

The weapon flashed in Theros' hands and gleamed like his armor did for a moment. When he handed it back, a rune on the woodwork shined gold and displayed the mark of Theros.

"The wood will never break," the god declared loudly for all to hear, "the steel will never need to be sharpened, and in dire need, call for it, Skharr, and it will come."

He took it and inspected the mark. "Thank you..."

His voice trailed off when he looked up again and realized that the god had vanished from where he had stood a second before. The people were still on their knees and whispered among themselves about where he had gone and where he had come from in the first place. He assumed that Theros had appeared as suddenly as he'd disappeared.

"Well," Tryam said and cleared his throat. "He certainly knows how to make an entrance."

"And an exit," Cassandra added.

Skharr narrowed his eyes at the boy. "You certainly do not seem surprised by the appearance of a god."

The emperor winked at him by way of response.

"Come on, barbarian." Cassandra caught his arm and pulled him to the gate as the guards pushed through the assembled group and began to draw away from them. "It's about time we begin."

"I was told you would need some goods in order to be well-supplied." Tryam motioned to the servants who lurked nearby and scrutinized the barbarians. "I'll need a pig slaughtered. On second thought, make that two."

CHAPTER SIXTEEN

They stood in an arena similar to the one in the Imperial City, complete with massive black marble columns to secure the stands in place for thousands to witness whatever entertainment was held on a particular day or week. Skharr had never seen the inside of the arena himself, although he remembered Tryam telling him he had fought there and been a champion in his division for a few years in a row.

Perhaps that was what the future held for him. From what he'd heard, the battle was meant to be bloody but not end in death, and those who fought regularly were rewarded with a great deal of coin and fame. It was a vulgar way to make a living, but he wasn't the type to be fussy about such things.

In this instance, however, the arena was empty. The marble columns gleamed with the midday sunlight, and every step was as clean as they had been when the arena was first erected with no sign of those who usually watched such sports.

"I would have thought that Janus would be here himself," Skharr muttered and studied the ax in his hand again. He almost didn't believe that he would swing the damn thing himself, but it was there in his hand and seemed as eager to shed blood as he was. "Given all the times I insulted him, I thought the godsbe-damned self-righteous lord high god would have some interest, at least, in watching me go through whatever gauntlet he has planned for the occasion."

Cassandra chuckled and drew her sword slowly.

He glanced sharply at her. "What amuses you?"

"Theros told me that Ahverna held a dagger to Janus' throat and made him swear that he would make no attempt to assassinate you during the trial. The dungeon would remain the way it was when others attempted it. Not that there have been many. The archivist said seven hundred and thirty-one men and women have claimed their right to the trials since they were instituted as a legal recourse for those facing execution. Thirty survived to this point. Needless to say, there is no real way to determine what could be waiting for you here, even if Janus made no changes."

The barbarian scowled and shook his head. "Well, I suppose that is good news."

"You don't need to sound so disappointed."

He couldn't help it. It seemed logical and reasonable that his years of insulting Janus would have guaranteed at least some effort from the god to kill him properly.

"Ahverna made him swear?" he asked.

"Yes."

"Ahverna? That was the name?"

She sighed dramatically. "And now you sound surprised. I would have assumed you were the one who entreated her to appeal on your behalf."

"I wouldn't even appeal to Theros, not for my life. For that of others maybe, but not mine."

Cassandra smirked. "Well, as it turned out, it wasn't your appeal that moved her. From what Theros said, it was one of her followers. A dwarf."

"Brahgen? The bold little fuck. Will wonders ever cease?"

"Probably not." She planted her sword in the sand and rested her hand on the pommel. "I will return to the service of Theros full time."

"It would appear you have already."

"What?" She looked startled.

"You're in your full plate. When we last fought together, you were dressed in something a great deal more…eye-catching."

She punched him hard in the shoulder.

He laughed. "Well? Weren't you?"

"Yes, I suppose I was."

"And you seemed to enjoy it too. With that in mind, it would take you asking for his permission to don your paladin's armor again. It's who you are."

"True." She sighed and turned to him. "One last kiss, yes? For luck?"

Skharr smirked and leaned closer to her. "For friendship."

"Fuck you."

"If you insist."

She pushed to her tiptoes and pressed her lips firmly to his, but a roar interrupted them.

"I wasn't…fucking finished!" she yelled, pulled her helm on, and fastened the strap. "I have some anger to unleash."

He nodded, flicked the ax into the air, and caught the haft deftly. "I'll be over here…practicing."

"Yes, you will."

She looked angry, although Skharr wasn't sure why. Still, she was a paladin in her own right and he was always happy to watch her fight. She had a way about her that would ensure that any of those who stood in the way of her sword would pay for it.

A gate on the far side of the arena was dragged open and he immediately recognized a scorpicore. Massive wings like a bat's were covered by a light fuzz of blue fur that extended to the rest of the creature. It had the body of a lion, and although he could see the leonine features in its face, the eyes were of a man.

This was an abomination created from the seed of the manticores of the mountains and the giant scorpions of the deserts. The evidence of the latter was in the thick, sinuous tail that extended from the creature's hindquarters. It swished from side to side the way a lion's would, but the tip held his attention. The appendage twisted into a stinger that carried one of the most lethal venoms known. It was able to kill a younger dragon, or so it was said.

Of course, much was said about scorpicores to increase their legend by the armies that used them as weapons. He could never be sure about the truth in wars like those. All he knew was that most armies would not risk open battle against the creatures. Who would against winged lions that flew on command?

Despite this, Cassandra did not look particularly horrified by the prospect. She advanced on the creature with her sword grasped firmly in both hands.

The beast used a running start and launched skyward in three bounds. It flapped its massive wings to kick a cloud of dust up before it was airborne but remained low as she attacked. The tail twisted and aimed a strike at her through the cloud of dust and sand.

The paladin was no fool and her reaction confirmed that she had fought creatures like it before. She dove and rolled to avoid the creature's claws and talons. Still on one knee, she swept her sword to sever the tip from the creature's tail and immediately continued into a swing to catch it as it flew past.

It screeched in pain, an unbearably human sound, and she missed her strike by inches but still clipped the wings at the base. Blood splashed from the strike and the scorpicore tumbled before it landed on its back. Cassandra reacted immediately and screamed something that sounded suspiciously barbarian as she attacked it. She shrugged its claws off as they struck her helm and breastplate and buried her sword into its neck. Still yelling, she twisted her blade until most of the head came off and she darted back to stare at it and confirm that it was well and truly dead.

"You weren't lying when you said you had some anger to vent," Skharr said with a grin. "Although it would certainly appear that you've fought scorpicores before."

"Never the scorpicores but their distant cousins. Manticores have a habit of taming prides of lions and using them to attack groups of travelers in the east. I've come across a handful of them."

The barbarian nodded and spun his ax in his hand. "Right, then. I think I should have a turn now unless you have more anger to deliver to the unfortunate creatures that fight for Janus."

"That particular well will never run dry. But I'll try to not lash out at you if that's what you're worried about."

"As a matter of fact, it was. Besides, I do need to bloody this weapon of mine. I can't have it said that you had all the fun in this trial while I left such an impressive ax to die of thirst."

She grinned and turned away as another roar signified the arrival of the beasts they had to deal with next. The gate that had released the scorpicore dropped down and another was raised slowly. Skharr could see movement in the shadows behind it and two trolls stumbled forward, tripped over themselves at first, and were blinded by the sunlight before they managed to stand. They nudged and pointed at the two companions opposite them. The creatures were not as foolish as they appeared, and he knew he was something of an expert in determining that.

They were dressed in the armor of their people and one carried a hammer and the other a cutlass. Both were small in comparison to some weapons he'd seen, but they were efficient. Given the thickness of their armor and the skin under it, the creatures were more than capable of rushing under arrows and spears to close the distance and physically crush anything that stood against them.

The barbarian was willing to put their power to the test. They were particularly large trolls, and he grinned as Cassandra stood beside him, her armor still dripping with the blood of the scorpicore.

"Have you ever fought trolls before?" he asked and spun his ax.

"Only a half-troll once." She grimaced at the memory. "He wasn't particularly fast and I was able to climb on his back and used a rope to fell him as he thrashed about. My sword was broken on one of the rocks growing on his skin, but although he fell, I couldn't bring myself to kill him. He was smarter than he looked, even though folk assumed him to be slow and dull. He was well-intentioned, so I let him live. I don't know what became of him afterward."

He pointed to their opponents. "Well, these are not well-intentioned."

The two combatants pushed forward and their stumbling and oafish nature fell away. They were powerful creatures, and when they rushed forward, their footsteps made the ground shake.

"They are like giant godsbedammed bulls," Skharr muttered. "They can gain a good speed but are slow to change direction."

"Fought a lot of bulls then, have you?"

"My fair share." He snorted mirthlessly. "Avoid the horns, strike as they pass, and you should survive."

Cassandra nodded and focused as their adversaries powered forward. The barbarian dove to the right and she to the left with perfect precision and the creatures skidded across the loose sand as they tried to regain the power of their charge. He avoided the strike of the hammer aimed at his skull and swung his ax to strike the creature's arm where there were splits in the armor around the elbow. His intention was to nick the creature and anger it, but the blade cut deeper than he expected.

The barbarian raised his eyebrows when the arm was severed at the elbow. The troll howled in pain, looked around, and grasped the half of an arm he had left and aimed it directly at his attacker as the thick black blood pumped out.

Skharr spluttered and protected his face as the warm blood splashed it. He swung his ax, knowing what would come next as the monster lunged at him. "Come on then, you piss-swilling sack of lard brain."

The ax bit and the weight of his opponent hurled him from his feet. He shoved him off and stood again quickly, the ax still in his hand as he brushed the blood from his face.

It had cut deeper than intended again and this time, the troll's head was almost severed by his strike. Only the thick skin and a few strands of muscle prevented it from coming off completely.

"It looks like Theros did a little more blessing on this than he needed to, eh?" He looked around when Cassandra didn't answer and scowled when she ducked away from the cutlass that the troll slashed at her. She was trying to brawl with the damn thing.

While she held her own well enough, she didn't keep her distance. The troll rushed her, swung his weapon, and caught the side of her helm. It was a glancing blow but she stumbled back.

"No...like a godsbedammed fucking bull. You pull away, let it charge and—" Skharr shook his head and took a moment to ensure that the first troll was dead before he ran forward to help her.

She was already on her feet and lifted her sword to block another attack, then scrambled away from another flurry of strikes.

"Pick on someone your own size, you overgrown maggot-brained fleshbag." He stepped in and swung the ax low at the creature's knee. Troll skin was as tough as boiled leather armor and harder to pierce, but the blade cut cleanly and severed the leg at the knee. The wounded troll stumbled forward and Cassandra was ready. She thrust her sword forward and it pierced the creature's eye and continued through to the other side.

"It looks like Theros—"

"Did a little more blessing on that ax than he needed to," she interrupted before he could repeat himself. "I heard you. I was merely a little too busy to reply."

"Did you see how it cut the godsbedammed creature's leg off?" Skharr hefted the weapon and flicked the blood from it. "I think I'm in love."

"I think you would find fucking that ax a little uncomfortable."

He grinned unashamedly. "It would be worth it. Until I accidentally cut my cock off."

"That would be a tragedy."

The gate dropped again, a sure sign that the trial would continue, with or without their attention. He grasped his weapon a little tighter and stared at the last gate. It was larger than the others and he could only imagine there was a reason for that.

"What do you think will come out of there?" Cassandra asked and wiped her sword.

"Something big," the barbarian answered. "Not a dragon, I don't think, but it will be something interesting. Trolls and Scorpicores are the type we would see Janus fighting with. There will be something new, something interesting to keep him entertained."

"Entertained?" She sounded incredulous.

"I've fought in the bastard's dungeons before. It is all for his entertainment, even this."

The woman didn't look like she approved of that, although there were too many other things for them to worry about as the gate began to open. Unlike the first two, which were portcullises, this one split open to reveal something large and hulking inside.

He narrowed his eyes as it moved in the darkness like it was trying to break free in the other direction before it decided to attack them. It was one way to settle on the battle, he reasoned but held his weapon firmly. Something that tried to escape instead of fight was intelligent, and those were the most dangerous beasts of all.

When it exhaled, flames emerged, almost like its lungs were

exposed to the air and the air itself was hot enough to feed the blaze.

It turned, finally committed to the fight, and he took a step back, his eyes wide as he raised his ax reflexively. From the look on Cassandra's face, she knew what it was as well.

"How the fuck did Janus get a real demon for his dungeon?" she whispered.

"Lesser demon." Correcting her didn't make him feel any better about what they faced.

"More than enough for any mortal to fight."

There were numerous stories of how the gods banished the demons and their spawn to the hellish realms to burn in the fires there for all eternity. The lesser demons were their soldiers, creatures that were known to be sent to level whole cities when they were called upon.

Maybe those stories were a little exaggerated, but Skharr could believe that men might abandon their posts on walls while watching the creature advance on them. Its head was horned and mostly little more than a skull.

It stared at them and fire gleamed out of its eyes and mouth as it panted and approached them while the fire within still burned. Most of the creature was skeletal, a fact easily visible when it stepped through the gate, stood on its hind legs, and sniffed the air before it settled in front of them.

In full light, Skharr could see it for what it was. It almost looked like a centaur but was at least fifteen feet tall. Its hind and middle legs were hooved like a goat's, but a third pair of limbs with hands and fingers like a man's jutted from its back. Behind these, a pair of wings flapped and waved slowly as it advanced and made it difficult to determine if it was capable of flying with those wings, or if they were as useless as the bone dragon's.

"Have you ever fought something like that?" A faint hint of anxiety edged her tone.

He shook his head. "Not in my lifetime. You?"

"I've only ever read about demons."

The barbarian decided not to share that he'd hoped she'd have knowledge to give them an edge. "I suppose this will be educational for both of us."

"Leave it to Janus to ass-fuck someone in the third trial with a demon."

He couldn't have said it better. Still, maybe he needed to try to sound positive. "Well, there's no point in letting the demon think we're scared of it. Let us get to the business of killing the butt-ugly fucking hellspawn."

Skharr flicked his blade and watched the demon catch sight of the weapon. It hissed and roared, although its breath impacted him more powerfully than the sound.

"I don't think it likes anything with a god's mark on it," he said and circled slowly away from the creature while Cassandra did the same in the opposite direction.

"I'll love my armor then," she answered. "Theros!"

"Theros!" Skharr bellowed in response as she sprinted to the other side of the arena.

He had no idea what she planned—if she had anything planned at all—but it was all for the best. The barbarian planted his ax in the sand and dropped to a knee as he drew his bow from his back along with four arrows from his quiver.

Three of those were placed in the sand alongside the ax, and he nocked the fourth, still on one knee. The demon appeared to have been distracted by the armor his companion wore.

Its hands snapped something from the flames that issued from its ribs, and he realized it was pulling weapons from within its body.

One looked like a sword, long and almost ridiculously thin, but he had a feeling it was more than capable of killing them both without an issue.

The other appeared to be a whip and the creature cracked it

and snaked it to where Cassandra was still moving to evade it and hold its focus.

Perhaps Theros knew it was the kind of thing that would get the beast's attention and therefore let them use the weapons as a way to keep the monster at bay and somehow control it. The arena was fairly large, but it would appear smaller when they faced a monster like that.

Skharr drew the arrow back and waited as the beast galloped toward the paladin. It opened its mouth with an eerily silent roar and she pushed the whip away with a tap of her sword and continued to run.

His first arrow flew, and he was already drawing a second without so much as looking to ensure that his first shot had hit. He already knew it would, but he needed the creature's attention drawn to him before it was able to corner her. It was an unsettling thought for anyone, but maybe she had the better armor to deal with it. His gambeson would likely not do so well against the monster attacking them.

The second arrow was already in the air by the time the first buried itself into the back of the creature's skull. He was surprised to see the arrows stick as he'd thought they would bounce off the monster's bones.

The second buried itself in its spine and stopped the demon in its charge. This time, its roar was perfectly audible as one of pain and it turned its attention to him.

"Yes, come on, you godsbedammed overheated bastard offspring of a hell-whore." Skharr drew back with the third arrow but waited until the demon's eyes were focused on him before he loosed it to burrow directly into its eye.

Although the arrow buried itself there, he knew better than to expect any real damage to result and sure enough, it remained in place for a moment before it caught fire and burned almost immediately.

He had its attention now, however. Cassandra used the time

to collect herself and appeared to ready herself for a battle. She pulled her spear from where she had carried it on her back.

It was the same weapon she'd used to kill the dragon and was a damn good spear too.

The barbarian released the last arrow and it thudded into the creature's skull. He would need to make a few new arrows now or he would start to run out. It was unacceptable for a DeathEater to be caught without any arrows for his bow.

"I'll have your puss-stinking demon blood on this ax today!" Skharr bellowed. "Theros!"

He rushed forward at the demon as it galloped toward him. Its wings flapped like it tried to fly but it could trap no air under the skeletal appendages. Perhaps with a little more power and speed, it might succeed. Or magic. He had no idea what kind of magic it might have.

But there was no running away from it. Tactical diversions would only help them for a limited time, and the longer they continued with the fight, the bigger the chance that they would tire. It seemed very likely that they would weaken before the demon as he wasn't sure they tired at all.

The creature launched into a concerted attack and the whip lashed at him first. He flung himself to the sand under the strike so it swept over him, then rolled immediately onto his feet and swung his weapon. The force of the impact juddered up his arm and into his shoulder but the ax shattered the creature's sword in a shower of sparks and hurled the demon back.

Something almost like power surged in Skharr's body as he bounded forward and arced his ax into the creature's legs. It cut directly through the bones but another heated roar made him stumble back.

The whip struck him before he could raise his defenses. "Fuck. By Janus' ripe, stinking, fucking hairy armpit—" His armor was caught in the flames for a moment and he swung his ax blindly. Again a shower of sparks erupted in response. He had nothing to fight fire with and staggered to gain a little distance as his gambeson was suddenly aflame.

He reacted instantly and the ax fell from his hand as he yanked the armor off as quickly as he could before it began to burn through to the flesh beneath. The fire burned hot, although he managed to avoid the worst of it with his hands. Unfortunately, the shirt had to go as well, which left him with nothing but skin from the waist up, a poor defense against the creature they faced.

It reminded him of Cassandra and how she often fought her battles wearing considerably less. Skharr turned to determine why the demon had made no attempt to attack him yet. The paladin uttered a loud cry as she drove her spear deep into the monster's chest from the side. It gave another roar as it whipped and tried to attack her as well.

As good a chance as they would ever have had presented itself, and the barbarian was determined to not waste it. He swept his ax up from the ground. The creature's focus was divided and for the moment, there was no way to know if it could pull more weapons out of its body should they allow it a moment to rest.

Skharr vaguely registered his primal scream when he swung the ax into the demon's spine below the neck as it prepared to attack Cassandra. Another roar issued from the beast but he pressed his assault despite the intensity of the heat on his knuckles. He drew back and hacked again. His companion did the same, and it appeared as though her spear inflicted as much damage on the creature as his ax did.

With one more strike, the head fell away, but the body continued to move and attack and it flung the paladin back, although her armor appeared none the worse for wear.

"Destroy the head!" she shouted as she scrambled to her feet. "Destroy it and the demon will be banished to where it came from."

Killing it would have been a preferable option, but he seemed to recall something about how the creatures could only be killed if it were done in the realm they called home. He was not sure he was willing to go to those lengths to kill the bastard. It didn't seem right in the end.

Still, he turned, his ax already brandished as he focused on the head. It snapped its jaws at him, roared, and burned with the same intense heat. He drove the ax into it repeatedly and continued the assault as it cracked and broke until there was little left but shattered pieces.

She had been right about the head. Once the fire in the skull had gone out, the rest of the body appeared to follow suit and sagged like all the magic was slowly escaping from it.

"So...they taught you how to beat the bastards in some paladin scroll, yes?"

"It is a part of any paladin's training regimen." Cassandra approached him and lowered to her haunches to study the skull closely. "But such a vague mention that I'd forgotten it. Demons have been banished from our realm and by all appearances, they don't like being here. I think everyone believes there is no point in teaching about them. This magic is...unsettling. Even being close to it makes me feel sick."

Skharr touched her shoulder. "We should leave this place before that happens, then."

"Yes...we should." She nodded to the gate where the demon had come through and he realized that it had already turned into a portal for them to use. "But first..."

She stood and rested both hands on his chest. He looked at the burns across his skin from where the whip had caught him. The pain hadn't even caught his attention, but as she started to heal the wounds, sensation returned and he gritted his teeth while she finished her work.

Once she was done, the burns were gone but the skin was still reddened.

"You look like a real barbarian now," she noted as they walked to the portal.

He grinned, unable to help himself. "Not quite. I'll need to find myself a set of mail undergarments first."

"Wouldn't that be a sight?"

Time seemed to have passed more quickly than it did in the trial and when they stepped out again, the sun had begun to set. He didn't think it had been more than an hour since they had stepped into the trial, yet several had passed in the palace.

Tryam, Elric, and the others were already waiting there for them, although Skharr could see that a small feast had been arranged for the group.

True to form, the barbarians ensured that there wasn't much food or wine left by the time they stepped into the palace grounds again.

"Here are the conquering heroes." Turan raised his glass. "In case you were wondering, we have decided to remain here for a while in honor of our fellow DeathEater."

"That, and your emperor feeds us well enough to justify it," another of the barbarians commented and drained his glass.

Skharr chuckled and shook his head. "I should have known. Then again, there's no point in turning down offers of accommodations, eh?"

"That is the true barbarian way," the chieftain pointed out. "What…in the hells happened to your gambeson?"

"The hells happened, oddly enough," he answered cryptically. "Now, assuming you have not devoured the whole of Tryam's larder, I find myself in need of a good meal. And a drink."

The barbarians cheered, although none noticed a hooded figure watching them again from the crowds. A second figure, one smaller like a child, also followed their movements as the party moved to the palace.

Neither of the two watchers noticed a third following at a safe distance, their gaze trained on the smaller of the two. It had been too long a day for all of them.

CHAPTER SEVENTEEN

His skin was still sensitive where the burns had already healed. Skharr groaned softly as he pulled on the gambeson that had been arranged for him but felt like he wore a bramble full of thorns for armor.

During his day of rest, he had seriously considered whether he should simply charge into battle bare-chested. It seemed the barbarian thing to do but he had no amulet to protect him like armor if he needed it. If something struck him in the chest, he would be wounded and possibly killed.

Instead, he'd needed to find armor that would fit him. Tryam helped, of course, and the armorers in the palace were only too agreeable to assist and had arranged a gambeson better than the one that he'd worn before.

"I would have arranged proper armor for you," the emperor told him as they walked clear of the palace. A handful of secret exits allowed them to slip past the throngs, who would not be able to determine if they were still there in the first place. The barbarian was a little annoyed that these secret passages had not been used before.

"Proper armor?"

"Aye, proper. Something in mail or even plate, if we'd had the time. But you are too fucking large so it would take weeks for anything decent to be properly fitted to someone of your size. A gambeson will have to do in this case."

He nodded and studied the markings that adorned the pillars on the side of the road. They were faded and difficult to read, but from the way certain figures raised their weapons, they appeared to depict an ancient battle he assumed would come into play during the trial he would take that day.

"I suppose there weren't many who volunteered to help on this particular trial," he muttered and looked around as they approached what appeared to be the entrance to a cavern. He could already make out the tell-tale signs of a portal waiting for them as the sun reached its peak.

"None we could find at least." Tryam's tone and expression betrayed something he did not want to make clear immediately. "Best of luck, Skharr. I know you'll make it through this one as well, although you would be the first to do it."

"There's always a first time for everything." The barbarian lowered his pack to check that he had everything he would need for the situation. His bow, sword, dagger, and ax were all he carried, although he wondered if he should find himself some kind of shield. It would likely mean he would have to put one of the weapons aside to make up for the weight—if he had to carry it all around himself, at least.

"Shame on you."

Skharr looked up sharply, his ax in hand and ready to strike. At some point, he might come to expect that Ahverna would be the one who snuck up on him at all times. When his guard was sufficiently compromised by this expectation, a real assassin would attack before he could regain his wits.

For the moment, however, there was no mistaking the leathers she wore or her icy blue eyes.

"Shame on me?" he asked and lowered his weapon.

Despite her stern expression, he sensed her amusement."Yes, shame on you for thinking that no one would be here to follow you into this next trial. It's like you have not paid attention to the impact you've made on the continent at all."

"I've fought on my own for a good many years now," he pointed out. "With…a few exceptions. There is no point in changing that now, don't you think?"

Her smile held a suggestion of mischief. "You would be surprised."

Skharr narrowed his eyes as his ears discerned the barest hint of someone moving closer behind him. He twisted and thrust his hand low to where he knew the collar of the dwarf's shirt would be. With a deft movement, he grasped it tightly and twisted to lift Brahgen enough for him to be unable to try to move away before he turned to study him.

He was small, even by dwarven standards. Not in height, of course, but he lacked the stocky, powerful frame of most of his kin. The barbarian had sometimes wondered if that meant there was a little halfling blood in him, but there was no real point in speculation at this point.

With the thick brown hair and beard he was growing, there was no question that he was mostly dwarf, even if there was a little something else stirred in by previous generations.

"It's nice to see you again, little one," he told his young friend. "I would appreciate it if you could return my purse to me whenever is convenient. When…did you take it?"

"When the emperor talked about your armor, you were distracted." The dwarf was cheerfully unconcerned in the large barbarian's grasp. "Frankly, you tend to not pay attention to what's happening around you when you speak to someone else. You might want to look into it."

Brahgen looked a little too smug as he handed him his coin purse, although maybe he was entitled to it. Or maybe Skharr's ego smarted a little too much from allowing the dwarf to rob him blind.

The discomfort was thrust aside when he realized that his friend looked like he was ready for battle. He held his dagger in hand and wore leathers that allowed him to move silently and provided some protection, most likely.

"It is good to see you again, Skharr."

"Likewise." He took the young dwarf's outstretched hand and grasped it firmly. "I see you and Ahverna have been working together."

"Aye, she ensured that I arrived here in time for this trial."

At the dwarf's statement, he frowned and tried to decide what the significance was. "This one in particular?"

"This is the trial of Silvania," Ahverna explained. "And it requires the deft hands of a real thief. You might be a powerful enough beast when it comes to certain kinds of robbery, but this one might prove to be more than you can handle alone. I thought the deft hands of my priest would be the best choice for the job."

"It's because she can no longer interfere directly," Brahgen explained and looked more than a little gleeful over the fact.

"Yes, quite." The goddess, on the other hand, seemed less pleased with the situation than her priest was. "Which means it is appropriate that your friend join you—with my blessings."

The last part made him raise an eyebrow, but she was already disappearing into thin air and appeared to gather the shadows around herself to do so.

"Come on, then, we have work to do." Brahgen motioned for the barbarian to join him and they approached the cavern entrance. "How did you find yourself in this mess?"

His snort captured his frustration and disdain. "Give me a dungeon any day of the year. Politics is far too dangerous for me."

"Ah. I see."

"The way I remember it, Ahverna preferred to do her own work," Skharr commented as they stepped through the portal.

The world twisted around them and altered everything for a moment.

When they emerged, they were in another cave, although this one did not look like it was constructed by dwarves. His cursory inspection suggested that it had been built at least a few hundred years earlier and it was still functional. A line on the wall indicated a small trench that followed the right side of the wall.

He retrieved steel and flint from his pouch and flicked a few sparks into the trench. It immediately illuminated the whole of the tunnel, both ahead of them and behind.

"How does it still work?" Brahgen asked and shook his head.

"Magic is a likely reason. If I had to guess, this would be some type of vault where someone very rich and very powerful could store something very precious to them. It is interesting that a thief would be the best candidate, don't you think?" Skharr asked and raised an eyebrow.

"I would assume that of all the people on the continent who know what these trials entail, Ahverna would be the most knowledgeable." The dwarf looked around the tunnel. "What do you think they have here?"

The barbarian studied his companion for a moment. "You don't believe me to be this stupid, do you?"

"What?"

He fixed the dwarf with a stern look. "A thief was sent in to steal something. She told you about something that must be taken from this dungeon. You need not tell me, but you should remember the priority of this trial is survival, after all."

"Now why would you need to remind me of that?" His companion sounded offended.

"A thief like you—"

"Will always put the life of his friend first like you did for me. But you are right. There is something in this place that Ahverna would like me to find and take if at all possible. Your life, however, will always take precedence."

"Your life too," Skharr reminded him. "Do not think of me as some greedy bastard who only thinks about what benefits me. I would not have approved of any joining me on these tasks—those who might die so I can live."

"I heard you were being a right hypocrite about all this."

He smirked and placed a hand on Brahgen's shoulder as they approached what appeared to be something blocking their path.

"All I am saying is that I would like the opportunity to look out for your life as you do mine."

His friend grinned at him. "Well, it looks like we will be looking out for each other again."

The barbarian decided it was time to change the subject. "How is that girl you had your eye on?"

"Quite well. We are engaged to be married before the month is out. It should have been this week, but I arranged with her to delay it until later. Given that you were instrumental in our betrothal, she understood and wished me well."

Skharr smiled. "I am happy for you, Brahgen."

"Yes, well, there is the matter of coming away from here alive. I suppose you have something to do with that."

The barbarian approached the barrier ahead of them and tilted his head as he studied the ground to ensure that no traps were waiting for them.

There was a moat beneath, and the light revealed only murky water that he had no intention to trust. He could see only one way across at this point—a narrow drawbridge that could only be let down from someone on the other side. The tunnel was too narrow for him to try to find an angle to shoot an arrow at a weak point to try to lower it.

Thankfully, it was made of wood and he thought of one way for them to get past, but he did need the dwarf to trust him.

"You're thinking about firing an arrow with a rope attached to it so that I can climb across, yes?" His companion sounded unperturbed at the notion.

He looked at Brahgen and grinned. "Unless you have any better ideas."

"How do we secure it on this end?"

"I'll hold it." He thought it was a perfectly practical solution given their sizes.

Brahgen shook his head. "And you'll pull the rope to secure it, thus weakening the arrow's hold on the wood across the line."

The dwarf made a good enough point and Skharr knew when to concede. "I don't suppose you have a grappling hook on you?"

"I thought you would never ask."

Again, his companion looked smug as he drew a grapple from his belt. The three hooks would ensure that it would have a chance to dig in even if the throw was not quite good enough. It appeared that he had wrapped the prongs with leather to ensure that it would not make any noise once it did catch on something.

"The only issue I find is that I do not think I would be able to toss it to the top, not from this far away given the angle." Brahgen shrugged apologetically.

Skharr scowled and took the grappling hook the dwarf offered him, along with the rope. There was no clean way to throw it to the top of the bridge—which begged the question of how it would come down—but he decided they would have to find that out once he was there.

"How do you think they open it without having someone on the other side of the bridge?" his companion asked with a frown.

"A spell of some kind," he suggested. "Or maybe there is a hidden lever on this side that would help."

"So, once I am on the other side, I must...uh, find a lever or something that would lower the bridge?"

The barbarian nodded. "I assume they would have one there. Or failing that, you'll be able to lower the mechanism manually."

"Right."

Skharr stepped close to the edge and began to spin the hook slowly with a short length of the rope as he approached the moat.

After a few looks to ensure that he would not slip and fall, he added more rope and let it droop into the moat before he made a final powerful swing and lobbed the grappling iron upward with all the effort he could manage.

It arced high and hovered for a moment before he yanked hard to guide it to the drawbridge and hook it firmly.

"This isn't your first time, is it?" the dwarf asked with a grin.

"Stop messing about and get to climbing."

Brahgen grasped the rope and proved to be a more than capable climber. He swung to the other side and used the bridge as leverage to climb easier. In less than a minute, he reached the top, pulled himself up, and peeked over. The barbarian leaned over the edge to see that the dwarf was trying to pull at the bridge as if to make room for him to slip through.

"Skharr, do you think you can reach the rope?"

He squinted to try to see better. "Not unless you expect me to climb on after you. What's the issue?"

"There's some give on the bridge, so it can be pulled open enough for me to slip through, but I haven't the power from my perch here. I'll try to—"

He grasped the rope and flicked it.

"Oh, fuck—"

Skharr leaned closer and made sure he was in no danger of falling into the moat. Brahgen held the hook to keep it rooted on the gate with one hand while he tried to work the rope with the other.

It was impressive and after a couple of attempts, the barbarian snapped the rope from the air but made sure he didn't pull the young dwarf off.

"Right then," he told his friend. "Make sure you're not hanging on the bridge when I tug. There's no way to know if it will fall when I do, and I won't explain to Ahverna how her high priest took a tumble into the water on my watch."

His companion looked like he was focused a little too hard on maintaining his perch on the wall, which prevented him from making any kind of retort. He did listen, however, and clambered as high as he could away from the gate before the barbarian began to tug on the rope.

Skharr made a few tentative efforts at first, but it was immediately clear that while there was some give to the bridge, it was still tough to pull. Before long, he leaned back and strained before he felt the bridge starting to give.

"All right...all right, I should be—oh, fuck!"

He looked up when the youth shouted, released the rope, and let the bridge raise again but the dwarf was already through and something thudded on the other side.

"Brahgen! Talk to me, you little bastard!"

"I'm...alive. My ego is a little bruised but I have no other injuries. How are you?"

"You almost—shit." The barbarian shook his head. "Get the godsbedammed bridge down before I hack my way across to fucking kill you."

A cheerful laugh was somewhat muted behind the wall. "It's good to know you care."

"Fuck you."

He could hear the dwarf still cackling on the other side and turned to move back a few steps to check that nothing was coming after them. Ever since the bone dragon, he intended to ensure that every step they took wouldn't lead them into a trap that would kill them.

Finally, the sound of the bridge lowering drew his attention and he turned to see that the bridge was extending well into the walkway. If he'd remained where he had been, it would have crushed him if not for the fact that it moved slowly enough that he could have avoided it. Pieces were held up by the frame of the tunnel, locked into place, and added support to the bridge while a section extended into the tunnel to ensure there was no chance it would fall into the moat.

Brahgen stood on the other side and while he looked a little ruffled and bruised in odd places, he was alive and none the worse for wear.

"It's nice to see you still alive," Skharr noted.

"Yes, we all know you're so very interested in my continued survival. Come on, there's something on the other side you'll want to look at."

The barbarian crossed the bridge and expected some kind of trap to be waiting for him, but none presented itself as he approached his companion on the other side. A closed door certainly looked promising for them, but he couldn't see any lock on the door itself. It was made of steel, and he had a feeling even his ax wouldn't cleave through it.

"What are you thinking here?" He looked around and noticed that Brahgen crouched next to what appeared to be a mouse hole at the base of the wall.

"I've seen these before. There's a keyhole in the bottom and they have a special device they snake in to unlock it. I can undo it, but it's too deep for me to reach."

Skharr scowled at it. "Do you have any ideas?"

His companion rubbed his hands together. "These are devised so that they can be lifted with certain tools. If repairs are necessary, locks changed, anything like that, they can be accessed without needing to break through the wall. Come over here and see if you can lift it."

He complied without protest. The dwarf was the expert in this case, which left him the role of being the muscle. It was one he'd often found himself in when he was younger but he'd left it behind as soon as he could given that the muscle was generally who got caught if everything went badly.

In this situation, that wasn't a consideration and he slipped his hand into the hole—very cautiously as he fully expected something to bite his fingers. Nothing did and he slowly began to pull the item he felt up. Interestingly, it felt like wooden slabs weighted down to keep them in place and disguised as the rest of the stone wall. While it was a decent weight, it was no great discomfort to hold it up while Brahgen leaned close to it and began to pick the lock.

"So what happened with you and Ahverna, then?" the barbarian asked after a few moments of silence.

"What do you mean?"

"She called you her priest."

"Did she?" Brahgen sounded a little distracted.

"Yes."

"Well, she was a demigoddess, but she now is a goddess. I'm not sure how, but I assume it means she'll call on me to do her work for her more often now."

He nodded but the dwarf was too focused to notice. "That is how it works. Still, I suppose it would have something to do with you as her priest. It's not every day that something like that happens."

"It isn't?"

"No." Skharr shook his head. It wasn't like he had any expertise in the matter either. "I suspect there is something involved in her moving into godhood. A demigoddess would not be allowed to alter her position in the hierarchy without something else happening in the background."

"What do you think it is?" The young dwarf sounded a little out of his depth.

"I'm fucked if I know. But I wouldn't be surprised to find that we are both pawns in all this."

Brahgen had nothing but a grunt to add to the conversation before something clicked into place.

"That should do it."

He held the lock until the dwarf was clear before he eased it down. His companion strode to the door and pushed it open without any real effort.

"How far do you think you would have come in this trial

without any help?" the dwarf asked with a grin as they stepped through the doorway.

"I would have died many times over without help in these trials, I think, but they appear to be designed for the companions I have with me. It's like they have minds of their own or something."

Brahgen shrugged as they stepped into the inner sanctum of the vault, where they immediately stopped to stare at something that looked like a scepter. Two golden wings flared around a massive black pearl at the top of a gleaming bronze staff.

"I suppose that is what Ahverna sent you to find?" Skharr asked as the dwarf approached it carefully.

"With your permission, of course. She did not tell me why, but she says you will need to walk the road or something to that effect." His eyes narrowed for a moment as he studied the staff. "I might have forgotten her precise words. A goddess appearing in the middle of my prayers did put me out of sorts."

"I'm supposed to trust the path," he answered with a scowl. "Other than my life, I wonder if there is any other treasure at the end of this—that I get to keep, at least."

His young companion smirked. "Put your hand on the pearl at the top. That'll be the portal that gets us out of here. Alive, amazingly."

Skharr grinned and placed his hand on the pearl, and the world immediately twisted as it did whenever they were in a portal. A second later, he sucked in deep breaths and looked around to orient himself. Again, it felt like time had passed slower in the dungeon and they now looked into the deep evening, the sun having set at least an hour before.

A crowd was waiting for them as well and cheered when they exited the portal, and the DeathEaters were there to greet them along with Tryam's guards.

"It's good to see you still alive, Skharr," Turan declared with a grin and offered him a horn of what appeared to be mead. "And I can see you took your biggest man with you on this one too."

"Have a care," he warned. "You're speaking to the high priest of Ahverna."

"There isn't much height to him."

Skharr nodded as the dwarf approached the DeathEater.

Brahgen regarded the chieftain calmly. "Appearances can be deceiving. The largest man can be the smallest, and the smallest halfling can be the largest, depending on their circumstances."

That seemed to make little sense, but the dwarf lifted Turan's coin purse as he patted the DeathEater on the chest, then tucked it deftly into his cloak.

"That is...odd wisdom," Turan muttered, not sure what to make of the words. He would discover his purse missing and likely know who had taken it too, but there was no need to tell him immediately.

"Come along now," one of the other DeathEaters called. "The emperor arranged a small feast for when you came out, although none of us are sure how he knew you would. Either way, there will be time for talk later."

"Lead the way," he demanded and they pushed through the gathered, cheering crowd. His eyes narrowed when he caught a glimpse of a hooded figure watching them, but as he focused his eyes on them, they seemed to fade into the background and immediately slipped out of sight. It made him wonder if he'd seen the figure at all or if it was merely a product of his paranoid mind.

CHAPTER EIGHTEEN

He'd forgotten how well his kin could enliven a place when they had reason to celebrate. Skharr wasn't sure how long it had been since he'd been in the company of so many DeathEaters, but Tryam had not been lying when he said they could consume the contents of a slaughterhouse and a meadery and still ask for dessert at the end.

Of course, he was the perfect embodiment of all these qualities, but he was generally the sole representative of his kin in any one place. More than one would prove to be a tenuous situation for any who might find themselves among them, especially if one happened to provide the food and drink.

Still, he felt a little better now than he had the day before. Thanks to Brahgen, he was less battered and beaten than he had been after the previous tests, and more of the healing potion had allowed him to spend most of the day recovering instead of being visited by the physician.

Unfortunately, no healing potion existed for what happened after a long night of drinking and revelry. He remembered most of it—which told him that he had not been too deep in his cups—

but staying up so late the day before he had to rush into another test was certainly not the finest idea he'd ever had.

He moved a little slower than usual and was bleary-eyed, even after the tisane provided by one of the cooks. The man had said that it sharpened the mind and strengthened the limbs. It seemed a little too good to be true, but he could feel a little more energy in his body although not enough to offset the effects of what he had drunk the night before.

A little fire fueled by combat would push it all aside if his experience counted for anything. Skharr steadied himself with a deep breath and turned to face the group escorting him. They used the secret passages again, and he knew it was the boy's doing. He had a bright enough mind to know that having folk follow his every movement through the palace would make it easier for intended assassins to keep track of him as well.

Elric waited for him at the entrance of the passage and grinned when he saw his exhausted look.

"I heard that you and your fellow DeathEaters had a particularly legendary evening," the lord commander said once he was in earshot and spoke in an intentionally loud tone.

The barbarian winced and rubbed his temple to ease the ache that had begun to throb.

"Legendary is one word for it," he muttered. "Another would be ill-advised."

"That is two words."

He groaned. "Maybe. I don't care. Please...lower your tone."

"Lower my tone?"

The man was practically shouting and he flashed him a glare that made the amused grin disappear almost immediately. No apologies were offered, however, and the lord commander pushed the frame of a six-foot-tall painting. It spun to reveal a door behind it.

"These passages were created to save the emperor's life in the case of a revolution," Elric explained as they stepped inside. "He would be allowed to slip away while the presumed mob was lost in the maze of the palace. The early emperors were rather terrified of their tyranny being questioned in such a manner, but the passages have mostly been used to move mistresses, lovers, and assassins through the palace instead of emperors. I've wanted to speak to Tryam about having them filled in, but I suppose they prove useful now that you have need of them."

Skharr offered no complaints. The passage was thankfully cool and the dim light of the torches lining it was more comfortable than what he faced in the open.

"Half my regiment is down this morning after challenging your kin to eating and drinking," the guard commander commented. "I suppose it should not surprise me that DeathEaters as a whole are more impressive specimens than most, but I always assumed you were one of a kind."

"I am," he retorted as they continued deeper into the passages. "You might want to consider bringing a handful of DeathEaters to toughen your men through example. Although if you look closely, I'll bet you will see the signs that the Clan are hurting as well. They are merely acting as though they do not feel it."

Elric nodded slowly. "I suppose there are signs, although they are not obvious. I might inquire as to whether a handful of them wish to remain even after your ordeal is over."

"You should speak to Turan," he suggested. "You might find he is open to an arrangement that would see the empire and the Clan exchange warriors for supplies or something of the like. It might help you as well as them."

"Interesting." The lord commander scratched at his beard pensively. "If any other were to suggest such a thing, I would think they were soft in the head."

"And now?"

"Well, I already know you are soft in the head." The man grinned. "But that does not mean it is a bad idea. I might have to speak to your chieftain on the matter."

Truthfully, Skharr hadn't thought Elric would be open to the idea. Maybe the empire was having difficulties. He knew they could stand to have a few DeathEaters to train their men and fight on the front lines too.

"Who does the boy have for me to fight alongside this time?" he asked and changed the subject.

"You know he only does this—"

"Because he cares. Perhaps a little too much. But I also know there are great games afoot—games Tryam has found himself tangled in and games with the gods."

"The gods too?" The lord commander shook his head. "Well, the hope is that you do not die on us, Skharr. This is a wicked test to fight in, by all accounts, but I suppose you are the most likely to live through it."

He noticed that the man had not answered his question and while it was a deft sidestep, it needed a little more finesse if he wanted to succeed in the political theater the Imperial City had become.

A short walk led them to a location outside the city borders. The door that was opened was part of the wall that surrounded the city. He emerged at the borders of a thick forest that had been cleared somewhat but had slowly begun to reclaim the territory.

What interested Skharr the most, of course, was the fact that only one person waited for him on the other side.

Tryam was in full plate armor and it suited him even though it didn't have quite the gleam and shine the barbarian had come to expect from the emperor these days. Still, it was well-made and fitted perfectly to his body. He wondered if it was the same armor he had used during his days in the arena, although the sword he carried was familiar.

"I guess you failed to find me a companion to follow me into this particular trial," Skharr remarked, his eyes narrowed. "Because I know you won't follow me in there."

"I told you he would agree with me," Elric commented and folded his arms.

"I will join you, barbarian." Tryam rolled his shoulders and appeared to move comfortably in his armor. "I am the best choice to accompany you on this particular test."

"Why?" he asked.

"It is Theros' test," the lord commander explained. "And it so happened that the god suggested Tryam join you a few days ago. While I disagreed, it is very difficult to argue with a god."

"The man has a point." The emperor motioned for Skharr to follow. "The portal is not too far away, but we cannot remain here chewing the fat until the end of the world."

This very practical reminder effectively ended the discussion. Elric returned to the wall while Skharr and Tryam proceeded to the portal. The barbarian had no idea what waited for them when it came to Theros' trial, but since Janus had been challenged to promise that he would not make his trial more difficult, his brother could not make his easier simply because he had a soft spot for the one taking it.

It was not a long way, fortunately, and the portal was already waiting for them near a small pond in the middle of the trees.

Once they were through, Skharr realized that he recognized where they were.

"Theros...is not the most creative of creatures," he stated and shouldered his bow for the moment. "Desert behind us, swamps ahead, with wrinkled ground between. This is where your dungeon was."

"The trials are the same, yes."

"Mind you, I do not think that is a bad thing. Gods might find themselves something better to do with their time than to create the dungeons where so many go to die. Still, I suppose it explains why you are the choice for this one. Although I suppose one does not need to be creative when a dragon guards the entrance of the dungeon."

Tryam tilted his head and smirked. "Well, I was informed that the dragon is no longer present."

"And how are we supposed to open the door?" He trusted his companion well enough but facing a dragon was never something he would be comfortable with.

"He assured me that the door is already open. The real trial is what you will find inside. But, if it isn't, I suppose we will have to find out what happens then."

The barbarian still wouldn't simply trust Theros' word on the matter. They would have to find a path through, however, and while he held his hand on his bow just in case, all they could do was to put one foot ahead of the other. And hope no dragon waited for them on the other side.

"I still do not think you joining me in this is a good idea," Skharr muttered once they had trudged along in silence for a few long minutes. "Not that I don't want your company, mind. But even if I were to survive, I would not want to know that you put your empire in peril for my sake."

"Then you'd best ensure I survive, then." The emperor sounded suitably commanding.

He grinned at the youth. "You know it only means I care for your safety as well, yes?"

"Naturally. But in all honesty, I welcome the opportunity to do something. Most of what is happening in the palace are spy craft and politics. I am learning the latter but the former is…well, beyond my ken. I don't think I'll ever understand how it all works and I have to trust others to help me."

"That can be the most difficult part." Skharr still watched the skies for any sign of a dragon approaching them. "Trusting others. Especially as emperor."

"Well, at least none are openly trying to kill me." Tryam did not look entirely trusting of Theros' word either. His sword was looped over his shoulder so he carried it on his back, but he was ready to drop it and draw it at a moment's notice. "We've continued to try to find out who might be trying to murder you, and a few promising leads have presented themselves. After the ordeal my sister went through with you, she has spearheaded that effort. I did not know you inspired such loyalty in her."

"I doubt that I do. She has her reasons for ensuring that I survive."

"Well…whatever those might be, she has worked tirelessly. We have found three smaller landed members of the gentry involved in the scheme thus far. Their lands are on the border between the empire and the Sareenans. It is good land, but it requires an investment of time. Instead, they have put efforts in to expand to our rivals' lands where they would find rivers and proper roads through which trade can pass. Their efforts would be in vain but for the unlikely scenario that the empire was to declare war on the Sareenans and immediately take control of the region to feed the army. This would place them in a prime position to make a great deal of coin from the influx of trade that would be required."

"It seems…an oddly mundane reason for them to decide to kill me."

Tryam nodded. "Less than a year ago when they started their infrastructure, war with our neighbors seemed all but certain, but tensions have since cooled and I am committed to peace on that front. There are even suggestions that I arrange a marriage between myself and the Jarl's daughter, who will reach marriageable age in a few years. The suggestion was that she spend a few years here so we can meet and be seen together and even learn about each other during that time before a marriage is proposed."

He turned to look at Skharr and thought that perhaps the barbarian was not entirely interested in discussing the complexities of political marriages. He did know something about them and he was far from disinterested, but the boy quickly changed the subject.

"Anyway, the three dukes and their warmongering have

paused those plans, and all we can do is assure them that there is no attempt on my part to break the peace we have brokered. It will be months still before talk of consolidating the peace can be approached. Until then, I will need to handle the three dukes myself. But there is other news."

Skharr turned to look at the young emperor, who appeared to weigh his words carefully as they approached the first of the small canyons that would lead into the tunnels a dragon used to call home.

"Well, there's no need to keep me in suspense. Out with it."

Tryam took a deep breath and nodded. "According to Micah, there are indications that the Patron God of Assassins is directly involved. More importantly, the Assassin who is hunting you has never come away without his kill, not in centuries."

That was never a good sign. Even worse was the fact that the Assassin's name was not known, only their skill. Regular folk loved to hear a famous name as the greatest killer of all time. When it came to the subtle art of assassination, however, he knew all too well that widespread fame was not the point. As long as the right people knew what could be bought, that was all that mattered.

At least he now had some idea of what he faced, even if he didn't yet know the who. "Is there anything else known about this assassin?"

Tryam shook his head regretfully. "Only that they appear to not have been active for many years now. Micah said she'd always assumed the Assassin was the fabrication of myth and legend."

"What made her change her mind?"

"Nothing she told me about. But the fact that she is taking these myths and legends seriously is enough for me to take notice. She has run my archivist ragged trying to find any details of this assassin in the hope that she can discover something that will help to identify them."

Micah was not one to lose herself to pointless stories, even though there was often a grain of truth mixed into them. Perhaps that was what she was looking for—some kind of pattern that might prove useful.

The canyon became tunnels and a few points of light came from above to reveal how treacherous the ground was. Still, from the way it was packed and looked as though it had not been disturbed for a while, it seemed Theros had told the truth about the dragon having left. Either that or it was hibernating, which dragons were known to do from time to time. He would not commit their lives to Theros' word.

Neither was Tryam by the looks of it. As they approached the area where he recalled the dragon's nest was situated, Skharr inched around the corner, his hand on his ax and ready to draw it if they saw the creature. He had no doubt that the bit would cut dragon scales, but the real problem was getting close enough to swing without being scorched.

He saw nothing and stepped from behind the corner, his weapon already in hand as he watched and waited with no result. The nest was empty and like the rest of the area, it appeared to have been abandoned for a while.

"I guess Theros told the truth," he muttered.

"It makes you wonder why you doubted in the first place."

Skharr fixed him with an unapologetic look. "Trust but verify anyway. Advice to live and survive by."

They approached the nest and the barbarian could see that the dragon's hoard had increased a great deal since they had been there last. He recognized most of the treasure from the one he and Cassandra had managed to kill and more. The piles of books and scrolls were also present.

They had assumed that the god would bring it all here where it could be kept safe, but there was no dragon to do the work.

Perhaps Theros was defending the spot himself while his dragon was away.

Tryam gestured at the pile. "Theros mentioned that we should probably loot as much as we can. He said it was the least he could do given how things went the last time we were here."

That was something, at least, and Skharr looked for a shield he could claim. His last had been shattered and he hadn't found the time to replace it yet. He saw nothing in his first hasty look and sighed as he began his usual process of collecting the smallest items of greatest value. These were gemstones, amulets, and various pieces of jewelry that could have some magic to them and would be worth a fortune to any mages he managed to find. Provided he survived that long, of course.

"Fuck!" Tryam exclaimed and jumped up from where he had collected items as well. "Skharr, I think this one belongs to you!"

His initial reaction was to be ready for an attack but he drew a deep breath, calmed himself, and approached the young emperor. The boy peered down at a ring—a simple golden band with no jewels or decorations—that appeared to glow in the shadows they were in.

"What makes you think it's mine?" he asked. "And what in the hell does an emperor need with treasure anyway?"

The emperor shrugged. "You never know when you'll find something in these troves that could prove to be priceless, the kind of thing you could never find anywhere else. And failing that, a little extra coin to spend never hurt anyone."

He made a good point and Skharr dropped to his haunches, collected the ring, and felt it almost pulse against his fingers. "Well, there's magic to it but no sign that it belongs to me."

"Well, it sure as fuck does not belong to me. It shocked me when I tried to pick it up but it did not do the same to you. That seems to spell out that it does not belong to me in every language known to sentient beings on the continent."

The logic was sound. He inspected it carefully and tried to determine what made it so special. He'd been told once that gold and silver were so valuable because they were innately better at retaining and transferring spells. Steel required the spells to be simple and in the form of runes, while the richer metals could take the more complex types without needing to have anything inscribed on them to retain the magical power.

It was therefore no surprise that nothing was carved into the gold, but it still did not answer the question of what the fucking hell it was supposed to be in the first place.

"Is it strange that I appreciate Theros letting me come through this again with you?" Tryam sounded almost wistful.

Skharr looked up from inspecting the piece in his hands and raised an eyebrow at the youth. "What makes you say that?"

The emperor sighed. "It's a reminder of where I've come from. I do try to remain as close to the ground as I can, but there is something about having folk kowtow around you at all times that is difficult to overcome. Some days, I find myself believing what the sycophants in the palace say to me—to my face, at least."

"I would suggest ordering Elric to slap you on a regular basis," he answered with a firm nod. "It will help to remind you that you are not a god made flesh—not yet, at least—and I am sure it would do wonders for his morale."

Tryam grinned. "That it would. Although he does have a wicked slap. I've seen him use it. He raps the men with the back of his hand with enough power to make them stumble."

"Well…that would keep you on the ground."

"True." The emperor shook his head, which suggested that he was very unwilling to encourage that kind of punishment despite the benefits. "What do you think of the ring?"

"It might not be mine," he answered and ran his fingers over it.

"It seems like it was meant for you, no?"

The barbarian slid it onto his pinkie, where it barely passed his nail. "It's for a lady or someone with thin, dainty fingers. I doubt it would fit on my smallest toe."

"Maybe it's meant to hang around your neck with a chain?" Tryam suggested as he collected one of the scrolls and opened it. "That you're meant to hold it for someone else. Ah, there we are."

"There who is?"

"It's for the archivist. Theros told me that she would need it for my benefit in the near future. And at this point, I think I am willing to trust him."

Skharr raised an eyebrow. "I never thought the gods were quite your style."

"Aye, but they are yours and Theros appears to do right by those who follow him."

"Eventually." He hefted his ax, the latest display of Theros' favor, and swung it a few times. He smiled as the steel sang as it cut through the air. "Oh."

"Oh?" Tryam frowned.

"Theros is not protecting us—or at least, not protecting only the two of us."

"What do you mean?" The young man looked at him in bemusement.

"He is protecting his dragon. We would not be able to sneak past it a second time, not without someone else approaching this place. We would have had to fight it and in doing so, either we or it would have died. Either way, it would leave the bastard without at least one valuable follower."

The emperor seemed unconvinced. "How...oh." He paused for a moment in thought. "I suppose you could have cut its head off with your ax."

Skharr nodded agreement. "Provided I was able to get close enough. It would not be easy, but easier than without it. Now... shall we sit around and play in the treasure or leave?"

"As much fun as I think a day away from the palace might be, I think we should find our way out of this dungeon."

They collected as much treasure as they could carry before they continued. It seemed a little like cheating but in the end, this was meant to be a matter of justice for the gods to decide, and Theros decided that his trial would involve considerable treasure and no dragon to battle.

After all, the god knew he was innocent of the crime of which he had been accused and thus forced into doing these trials.

"I suppose Theros doesn't want the emperor to be killed fighting a dragon either," Skharr muttered as they wound through the pockmarked tunnels and eventually reached the surface.

"He'll catch hell for this with the other gods," Tryam noted. "If Janus was not allowed to make your trial more difficult, Theros most certainly would not have been allowed to make his easier."

"Something tells me he is playing a longer game than merely our survival," he replied as they climbed over the loose soil that led them to the full embrace of the sunlight.

He could tell something was amiss almost immediately and his gaze scanned the area at the sound of something approaching the entrance they were using.

The creatures appeared to be reptilian. They looked almost like crocodiles, although they stood on their hind legs and their forelimbs had three elongated fingers that they used to carry roughly hewn spears. While they wore scraps of clothes as a sign that they had some concept of modesty, most of their leathery skin was bared to the sun and showed no indication that they were in any way uncomfortable in it.

A pack of about a dozen of the creatures appeared to be setting up camp close to the entrance to the cave and seemed as surprised to see the two adventurers as the humans were to see them.

"What in the living fuck?" Tryam whispered, his sword already off his shoulder and his hand on the hilt.

"Kobolds," Skharr explained and grasped his ax. "Reptilians that likely call the nearby swamps home. They are possibly here to pay their respects to the dragon that lives below. If they do not see us as a threat, they might leave us be. On the other hand—"

He had no time to finish his sentence as one of the creatures hissed and flung its spear at him without so much as a warning.

The barbarian swayed to the side and the weapon sailed past him into the tunnels they had walked through. Another rushed toward him with a spiked club brandished aggressively.

If he were to place a wager, Skharr would have suggested that they saw the larger human as the greater threat.

In this case, they would have been right. "My blade is thirsty, you swamp-clogged fucking scaly sludge brains."

The ax was already in his hand and felt almost like it was eager to jump into battle with him as he darted away from the wild swing that would have broken his shoulder at the very least. He snarled as he lunged forward and his blade sliced through the creature's neck. Its leathery skin was likely better armor than boiled leather, but it was no match for the weapon in his hand. Its head was severed cleanly.

When another surged forward wielding what appeared to be a crude iron sword, Tryam slid his blade over the creature's guard and opened its throat. The boy had improved all aspects of his fighting abilities, which included his footwork as he circled the kobold he'd killed like he was a dancer and slashed his blade at the one that came in behind.

The barbarian drew his dagger and launched it at the one that tried to sneak up on him from the rear. It caught it in the chest—not his finest throw, but it worked out well enough and the kobold stumbled away.

Tryam showed no sign of stopping. With the blood of two more of the kobolds on his blade, he lunged into the rest of them without so much as a pause.

He had confidence at least, and Skharr intended to make sure it was not misplaced. Charging into the kobolds did not seem like the kind of action he would consider wise, but they were as surprised to be in the fight as he was. They were both lightly armed and lightly armored as well.

It did not take long before those who remained began to turn tail and run. Any thought that they could pursue the creatures ceased when they dropped on all fours and raced away at about the speed of a galloping horse.

"It wouldn't be like old times if we didn't kill a monster or two, I suppose," Tryam said and sucked in a deep breath as he cleaned the blood from his sword. He did strike an imposing figure, armored and prepared for battle and already splashed with the blood of his enemies.

"I suppose so," Skharr conceded, although his thought was interrupted when a portal opened in front of them. "I hope you thoroughly enjoyed your day away from the palace. It would appear we have to return already."

"It was enjoyable enough. I might start to leave the palace in armor that covers my features, travel the land, and do good."

The barbarian snorted but when he spoke, his tone was serious. "You would do more good as emperor, you know."

Tryam nodded but his expression was regretful. "True, but it all feels so distant. Something about performing the work with my own two hands is satisfying."

CHAPTER NINETEEN

"You've got to let us in. The sun hasn't even set yet!" This and other protests were shouted by those who reached the city too late to gain entry.

"The gates close when the sun sets. It don't mean we need to let anyone get crushed by the bloody gates while we close them. Now get the fuck back!"

Guarding the gate was meant to be a comfortable job. Not quite as good as they had it while guarding the palace or the granaries, but the coin made up for it.

Seth found that being a close friend of the division captain served him well. He was confined to maintaining order at the western gate of the Imperial City. More than a few traders wanted to bring restricted items into the city and were willing to pay for the guards to look the other way.

Corruption was rather rampant and possibly even encouraged, but the traders knew he asked the best prices compared to the guards manning the other sections of the wall.

Or, at least, those who traveled through the city often. The new arrivals tended to not know the going price for entry into the city with illegal goods was and were generally charged a fee for their first time. The coin was divided evenly among the guards who held the line with him.

Currently, many newcomers visited the city. All the guards knew why they came, of course. It was a circus in the city at the moment and the yearly chariot races at the arena commanded a great deal of attention.

Added to that was the barbarian undergoing the trials that had the attention of the locals as well. Seth had no idea what the appeal was, but it seemed he was rather famous and folk wanted to be present when he went through the Seven Trials or died in the attempt. It was history in the making, and those who had little else to do while crops matured in the fields wanted to be present for it.

At first, he'd appreciated the additional income, but there could be too much of a good thing. Every day for the past week, folk had clogged the gates until sundown and even tried to force their way in when it was time for them to close.

Guarding the gate had begun to seem a little too much like hard work by this point.

"Oy! Who's in charge of the guard here?"

He looked up from the papers of the last few to pass through, narrowed his eyes, and shielded them with a hand so he could see who had asked the question.

A tall woman stared at him, her brown hair bound in a tight braid. Her clothes were travel-worn but of good cloth, and the saber she carried at her hip was particularly eye-catching. She had the look of a warrior, which included the warhorse she was riding.

"I am," Seth answered. "Who be you? We're closing the gates."

"I can see that. I need to get in before you do."

"The last folk going in have gone. You'll have to make camp outside the walls along with the rest of them." He scowled and shook his head. "Sorry. I can't break the rules for you without breaking them for the others."

"I am Captain Sera Ferat, half-sister to the emperor, and I need an escort for myself and my comrades to take us to the throne immediately."

He realized there were two men with her, also on horseback and looking like they were ready for battle, although their weapons were not quite as impressive as hers.

Seth took a step forward and motioned for the men to pause in their work of closing the gates. "Even if you was to head in there, you won't find the emperor sitting on the throne. Hells, most aren't where they should be."

She shifted in her saddle and looked annoyed and about as tired as he felt. "Why?"

"It's like a fucking festival in there, is why. Bad enough that folk are here for the chariot races but now, we's got some bastard taking the Seven Trials who folk want to see. You'd think it would be horrible, but the city can't get enough of it."

The captain dismounted fluidly, patted her horse on the neck, and spoke softly to it before she approached him.

"It's true then? Skharr DeathEater is taking the trials." She waited so he had to answer.

"True as the price of gold." He narrowed his eyes. "What'd you say your name was again?"

"Her name," another woman's voice interrupted as a cloaked figure approached with two of the Emperor's Eagles on horse-back, "is the honorable Captain Sera Ferat."

The hooded woman, who had mingled with the other folk near the gate, pulled her cloak back to reveal a face that had become only too familiar to the guards in the city over the past week or so. She was one of the emperor's new confidants and his sister as well, according to the whispers.

As he expected, there was a resemblance between the two. Dame Ferat had a harder edge to her but they were most certainly kin.

"Dame Ferat," Seth said as loudly as he could to catch the

attention of the rest of the men and ensure that they were listening as well. "We wasn't told to expect you."

"And that is the way it is meant to be, my good man." Her smile made him uncomfortable and he took a step back without even thinking about it.

"She's…your sister then, is she?"

"Yes." Dame Ferat waved the Eagles to where she stood. "And I'll escort her to the emperor and find accommodations for her two companions. Now open the gate and allow us to pass."

"Right away!" Rules could not be broken for simply anyone, but she was sufficiently important to warrant it.

As he directed his men to reverse about fifteen minutes of handling the gears meant to hold the gates opened or closed, he could hear the two women speaking.

"Micah? What in the living fuck are you doing here?" The newcomer looked startled.

"Waiting for your late ass." Micah sighed softly and shook her head. "I spread word as far as it would go in hopes that it would eventually find you. Now, get back on your horse before the sun comes up and they open the gate for you anyway. It wouldn't do for you to miss your entrance."

"My entrance?" Sera looked blankly at her.

"Gods, you can be as dense as the barbarian sometimes." She grinned and stepped forward to embrace her sister warmly. "It is good to see you but catching up will have to wait until you've met our brother."

"Of course." Sera turned, mounted smoothly, and gestured for her two companions to join her as they approached the gate with their escort of the Emperor's Eagles.

Micah managed to find a horse, although Seth couldn't fathom where she'd conjured it from, and they moved through once the gates were open enough for horses.

"Who in the bloody hells was that, Captain?"

"Mind your fucking tone," Seth snapped at the guard and

glowered at a few hopefuls who walked closer, thinking they could still get through the gate as well. "The emperor's new spymaster has eyes everywhere. There's no point in getting on her foul side. Shut the gates so we can head on home."

It had been a while since she'd seen her sister. Micah had always been a little jealous that Sera had been sent to train at the feet of the blademasters. It added a certain poise and presence to her.

Still, she could see that the woman was studying the papers presented with a hint of doubt.

"An assassin like that would not be able to keep himself a secret for so long," she said and put the scroll down. "How have we not heard of him before?"

"Honestly, I can't even tell if the Assassin is a he," Micah answered and glanced at the door to ensure that they would not be interrupted while the two sisters got reacquainted and focused on what they needed to discuss. Sera looked like she had been riding nonstop for days on end to reach them, which was always something Micah liked to see in the folk helping her.

"If the truth be told, I've heard whispers of this assassin before and dismissed them as myths," she continued, "but there was always a pattern in their kills. Never killing the person directly but seeing to it that death was delivered by another's blade, and always with second or third considerations in mind—generally political. I would not be surprised if old families know how to contact them, likely as some kind of offering through one of the temples. I've tried to find out if any large offerings or promises have been arranged, but it is rather difficult to persuade the priests to talk. Bribes work better than threats with them, but it is still slow work."

"I've loaned the use of the guard for the purpose," Elric interjected. "And you've worked faster than our spymaster."

"He's worked a certain way for many years," Micah explained. "There is nothing wrong with that. Combined minds have worked faster, that is all."

Sera shook her head and her hand rested on her sword in the way that made Elric very concerned by the look of him.

"How did Skharr get involved in so fucking much?"

"Sheer fucking talent," she answered with a smirk. "But in this case, I am sure he bears part of the guilt. He has helped too many people and harmed too many others. Besides, our brother has been known to use him as a blunt instrument a few times. This has made him the perfect instrument to knock the emperor down a peg or two without directly attacking by removing one of his more offensive and offending pieces from the board. If I might make a metaphor of the game."

"You've never allowed anything to stop you before," her sister answered with a scowl. "I'll admit that I'm shocked to find you here. I didn't think you cared so much about the barbarian."

"You can thank the Eagles, if you like. They have a way of arriving and taking you places if it's what the emperor requires."

The two Eagles at the door snickered. It had been interesting to travel with them, and she'd made a point to request them at the forefront of any efforts that required a guard's presence.

"And how does the gate guard know of you?" It seemed the captain in her always had a million questions.

Micah knew better than to leave them unanswered. "I expected you to show your morose features sooner or later. I couldn't locate you when you disappeared after your caravan last made camp inside a city's walls. You were in areas where my tendrils do not reach."

"Ah." Sera grunted and shook her head. "Well then, I suppose we shouldn't keep the emperor waiting."

"He might want to wait a little longer." Micah grimaced almost apologetically but not quite. "I don't mean to insult you, but your horse has left enough of a stench on you that you might find it advisable to be a little late."

The captain paused, raised her arm, and sniffed her armpits with a grimace. "Point taken. I might need a bath and a fresh change of clothes."

"They are already arranged and waiting for you. Meeting our half-brother for the first time should not be done on a whim."

That seemed to catch Sera's attention. "It sounds as though you have plans to remain here."

Micah guided her sister into a room where a large brass bath was filled with steaming, rose-scented water and a fresh set of clothes was already waiting. She appeared more than willing to wash her as well.

She declined the offer, however, and it wasn't long before she pulled her fresh clothes on.

"I guess I shouldn't ask how you know my size."

Her sister grinned. "I've spoken to your tailors over the years. I would not have you improperly dressed if it is ever in my power to help. And it helps that you do not have the dust from the road in your cracks."

"You're crass," Sera answered, loosened her hair, and brushed the knots out before she braided it.

"And yet it's true," Micah countered. "Besides, when I speak to guards, I speak their language."

"I see. Would you like me to speak a little more like a lady as I slap your ass around?"

"Well, not you...or your barbarian." Micah grinned as her sister's eyes flared when she paused. "You are too easy to rile. I'm amazed that you're still alive and have not been killed in some kind of honor duel before now."

"There have been many who tried, but not the type who would succeed against a trained blademaster, sister of mine. Although I suppose that even the slow of blade and wit would eventually find success if they had luck on their side, but fortune has been known to favor the prepared more."

"Why do you jest when you know I'm being serious?" Micah mock pouted but a trace of irritation threaded her words.

"I'm jesting because you are being serious. At this point, if we were to fret over every threat we encountered, we would worry ourselves into a grave with no help from those who would see us dead."

Micah grinned, patted her on the shoulder, and studied her critically before she decided she was about as presentable as she would ever be. The medallion and sword she was honor-bound to wear at all times added a certain regal look to her that would have been absent otherwise.

"Come along now. Our brother would like a word with you."

"You keep calling him that." Sera almost sounded offended.

"Because it is true. And because the walls have ears. It never hurts to remind those who might be listening that we are related to the emperor."

"You always think ahead, don't you?"

Her sister grinned and chose to take it as a compliment. "You say that like it's a bad thing. Like it has not kept both of us alive for decades."

"True enough, I suppose."

Micah directed her through the maze of a palace that their brother called home before she approached a door guarded by two of the Elites.

Neither appeared happy that Sera would be in the same room as the emperor with a sword at her hip, but her sister had already warned Tryam and he'd told his men there would be no contesting his sister's approach, no matter what the circumstances.

It would be a scandal if Sera were to assassinate Tryam, of course, but in that case, she would have an even better relationship with the emperor who took his place. She would have to in order to avoid any talk of a regicide trial.

The guards opened the door for her. Tryam was already waiting, seated behind his desk as he usually was when he met with her. His loyal attack dog Elric stood alongside and the man's gaze, like the guards, immediately went to the sword Sera had at her hip. He too had been properly admonished regarding how the emperor's sister was to be treated.

Tryam rose to his feet when he saw her and smiled broadly as he circled the desk with his arms outstretched.

"Captain Sera Ferat. We have met before under very different circumstances, but I am honored to finally meet you officially," he said and she immediately stiffened in surprise when he embraced her like they were friends. "I don't suppose you would understand, but I have a certain yearning for family, although I do understand if it is not shared."

She didn't answer until he'd taken a step back and she looked like she was trying to determine if he was being genuine or not. Her thoughts could almost be read through the expressions that crossed her face, but she appeared to finally decide that her brother was not trying to trap her into anything.

It was interesting to see the two of them together. While young, Tryam had the build of a warrior, with powerful, broad shoulders and a slim waist. Sera looked much the same although more slim, lithe, and agile.

How Micah could be related to these honorable warriors was a question for another time, she decided.

"I would not say it is not shared," Sera answered, still a little confused but smiling despite this. "I merely did not expect to be greeted with such warmth. As I recall, my sister and I were instructed to never return to the Imperial City after our mother was sent away."

"Another time, and another emperor besides," Tryam answered

with a dismissive wave of his hand, which prompted a few servants to quickly fill a few goblets with wine and hand them to all present. Elric declined with a polite smile. Micah assumed the man still did not quite trust the two of them yet. "Besides, I have learned to appreciate having your sister alongside me as well, and I can only assume that having you here with her will improve her focus."

The blademaster narrowed her eyes. "This is my sister we are talking about? Just to be sure."

"Fuck you," Micah protested, which prompted a laugh from Tyram.

"I'll not deny that she can be a handful at times, but that is what I need for someone in her position."

"That position being?" Sera asked and raised an eyebrow.

"My spymaster, of course."

That seemed to make the captain more perplexed and perhaps even more suspicious than before, although she knew better than to voice it while speaking to someone like the emperor.

Inevitably, she began her questions. "So, you two have been working together already?"

"Not for long," Micah admitted. "I only met him for the first time when I was summoned to help Skharr. Thus far, as I've already shared with you, we've attempted to uncover the identity of those who have tried to kill the bastard as well as those who might profit from it."

"There is the matter of you entering one of the trials with said bastard," Tryam stated and sipped his drink as he watched them and their interactions carefully. "Putting your life in a great deal of peril from what you told me of it."

"You did that?" Sera asked. "For Skharr?"

"For you," her sister clarified with a deep scowl. "I could not care less about the fate of the barbarian, but I have a soft spot when it comes to you."

The captain nodded slowly. Micah did understand that she was presenting her sister with a great deal of information that she would need time to process, but she was doing a decent enough job of it.

"I suppose I owe you an apology," the blademaster said finally with a soft sigh. "And my heartfelt thanks for helping to keep my friend alive."

Micah studied her for a moment. "The friend who, when you found out about all of this, you immediately set out to race your horses to near death to reach the capital. That friend?"

"Yes."

"Even going so far as to threaten to attack if they failed to let you through the gate?"

Sera looked decidedly flushed and defensive. "Well, they were closing it."

"You don't think you could have waited outside the gate with the rest of the folk who were a little late in arriving at the city?"

"What are you suggesting?"

"Nothing." Micah shrugged. "Merely that your friends are lucky to have someone like you who would go to such lengths to ensure that they were safe."

She wasn't sure if she was making her subtext clear enough, but she couldn't push it any more at this point, not without being too obvious about it. Sera saw Skharr as something more than a friend, although the precise nature of their relationship was not quite defined. Her sister was still unsure if the two had fucked yet, but it was only a matter of time—assuming the barbarian didn't die before it could happen.

Still, Tryam was watching and he studied Sera carefully as her face flushed before he looked away, having seen all he needed on the matter.

"Well, then," he said and took a sip from his cup. He had been drinking more lately, and Micah knew she wasn't the only one that had noticed. The only question that remained was how to address the matter with an emperor in good standing. "Skharr will undertake his sixth trial soon. He's survived five so far with the help of his friends, but the sixth seems to be the most dangerous."

"How do you mean?" Sera asked.

"It's a trial of sacrifice," Micah explained. "No one knows what that means because none have survived thus far in the trials. The assumption is that someone will have to give up their life."

Her sister looked relieved, almost as if laying her life down was preferable to other uncomfortable considerations. "That's a given, I suppose. I know Skharr would do the same for me, so I would be willing to help him with that."

Micah doubted Tryam needed any other markers to confirm that Sera was the woman for the job.

"Why would you do that?" she asked.

"Because he would do the same for me." There was no hesitation in the blademaster's response.

As stubborn as a mule, her sister was.

"True enough," Tryam admitted. "And that means the barbarian would rather go through the fucking trials alone and die than have someone go with him. He has the sense to not stop folk from helping him when they are already there, but if he were to know that someone he cares for put their lives at risk for him... Well, I like to think I know the man well enough, and my thought is that he would attempt to escape and fuck the consequences. We cannot allow that to happen."

Sera nodded. "I see. We'll have to keep my presence here a secret until the last minute when he has no option but to go into battle with me."

"It is what we have done thus far," Micah explained. "I think Skharr knows he is being manipulated and might have an endgame to play out but for the moment, he is fighting the way we need him to."

"I have the feeling that he would physically stop you from coming in if he knew this was a sacrificial trial as well," Tryam added. "Which is why we are allowing him to remain in the dark until he absolutely must know. Besides, we wouldn't want to disturb his day of rest before he enters the next trials. It might ruin sleep."

Sera raised an eyebrow. "His?"

"Everyone's," Micah interjected. "His, the guards when he is complaining, or yours if you are next. I am sure he could argue with you all night long and ensure that no sleep is had in the palace."

Her sister grinned and shook her head like she had thought of another example of the barbarian's stubbornness, but she didn't look like she would share it.

"Well, with that in mind, I suppose I should find some rest as well," she said and squared her shoulders. "I've been riding for days now, and a few hours of sleep would be appreciated."

"Granted," Tryam answered with a smile. "The guards outside will show you to quarters that have been prepared for you. If you would allow me, I need to have a word with your sister before she can join you."

"Extend it to a whole conversation." Sera patted Micah on the shoulder. "I'll see you soon."

She left the room and Micah waited until she knew that she was well out of earshot before she turned her attention to her brother.

"You do realize we could be sending her to her death?" Tryam asked, drained his goblet, and gestured for it to be refilled.

She sighed slowly and rubbed her eyes for a moment. "Of course. But I have to trust the word of a goddess that Sera has the ability to slip through this test in a way that would allow both to survive."

"You have trouble believing the word of a goddess?"

"I have trouble trusting everyone, you included, but I am working on it." She grinned when she saw him cough up some of the wine he had in his mouth. "But I saw how Ahverna looked at Skharr as well. Somehow, that hulking barbarian got to her the same way he got to my sister. In fact, I would bet that he's introduced her to his dragon to use the popular euphemism. I would bet Sera's life on it, at least."

The emperor shook his head. "Enough of that for the moment. Now...what have you learned about those three bastards?"

"I love it when you talk business." She nodded, clapped briskly, and focused on the papers on his desk. "Here are my thoughts on the matter..."

CHAPTER TWENTY

"I did not think the guards were allowed to join the betting," Skharr commented and studied those in his escort. "I assumed you had some great talk of how honorable and ethical you are meant to be."

One of them snorted and ventured a response. "Well, yes, there is some of that but in the end, what we do on our own time isn't anyone's business, is it?"

"Aside from committing crimes or speaking out against the emperor, of course."

The guard considered that for a moment. "Right. Most of what we do on our own time is not anyone's business is what I meant to say."

"Of course." He accepted that at face value given that his curiosity was piqued. "Out of interest, what odds am I pulling in?"

"They were higher when you started," another responded. "Almost a hundred to one. Before the first tests, Olive put eight gold coins on your surviving the full trial. If you do, she'll make more than she earns in a year, and they won't bother to give one of the emperor's Elites any trouble about her payout. All she needs is for you to—"

"Survive." He nodded. "Of course. What are the odds now that I am...is it the sixth?"

"Aye, sixth. Still high, from what I hear. I made my wager of seven silvers when the odds were still over fifty to one. Now they are closer to twenty. None have ever survived this far into the trials, but all that means is that you do not have any idea of what you will face. As such, it will be more difficult."

The man made a fair point with that, although Skharr was happy to know that he was at least making a decent amount of coin for those who believed in him to succeed. He had begun to have his doubts, however.

It was not lost on him that it did not appear that he was being led to any of the passages they had used in the past. He was being guided to where the rest of the people gathered. The path ahead was not cleared, so those people they encountered watched him with eyes as wide as serving platters as they were politely but firmly moved out of the way.

Elric was the last one to join their little entourage, and the moment he appeared, the rest of the guards stiffened and looked around to ensure that nothing and no one was following them.

"All clear so far?" The lord commander looked like he was a little tense.

"Nothing to report, sir."

"We're told that an attempt will be made today. Keep your eyes open."

The lord commander winked at Skharr before motioning for his men to continue as he fell into step with them.

Maybe there was another reason why the guards probably should not have been in a position where they could make money on whether or not he survived. If they happened to make the wager that he would die, they would have a conflict of interest given that they could make some coin if they did not do their jobs.

The barbarian had some trust in his ability to defend himself, though. If he was used as bait, they might as well have him move through the palace with either a small guard, only Elric, or on his own if they wanted to make him an irresistible target. Of course, if the Assassin was as good as Micah assumed them to be, the trap could not be more obvious, although one so skilled might think they could survive the trap if their target was presented so clearly.

Despite his dislike of all manner of intrigue and plotting, he was inadvertently but unequivocally involved. It was annoying how it appeared to find him, but he was committed by this point. He was too far into this and wouldn't withdraw unless he was sure that it would prove to be no danger to his friends.

That was the moment when Skharr realized that Elric carried his trusty blade like it was his own, held in such a way that it would be easy for him to grasp.

The lord commander grinned when he saw that he had noticed.

"A fight, then?" the barbarian asked. "Good. I guess too many think I'll win this by points."

"Those who arranged for you to die are becoming nervous," the man explained in a low tone. "If you survive the trials, all they have done will be for naught, from what I hear. And you have the whole capital behind you. If I were to guess, I would say it was certainly not the way they imagined all this would play out."

Skharr nodded. "I think they assumed I would fight to avoid arrest and so force Tryam to kill me."

"It was a good guess. Even I assumed your first reaction would be a violent one."

The barbarian grinned. "Well, nothing plays out simply when the gods are involved. For what it is worth, I would have preferred it if they kept out of this mess."

"Not I. They've helped too much at this point, but it shows that there is always a bigger game than what we think. Even when the emperor is involved."

"Have they learned anything?" Skharr couldn't help a little levity.

"Who—Tryam?"

He grinned and gestured expansively. "The gods."

"Who the fuck knows?" Elric motioned for the rest of the guards to form up as they began to approach areas of the palace where there was more movement. "They keep their own counsel."

He was right enough about that, although Skharr didn't like knowing that more parties were aware and invested in the outcome than he could ever know.

Even worse, it was distracting. Having to think about how many different people would have something to gain from his success or failure would always weigh on his mind.

More people had begun to arrive. This was a public area of the palace, where those who had followed his movements over the past week or so were gathered.

There were far too many of them. That much was clear immediately as they pressed in while they shouted at him and tried to gain his attention. He couldn't make out any particular words and they were pushed back by the guards.

The press slowed the group and made it difficult for them to move forward. Despite the seemingly natural ebb and flow of the crowd, it felt intentional. He had planned enough of these to know that if there was ever a time for an attack, it would be now.

He snapped his hand forward and drew his dagger from Elric's belt as one of those who shoved against the guards flashed steel in his hands.

The gathering turned to chaos in seconds and the assassin immediately drove his blade into the guard's gut and pushed him into the others, and he was not the only one. Skharr identified three others who immediately attacked the escort, and four of them were felled before they could even draw their weapons. The assailants pushed forward to where he waited for them.

Others stepped out of the crowd with their daggers in hand,

and he knew even more waited in the background, likely with crossbows to try to find a shot on their target in the chaos.

One of the assassins had a clear path to him and squeezed past the guards who still tried to form up around him. The blade in his hand caught the light for a moment. He had to admire the man's courage that drove him forward like he expected him to be another lordling hiding behind his guards.

The dagger was thrust at his chest but he was ready for it and moved out of the way, sidestepped the stab, and hammered his arm on the assassin's wrist. A sharp crack was followed by a cry of pain from the man, who dropped his blade. It clattered on the floor as Skharr grasped him by the collar and lifted him off his feet.

Instinct told him it was a better idea than simply stabbing the man and throwing him aside. He had no shield and if they intended to fire crossbow bolts at him, he had to improvise.

His suspicions were justified when the soft twang warned him that bolts were incoming. He wasn't sure where they came from, but the way the assassin in his hands jerked and jolted twice, it seemed he was holding his meat shield in the right direction.

The man had fought to try to free himself, but his body immediately went limp in the barbarian's arms and he hurled him away. Two bolts protruded from his back and the sharp-shooters were now visible. They likely had been told to wait for the innocent folk to flee and take the first opportunity, or they would have known to wait to strike when the guards were out of the way as well.

Then again, Skharr was tall enough that he stood above the guards in front of him, and the assassins had likely not thought that he would use one of them as a shield.

He hefted his dagger and scanned the courtyard, which was now empty. The two crossbowmen struggled to reload their weapons as quickly as possible.

While he couldn't handle both in time, one less bolt would be a boon, at least. He leaned forward, whipped his arm out, and launched his dagger.

It cut a smooth trajectory and spun gracefully before it buried itself in the assassin's chest—a good throw, he decided with satisfaction as the man stumbled back. He pulled the blade out almost immediately and staggered before he fell as blood gushed from the wound he had opened further. If he'd left the weapon in, he would probably have survived, but maybe these assassins had no intention to be taken alive.

Once the guards had formed up and prepared for the attack, many of the assassins were felled and cut down, but almost a dozen more were ready to attack. By the looks of them, they had sent the weak and the ill-prepared to attack first and thin the numbers. The others wore proper armor and leathers and looked like they were ready to overpower the guards before reinforcements could be called in.

Skharr did not intend to allow that to happen. He dropped to one knee, dragged the bolts out from where they were buried in the lone assassin, and rushed to where he could see Elric was tangled with one of the pawns. The man bled from at least three deep wounds, but he still held onto the lord commander to distract him from the one who rushed in from behind.

They would have to find out who sent assassins who were so willing to be killed so someone else could complete the assassination successfully.

And since they were still inside the palace and would be swarmed by Elites in seconds, even the skilled fighters would likely end up dead.

The barbarian assumed that the Elites would try to take as many of them alive as possible, which in turn meant the assassins had been instructed to end their own lives once their task was done.

Unless he ended their lives for them. It seemed the decent

thing to do. They had provided him with some engaging combat, after all.

He rushed at the man who tried to catch Elric off-guard and roared as he hammered the first bolt through his arm. It stopped his short sword from reaching its intended target and he shoulder-charged the man to drive him off course.

The wound was not lethal but the assassin clutched his hand as if it had seized. His mouth began to foam and he sagged, then fell as his whole body convulsed and shuddered.

It could only be poison, although Skharr was not sure which kind.

"A good fight, wouldn't you say?" Elric asked and looked at him with a grin. "Thanks."

The barbarian chuckled and shook his head. "You and your men are defending my life and you feel you need to thank me for returning the favor? Either way, it seemed like a waste of perfectly good poison."

"I don't know. It felt like the polite thing to do."

Before he could answer, three more of the assassins pushed past the line of guards and Elric reacted to almost sever the head of the first one. He reversed his blade quickly to slash the throat of the second before he could bound over his fallen comrade.

The third was quicker and smaller—a full-blooded elf, given how she moved—and her face was covered. Perhaps she was a blood elf, although he wouldn't wait for her to take her mask off to show him. Her gaze was fixed on Elric, so she probably intended to kill him with a slash from her poisoned blade before she attacked Skharr. If the barbarian had backed away and tried to save his own life, she would have had a chance.

He knew better and surged forward and lowered his shoulder to hammer into the assassin around her midsection. He expected to feel her blade slice into him but instead, her body jerked and he realized he had escaped being hit with another crossbow bolt.

Luck had played its part, and he wondered if there was some godly interference.

Then again, he would never be an easy target for the crossbowmen, especially since more of the guards raced in to help. The assassin had only one shot left but had wasted it and killed one of his comrades instead of him. All in all, the entire attack was a rushed attempt by those who were certainly not the best in their field. Despite this, however, they had still almost managed it, even when the guards expected the attack.

More bootsteps announced the arrival of reinforcements and a handful of the assassins who were still alive immediately turned their blades on themselves rather than risk being captured alive.

It wasn't quite the end they had hoped for, and Skharr knew that Micah would likely blame their lack of any live assassins on him somehow.

Still, better them than him. He heaved a sigh and checked his body for any injuries. "Check yourselves for cuts, no matter how small. They used poisoned blades and time is of the essence."

The guards nodded and all immediately checked to ensure there were no wounds that would kill them as surely as a dagger to the heart. Most had none thanks to their armor, but the few who had been wounded early in the fighting were already dead.

Not too many, however. He could be happy about that, at least, but he still didn't like it that someone with so much in the way of resources was so intent on killing him. At any other point of his life, he would have saddled Horse with all the resources he could carry and left, avoiding the major roads so that he could move without stopping until he reached an area where folk didn't want him dead.

It would not have been the first time he did that. At one point, he had even run out of food and needed to stop for a few days so he could hunt, fish, and gather enough for him to be able to continue his journey.

That hadn't been his finest hour, but it was still better than what he had to endure at the moment.

"Barbarian," Elric called as he cleaned the blood from his sword, "you'll have to leave soon or my men will start taking after you."

Skharr grinned and retrieved his dagger from the chest of the fallen crossbowman. "There will always be a little barbarian in every person. It's only a matter of how often they let it out, if at all."

All the assassins were dead. More than a few of them showed signs of seizure and foam that indicated they had poisoned themselves to ensure they were not taken alive. Even so, he had a trial to attend, and any investigation would have to wait until he returned.

Or until the trial did its work and killed him.

Now that he was no longer bait, they were able to move at a rapid pace. Most of the common folk had run for their lives and thankfully, none of them had been caught in the fighting.

He was led through a few narrow passages to where more guards were waiting. They had no doubt already heard about the assassination attempt and stood with their weapons already drawn and ready for an attack.

The barbarian scowled when he saw Sera with them. She had her sword drawn as well.

He stopped short and regarded her with undisguised irritation. "What in the seven fucking hells are you doing here?"

"Is that the kind of thanks I can expect for helping you?" Her smile belied the hint of offense in her tone.

"You're fucking right it is. Now answer the godsbedammed question."

She rolled her eyes and twirled her saber in her hand, and a small smirk appeared on her features. He hoped she understood that while he was more than happy to see her, he did not want anyone else to be mixed up in his mess.

"I'm here to help a barbarian idiot," the captain answered. "And if you have any objections, you'll find they have a very warm and comfortable if dark home up your ass."

"And again, your friends appear to impress." The rough interjection prevented his response.

Skharr turned to his DeathEater comrades who approached. None of them had their weapons in hand and by all appearances, they appeared to be drunk, full, and happy enough. It was almost like they did not know or care that assassins wandered the palace.

The one and only the sign he needed for reassurance was that each one had his bow strung and ready for a fight.

They carried his weapons to him and he equipped himself quickly before Turan handed him the ax.

"Keep it up, big'un," the chieftain whispered. "The food is plentiful and the fights make it all worth it."

"Get on out of here, you big oaf. I'm sure there are enough cooks and loose women for you to catch the attention of," Skharr muttered and shook his head when Turan raised his hands in surrender and gestured for the barbarians to leave.

Each one stepped forward to pat him on the shoulder in the familiar gesture of wishing him good luck before they moved away.

Everything about it told him the barbarians were out looking for an assassin to kill, likely in as spectacular a fashion as possible to ensure a message was sent to any who wanted to do him any harm.

He was encouraged by their support, but he doubted that any of the assassins were left for them to kill. Still, Micah could probably make use of their enthusiasm.

In that moment, he realized that Sera was watching him carefully.

"What?" He raised an eyebrow at her.

"No comments?"

"About you heading out with me?" Skharr sighed and shrugged reluctantly. "I would if I had a choice. But you are your own person and you do this because of...well, I assume the reasons are stupid. But stopping you isn't something I care to try. Instead, we will win this and you can tell me about how I should retire to a mountain far away from civilized company or something of the sort."

"Continue dreaming." She chuckled. "Come on, barbarian. You've had all the bloodletting so far and I intend to join the action."

"Those words will always warm my heart."

They headed off and the chieftain watched them as Elric stepped beside him.

"How does he know all these women warriors?"

The guard commander shrugged. "Beats me. Although I understand from Tryam that the women in a queen's fortress practically threw themselves at him for a few dungeon stories."

Turan shook his head. "Perhaps we should all aspire to be Skharr when we eventually grow up."

CHAPTER TWENTY-ONE

The fog showed no sign that it would lift. It permeated his clothes and made him feel like he was sweating.

His first thought was that it was almost like they were in some kind of swamp, except that Skharr could make out the dim forms of trees in the grayness that surrounded them on all sides. No mud sucked at his boots, which told him they were on firm ground for the moment, at least.

"A trap?" Sera asked, her sword already drawn.

He studied their surroundings uneasily. "Most likely."

It would be best if she handled anything that came close. He was confident in his abilities, of course, but knew she was still better in combat at shorter distances. This also left him free to cover longer distances. He drew his bow off his shoulders and waited with an arrow in hand.

The stillness around them made him think he would be able to hear anything that approached them. Of course, the real fear was that something could approach them even in the silence without making a sound.

"Well, there's nothing else for it," Skharr muttered, nocked his arrow, and nodded for them to move forward.

They couldn't see much beyond five feet ahead before the mist grew too thick. They would have to rely on the sounds of everything around them to have any hope of detecting a trap or attack ahead of them.

As they moved cautiously along the path, nothing emerged to harass them. A few creaks and squawks issued from insects and birds in the trees around them, but nothing suggested an ambush or that they were walking into danger.

In silence, they continued. He would not let himself be drawn into a fight in the mist if he could avoid it but couldn't help being suspicious at the almost unnatural calm. His shoulders were tense and he forced himself to relax but remain vigilant as he looked at the landscape around them.

Nothing moved, not even a breath of wind, and it wasn't long before a rivulet of sweat began to inch down his back. He frowned when he noticed a shadow ahead of them.

His initial fear that they were approaching a massive monster was quickly put to rest. Instead, he stared at a pale white building that looked much like a mausoleum. It was made entirely of pure white marble, although the mist made it appear a ghastly gray. Skharr studied the building for a moment and paused at the steps leading to the entrance.

Sera displayed the same reticence although she took the first step.

"There's nothing else for it," she said, grinned, and motioned for them to ascend.

Exactly twenty steps brought them to the top. It seemed like the mist continued inside the doors—which were also made of marble—and everything was open as if waiting for them.

Inside, a ring of seats was positioned around the building and it began to look a little more like a temple than a mausoleum. The center was left open and contained no seats like everything was arranged to enable people to watch what was happening. An altar of black marble there contrasted sharply with the white everything else was made of.

"That…looks like an altar," Skharr noted as he approached it.

"It is."

"It seems like we might have to kill something to put on it." He gestured irritably at the deserted space around them. "Do we have to head into the mist to find a monster to slay so it can be placed there?"

His companion looked thoughtful. "I don't…no, I don't think that is what it is meant to be."

He narrowed his eyes and approached the smooth, flat surface. A handful of inscriptions on the black marble caught his attention. He couldn't read the languages, which was odd on its own, but it seemed Sera could. She ran her fingers over one of the inscriptions and muttered like it was a language she hadn't heard or spoken in years.

"Do you understand this?"

She nodded but her face had captured a frown. "It's an old form of elfish but not any of the higher dialects. I don't think I've ever read any of these in particular."

"But you can read it?" He knew he was pushing her but if she couldn't, they would have a real problem.

Her gaze fixed on the carved writing, she extended a flat hand and moved it from side to side. "The…portal, I think—or maybe the door through the…test, maybe, requires a lamb."

He snorted in disbelief. "We need a sheep? How in the fuck should we have known that before we came in?"

"It's…not a literal lamb. Lamb is used in many elvish languages as a metaphor because they are used in most sacrifices before battle. So…I assume it is a metaphor."

"A sacrifice?"

Sera nodded before she focused on the inscription. "One can give only once and it is worth all to them. Let…blood—or maybe life—drain through the channels on the edge of the altar and…

uh, let life be lifted by the lamb. I think that was supposed to be a rhyme in the dialect. "

Skharr needed more time to determine what was being said but once he did, he shook his head. "No."

"What?"

He needed no help to make this particular decision. "This is bullshit. It's one thing for a companion's life to be risked for these trials, but there's no way in heaven or hells that I'll take part in a trial that requires a companion to sacrifice their life for mine."

She studied him closely and did not present any other argument as he shook his head and shouldered his bow. It was clear enough that they would not face something his weapons would be needed for.

Her silence told him volumes. For one thing, it said she already knew a sacrifice would be involved in this trial, and he knew she was offering that regardless of his arguments. She was her own person, of course, but so was he.

He pointed his finger at her. "Listen here, Sera Ferat. It will not happen. I care too much to kill my friend. Hells, I'll slit my own throat before I sacrifice you to...to a fucking godsbe-dammed demon or whatever."

Sera didn't look like she believed him and he drew the dagger he'd used to kill one of the assassins and pressed it to his throat.

He'd never considered suicide as a way to end it all, but it wasn't regarded as a dishonorable way to go. At the same time, he was aware that if he died, she would die too, but at least he would not have to live with having let her die for him.

Maybe that was a selfish decision on his part and if there was an afterlife, she would undoubtedly hold it against him forever.

It was a terrible idea, in all honesty.

"Stop, Skharr," she said quietly, smirked, and shook her head. "There is another way."

"What other way?" the barbarian demanded but lowered his

dagger. "This is worse than what even Janus usually does. Although I wouldn't put it past the bastard to kill my friend."

"No." She shook her head and slid her sword into its sheath. "I —fucking hells, Micah, when I get out of this, I will choke you."

Confusion began to overtake his frustration. "What does Micah have to do with this?"

"Because she knows!" Sera slapped the altar. "She knows, and I know, and now...I have to share it with you."

Skharr felt like people were playing games with him, and he didn't like it.

"What...share what?" he asked in exasperation.

She turned to look at him and he realized she was blushing furiously. That, if nothing else, indicated that she had no intention to let herself be killed by this trial and she certainly wouldn't let him die either.

"Well...I am not a simple girl, mind, but I am not a woman, strictly speaking."

The barbarian tilted his head and tried to wrap his mind around what she was trying to tell him. "You're...not a woman?"

Sera sighed and tried to think of a better way to describe it. "What do you see when you look at me?"

It seemed like she was trying to trick him, or it would have if she didn't look as out of sorts as he felt.

She stared expectantly at him so he felt compelled to answer. "A...a warrior. A woman. A worthy friend."

"Anything else?"

He scowled. "I feel as though I am having another trial already."

"Answer the question."

At that, he took a step forward and held his knife up. "Sera, I have been your friend for a long time. You've saved my life about as many times as I've saved yours."

That wasn't the answer she was looking for and she pursed her lips.

"Do you remember when we were on the road and that crass rogue who tried to stop us with a tree suggested that he wanted to have this way with me?"

"He did a good deal more than suggest it. It was why I shot him."

"Well, I might have..." She paused and toyed with the filigree of her sword. "That was the moment I fell for you."

"Fell...for me?"

Skharr had a habit of playing the barbarian when out and about and often looked and sounded as dull-witted as he could so folk didn't think they had to worry much about his brains. This, however, was the first time in a long time that he felt genuinely stupid.

"Yes. Fell. For you."

"You're one step from the emperor's throne," he reminded her. "I'm a barbarian."

"And yet you have ladies from Verenvan to the capital city dropping their undergarments at the mere mention of your name —and even willing to pay you a gold coin for the effort."

He gestured dismissively. "As it turned out, there were political machinations involved there as well. But I don't do that."

"You did."

He sheathed his dagger. She had made this far more complex than it needed to be. Perhaps it was more important to her, which was what the sacrifice needed. If she saw it as only some physical pleasure and release, she would not have been the right one for the trial.

His reply was important and he phrased it carefully. "It's not as though I had an oath and my promise, or a ring on my finger. Being paid for a night of passion is not a terrible thing if it didn't come with fighting to the death. Eventually, they would find a more powerful or better swordsman and I would fail. If I fall, I'd rather it be for someone I cared about."

She fixed him with wide eyes. "Like?"

"Well…you." He indulged another deep scowl. "And you must know I've never found my way between your thighs, so you'll know it isn't only…"

"You thinking with your dragon?" A small smile tugged at the corners of her mouth.

It was his turn to turn a light shade of red. "Folk talk too much."

"But this"—she pointed to the altar—"has two meanings. One is certainly the obvious choice, and if you think about it, this is the sixth trial. If someone has made it this far."

This, at least, was easy to answer. "Which has not happened before."

"Then something special is happening. Whoever concocted this trial wants someone to sacrifice something special. Truly special."

Again, he spoke what he thought was obvious. "Their life."

"It could be, provided one puts a great deal of value on their own life. Or…" She took a step closer to him. "Perhaps a woman who truly loves a man would be willing to give up her…virtue, as it were, for him. If he understood what that sacrifice meant for him and him alone."

"Sera…" His mouth was suddenly dry and Skharr realized that he was at a loss for words. What exactly should a man say to something like that? "I…I wasn't serious about the demon. Although I meant the rest of it." He wasn't sure where that pointless comment came from, but he needed to respond to her somehow.

"As do I." Her calm expression reassured him. "If we were to face a demon, I could demand that you take me and my conscience would be clean. I would sacrifice my desire to be… special with one I love to protect you from a demon. Why would I not be willing to give myself up in that manner now?"

She was articulate, he had to give her that, and the way she inched closer to him was a little more than he was prepared for.

"If the truth be told," he said finally and drew a deep breath, "Sera Ferat, I am not fucking worthy. You only know the Skharr who came from his farm to fight for coin. The man I was before that farm had an incredibly black heart."

"Damn right you are not worthy, but I still love you. That makes all the difference, Skharr DeathEater." She patted him on the chest to emphasize each syllable of his name. "I will admit between you and me that I have certain...feelings for a barbarian —a man who can protect me and cares for me as a person instead of for what I might give them. One who sees who I have become and can battle me toe-to-toe. A man who appreciates my mind as well as makes me feel special when he watches me move."

Skharr looked away and scratched his beard. "I...didn't think you'd noticed that. And I have tried not to do so."

Sera nodded, her hand still resting on his chest as she appeared to use the moment of silence to gather her thoughts, something that had not been allowed her since the moment all this started.

He opened his mouth to say something in the same moment that she spoke. It was for the best, as he had no idea what to say and he likely would have blurted something that annoyed exceedingly.

"But now I am willing to fully admit that I want you, Skharr. I want your attention, barbarian. If you walk away from these trials and head into your sunset, I will accept that. I admit my feelings and that is as much my sacrifice as anything else."

For some reason, his mind turned to Ahverna and how she had mentioned that it was likely the last time she could be with him. He'd not understood what she was talking about but his mind had not been on words at the time.

Cassandra had made the decision to bind herself to Theros again. There were no other ties to keep him. If he didn't know better, he could almost believe the gods had begun to meddle in his love life now, and there wasn't a damn thing he could do about it.

"Can you—a princess—truly handle a barbarian?" Skharr asked and placed his hand over hers. "Honestly, I always had the feeling that you believed me to be...beneath you."

"I have often considered that, I suppose." She laughed softly as her fingers closed around his shirt and she tugged him closer. "But your big-assed buckle is a bitch. Get your clothes off, and I would ask you to go slowly to begin with."

It seemed like she had misunderstood him, although he couldn't tell if that was intentional on her part or not. Either way, she had committed herself and any attempt by him to second-guess what she was doing would not end well for either of them.

Her tugging grew more insistent and he helped her to drag his shirt over his head and fling it aside. He undid his belt, removed his weapons and equipment, and let them fall with about the same amount of care as he had shown the shirt. There would be time for him to collect it all later.

He hoped. Sera began to remove her clothes. There was an efficiency about her movements that Skharr had no issues with watching. She had kicked her boots off and lowered her breeches along with her undergarments by the time he was done with his belt, and a wild, excited look captured her face as she grinned at him.

"You're watching me again," she whispered and licked her lips, and he looked into her eyes again.

He had no intention to offer a rebuttal despite his instinct to do so. Instead, he approached her, leaned down to cradle her cheeks in his hand, and pressed his lips to hers as tenderly as he could. Something in him wanted to go about it quickly and take her in a manly fashion, but a slow approach allowed him to savor the taste of her lips and was certainly worth it.

Sera, naturally, disagreed. She grasped his hair and his shoulders, pulled herself up, and wrapped her thighs around him. He lifted her a little higher so her legs wound around his waist, and she cupped his chin to press her lips hungrily to his again.

Skharr moved to the altar and settled her carefully on it as she giggled against him.

"It's cold," she managed to say by way of explanation as she shifted a little on the marble, inched back, and moved her hands to his trousers.

Her efficiency manifested again and she pushed his trousers down in moments and slid her hand to where she could feel him press against her. He slid his hands over her hips and pulled her a little closer, but it seemed like her full attention was on what she had in her hands.

"That is one hell of a sacrificial weapon," she whispered but still sounded excited. "I imagine it might hurt a little at first."

"Not necessarily," Skharr replied softly, stroked her cheek, and leaned forward to kiss her neck tenderly. "I'd like to make this special for both of us."

"You would?" She caught her breath as he kissed and nibbled over her collarbone, then shivered against him when his lips and tongue caressed her bare nipple lightly. "I understand it is special for me but..."

Skharr looked up and smiled as he pressed a light kiss to her lips. "As odd as it may sound, I've never been with...well, a friend who...who hadn't already—"

"Who was a virgin, you mean? Are you telling me that you've never visited one of those vestal temples for a special offering?"

"A what?" He frowned in momentary confusion.

"Never mind." She grinned, leaned closer to kiss him, and ran her fingers through his beard. "Out of curiosity—"

"A lady of the night," Skharr interjected immediately and trailed his fingers over her stomach to spread her thighs a little more as his middle and forefingers stroked her tenderly. "In a small town, after earning my first coin as a mercenary. Nothing particularly special."

"Well, you can only give your virginity once, but perhaps you can give yourself fully to a friend—"

"No." He placed a finger on her lips to stop her. "Someone I love. I would die for you, Sera."

"I know but I would still prefer it if you were alive. It makes this part so much more enjoyable." Sera pressed her lips to his chest, looked up, and grinned as she ran her tongue over his bare skin and moaned softly as his fingers continued their work between her thighs. "Now, stop talking. I want you for as many hours as we have in here—wait."

"What?" Skharr paused and stared into her eyes to ensure that everything was all right.

"If the portal opens to let us out, do you think anyone could see us?"

The barbarian looked around hastily. She made a fair point and he wasn't quite sure what could or could not be seen through them.

"Perhaps it'll only open once we're finished with the altar," he suggested.

She appeared to think about it for a moment but turned her attention to him, moved her hand behind him, and grasped his ass to draw him closer to her.

"Fuck it," she whispered. "Let them watch a princess take a real man."

It had not been her finest idea. Micah had trusted the word of the gods and being stuck in a situation she had no control over made her anxious and nervous.

Perhaps she should have gone in with Skharr. The chances were that she could find something she loved that could be sacrificed.

"If she dies, I'll kill him myself."

Thankfully, her mutterings were lost in the crowd that had gathered as close to the cave as the guards would allow. Many of them had wagered coin on whether the barbarian would be able to endure all seven trials and emerge unscathed. Those who had made the bet early likely felt rather proud of themselves by this point.

Unfortunately, she did not share their confidence. Yes, he had survived the trials longer than anyone else, but it was no guarantee that he would survive the last two. Hell, she'd sent the man in with her sister on the word of a goddess who, for all she knew, wanted to remove all competition for his affections.

The guards had reacted well to the attempt on Skharr's life, however. The Elites stood at attention, their pikes lowered and directed at the populace. Any who approached were immediately warned that this would be considered an act of aggression and the Elites would retaliate.

Only one warning had been needed, and those Elites with crossbows in the back were ready to eliminate any who might test the patience of those on the front line.

Whispers broke her out of her reverie and she looked up as the portal flared and jerked as it usually did to warn of something coming through from the other side.

It indicated that Skharr had survived, but her heart leapt to her throat and thudded uncomfortably. Her anxiety made her take a step forward, impatient to see who would emerge.

The barbarian came through first. He looked a little sweaty and flushed, but for all she knew, it was because he'd had to watch someone he cared for deeply die.

"Son of a whore," she whispered and drew her dagger, then noticed that Tryam was celebrating along with those in the crowd.

Celebratory shouts swept through the ranks when they saw another figure leave the portal.

Sera looked a little flushed as well. She rested one hand on the hilt of her sword and looked nervous.

"That fucking shit." Micah scowled. "She is walking a little odd, isn't she?"

She sheathed her dagger and suppressed the urge to push through the guards. Tryam's eyes were narrowed as well and she was sure he had noticed the same oddity she had seen.

The crowd gave themselves to celebration as if they had survived the trials, although perhaps those who were most enthusiastic had some coin on the venture.

Tryam greeted the barbarian with a warm hug. Micah would have advised against such displays of affection, but it wasn't like people didn't know that he favored the barbarian.

Still, she chose not to remain beside the emperor, not with so many people there to see it. She smirked, drew away from the celebration, and disappeared into the crowd. Sera wasn't an idiot, and she would have made the connection as to why her sister knew she was the right companion for this trial.

"You don't look like you encountered much fighting," the emperor stated as he pulled away from Skharr. "Warm, though, like you were put through a great exertion. Too much running, I suppose."

"You could say that."

The barbarian acted laconic again, although Tryam couldn't tell if it was simply because he wanted to maintain the illusion for the rest of the people. Or perhaps he merely didn't want to talk. From the blush on Sera's face when he mentioned the exertion, he could tell that something had indeed been sacrificed. Micah hadn't explained but it seemed plain enough. And in the end, there was no use in prying, especially not out in the open.

"Clear the way. I would return to the palace," he ordered and the Elites immediately carved a path through the celebrating bystanders. "Come with us, Skharr. We won't need the seventh test."

The emperor spoke in a low tone easily drowned out by the people celebrating all around them.

"What do you mean?" Sera asked and leaned closer.

"We will speak of it in the throne room. Make haste."

There was no point in keeping anyone waiting or talking about it with the rest of the empire listening.

Thankfully, the people were more than willing to make way. Word of the attempt on Skharr's life had spread like wildfire, and while they were happy to see he had survived, they were more than anxious to ensure that they were not taken for assassins themselves.

Their escort led them briskly to the smaller throne room. While it wasn't the main one, it was where most of the real business was allowed to happen.

Tryam marched up the steps to his throne, settled himself comfortably, and gestured for the rest of the party to be brought in.

There were more than enough of them, but he wanted to ensure that nothing was left to chance.

"What's happening here?" Skharr asked as he studied the room.

"All in good time." Tryam nodded to the guards.

The side doors opened to admit the Sareenan diplomats, who swept in with a group of their official guards. Elric had insisted on it to ensure that they had no doubts about the loyalties of the men who would defend them.

From the other side, another group entered. His grim-faced Elites dragged three men in. They were gagged and in chains, although they still tried to voice their vociferous protests.

"I thank you for taking the time to meet me on such short notice," Tryam stated as the Sareenans were shown to their seats and the dukes were forced to their knees. "After the assassins were killed, drastic action had to be taken. It would seem a few former members of my gentry are responsible for the mess we find ourselves in. They conspired together to go against my wishes and start a war I do not want. To accomplish this, they enlisted a nigh-mythological assassin whom they paid and the Patron God of Assassins, who we feared was lost to time."

Skharr didn't look happy about any of this, but he at least knew to keep his mouth shut. His annoyed expression, however, said all that needed to be said.

Sera appeared to have regained her composure and stood silently and as placid as a statue, her hand on the hilt of her sword.

"From what we have been told," the emperor continued, "this assassin is an extension of the god in question. Nevertheless, he would have failed since Skharr will have been proven to be not guilty."

"Fuck that." The barbarian growled and stepped forward. "I'll not have an assassin go after me, nor will I allow anyone I care for to be caught between me and them."

The Sareenans looked surprised, although Tryam couldn't tell if it was because of the outburst or how eloquent it was. They still thought the man was practically a mute.

He turned to look at Sera for a moment, who still showed no sign of any emotion.

"Never," Skharr insisted and this time, he spoke in a lower, less confrontational tone.

"I think I can help with that." The voice carried through the chamber and most of the Sareenan guard reached for their weapons as Ahverna made her presence known. She stepped out from the shadows that had suddenly gathered in the corner of the room. "But I'll tell you now that this assassin is as sly as a fox and will not be easy to kill."

"When are they ever?" Skharr growled belligerently. "Put me in the same room with…him, I assume? I'll rip his eyeballs out."

"Him…and an it, as it turns out," Ahverna answered, well aware of the fact that she was being more cryptic than usual. "I'm afraid I cannot say much more."

"Fucking gods," the barbarian muttered and shook his head.

She sighed dramatically. "You don't know the half of it. There are so many rules and honestly, it's confining."

"For a reason, by my estimate," Tryam interjected.

The Sareenans appeared to not care much about the presence of a goddess and discussed something quietly between themselves.

"The two of us will not lose you to this assassin," Sera commented as she approached Skharr.

"It's cute," Ahverna said with a small smile. "Or do I mean disgusting? No, cute, certainly. Truly, that is what I think."

He didn't look like he was in the mood to deal with whatever Ahverna was talking about. Instead, his attention turned to the three dukes and he strode closer to them with a look that immediately stopped their attempted shouts as they stared at the giant of a barbarian.

"Do not think I've forgotten you. I haven't forgotten your disrespect either." His tone was cold with controlled anger.

Tryam smirked. "I've heard the barbarian has a habit of impaling those he hates with burning posts before he tears their arms off. Rumors and myths, surely, and yet…I'd very much like to discover if there is any truth to them."

Skharr turned to face the emperor and an oddly subdued look slid onto his face.

"Where did you learn that?"

"I have considerable gold," the young ruler answered with a smile. "And I am very interested in learning all I can about you."

"We'll have a talk about this later as well," Skharr retorted.

"Right, then." Ahverna stated and clapped briskly. "I suppose I'll take the three of you?"

Tryam turned as Micah entered the room with her arms folded. Her expression suggested there was something to add to the discussion.

"Only two," Skharr answered. "Sera and I should be enough for this."

Even the captain looked surprised by that but wasn't unwilling, at least.

"Oh, shit," Micah whispered and approached the throne, although it didn't seem like she spoke to anyone in particular. "Life just went sideways."

Sareenans displayed little interest in anything else happening in the room and continued with their low-voiced conversation as Skharr, Sera, and Ahverna disappeared.

"Emperor Tryam, we will send word to the Jarl," the diplomat finally stated and stood slowly from his seat. "I think your explanation is acceptable, but I cannot speak without his consent."

"Send the Jarl my deepest respect and condolences. I am told the honored dead was close to him."

"Both are graciously accepted."

Tryam turned to Micah, who still looked somewhat agitated that her sister had left her behind. "I have a feeling you had something you wanted to say to me. What was that about three?"

She shook her head. "We need to talk—without any ears."

"Well, you might as well talk." Tryam stood from his throne. "These three won't be able to speak of much from the grave, after all. We might as well kill them."

"And deprive the barbarian of his justice?" Elric asked.

That caused a great many muffled shouts from the dukes, who were still gagged but begged for mercy all the same. The emperor thought he could detect a hint of a smirk on his lord commander's face.

"Why do I have the feeling the two of you have been at this for a while now?" Micah asked and looked from one to the other, her eyebrow raised.

"Who, us?" the emperor asked with a chuckle. "See them secured in chains. Honored guests from Sareena, I will speak to you soon enough and my council will update you on the punishments we will enforce. Suffice it to say that those at the top will be punished and lose their lands, if not their lives."

The Sareenan diplomat bowed deeply. "And who will be put in their place? If we have three royals with the same attitudes, it will matter little. Replacing an old goat with a young goat will leave a man with an old goat all the same, as they say in my land."

Tryam managed to avoid a smile that might create the wrong impression. "I've never tended goats myself, but I assume you speak the truth. Either way, I promise they will not be three with the same sympathies to cause mischief on our border. Now, if you will excuse me?"

"Of course."

He descended from the throne and gestured for Micah and Elric to follow him with a small contingent of guards.

CHAPTER TWENTY-TWO

"What did she mean by three?" Skharr asked.

His companion looked at him in confusion. "I... maybe she wanted Micah to come with us?"

"It didn't seem like it. As I recall, she looked at you when she said it."

"Does it matter?" Sera looked around. "Where the fuck are we?"

"The mountains."

"As if that isn't obvious enough." She shivered slightly. "Which mountains? And why did she bring us here?"

"I assume my would-be assassin is somewhere around here." Skharr looked up the mountain face and breathed deeply. "Oh... fuck me, this is not good."

"What?" Sera looked around and sniffed the air as well. Her eyes widened as she drew her blade. "Oh. Shit."

"Yes." Skharr carried no weapons, although there was no reason to worry about it yet. "A dragon lives in these parts. We'd do well to be cautious of it."

She nodded and motioned for him to lead this time as they began to ascend the path. It appeared to wind around the mountain range, likely an old trade road that had long since been abandoned given the condition of it. While it had once been wide enough for carts and carriages to be pulled two abreast if needed, it was now barely safe for even a horse to walk on it.

Still, two people on foot were safe enough, and he maintained a good pace. He moved quickly and his gaze constantly searched between the sky and the mountain face to ensure that nothing could assail them from above. He didn't disregard the fact that the dragon might attack them from below but as a rule, the creatures preferred to nest in the heights and the peaks of mountains.

The path came to a sudden end and opened onto a flat space that led directly into the mountains. The barbarian couldn't tell if a tunnel or merely a cave shadowed the rockface, but he was distracted from his survey when they realized they were not alone.

A hooded figure sat on a rock close to the cave's entrance and a fire that crackled and burned brightly.

Its gaze turned directly to them, and its eyes narrowed to study them in silence for a moment, although it did not seem particularly surprised by their presence. Instead, it appeared to gauge them intently as they came to a halt some ten paces away.

"It's hard to find pinewood this high up," Skharr noted. "And even harder to bring it this far, I think, and with no horse besides."

The figure stood slowly. It was slim but almost as tall as he was, although it looked like something was hidden under the cloak.

"Ssssssso," it hissed. "My mark comessss to me. Thissssss is a firssst."

The barbarian drew a deep breath and folded his arms over his chest. "The world always sees the first of something. And the last of another."

"I sssssee the woman with child has brought a ssssword. But...where issss your blade? Or do you plan to beat me with your bare fissssstsssss? Or bite my fingerssss off? Barbarianssss do have a reputation for their beasssstly naturesssss."

He grinned and glanced at Sera. He didn't know what the creature meant when it said Sera was with child, but now wasn't the time to think about it.

"Some mighty tool of the gods you are," he answered with a chuckle. "And yet you are still a simpleton. I'll have my ax now!"

The ax was gone.

It had been delivered to him the moment Skharr returned from his trial, although it noticeably lacked any blood of the fallen. Of course, he might have cleaned it, although barbarians were generally not the type to clean their blades when they returned from battle.

There were questions as to what in the hells had happened during the trial, but no details were provided. Skharr had been hurried away by the emperor, although he'd had his weapons removed and delivered to the appropriate parties. The ax had been returned safely to his hands.

"Where has the fucking ax gone?"

His tone of voice immediately sobered the other DeathEaters in his party, and from one moment to the next, they changed from the carefree, fun-loving brutes who had begun to gain more popularity in the city into the hardened, calloused battle veterans he had chosen for precisely that reason.

Weapons were grasped and drawn, the music stopped, and they all looked around to try to find the thief. Screams issued from the people who were being searched and removed.

"What is the meaning of this?" One of the Elites stepped forward but studied the barbarians warily and tried to determine if he and his men were in any danger.

"Someone's stolen the Ax of Skharr DeathEater!" Turan

growled his rage. "Now, either join us to find it or get the fuck out of our way!"

"We will join you." He motioned for more of the guards to approach and directed them quickly to start looking for the thief. "It cannot have gone far."

"You're wrong about that." The ancient was a little more familiar, and Turan knew him immediately. Theros liked to portray himself as an old man, likely for the same reason that Skharr liked to portray himself as an oafish buffoon.

Cassandra stood beside him in full armor and ready for battle. A rent in the air around them left no mystery as to how they had arrived out of nowhere.

"Skharr had need of the ax," Cassandra explained. "And he will need help before too long."

"When does Skharr ever need help?" Turan asked with a scowl. "He's fought gods and dragons before."

"And he will fight a little of both this time," she answered. "There will be a need for health potions."

"Aren't you a paladin?" one of the barbarians quipped and gestured to her with his weapon. "Or will you go into battle as the Barbarian Princess?"

"Continue making that wish and it might come true—if you find a djinn."

"Of course I wish it," the man laughed. "Every barbarian wishes to see their princess in all her...glory."

Theros fixed the man who spoke with a gimlet stare that made it difficult for him to continue his joke.

"Barbarians," Cassandra declared before any of the tensions she could see rising distracted them from the matter at hand. "Let's go to battle."

"Our princess speaks our language," Turan shouted, brandished his blade high, and raised a cheer from the group as another tear appeared ahead of them. A handful of the Elites hurried forward to join the warriors.

"We have to make sure they aren't getting into trouble," one of them offered by way of explanation.

Theros rolled his eyes. "I want it said that I had nothing to do with this."

That didn't sound like the lord high god, but now was not the time to question it.

If Skharr needed their help to battle a god and a dragon—or some combination of both—he would have it. Perhaps the next song would feature all those who committed to the event too.

He wasn't sure what kind of faith he had in whatever blessing Theros had put into the ax, but as his fingers closed over the haft, he nodded at the comforting weight of the weapon in his hand. Fortunately, he'd never removed his sword and dagger after the trial so he had those as well if he needed them.

"You have to love a god who stays true to his word," Skharr said, grinned, and twirled the weapon to reacquaint himself with its strength and perfect balance. "You were saying?"

"Ah…the Axssss." Its voice spat almost like a snake as its gaze studied the weapon in his hands. "Truly devioussss."

He faced it resolutely. "Not quite as devious as attempting to manipulate my friend the emperor into assassinating me on your behalf."

"True enough, and yet ssssssimple had you fought back. But in the end, all your battling, all your sssssstrife….issssss for naught. You will die jussssst the ssssame."

The creature spoke like a snake and when it pulled its cloak free, the barbarian realized why. Its mouth was long and ended in a snout that looked suspiciously like a snake's, complete with a forked tongue and fangs that protruded from the top half of its jaw.

It was unsettling to look at, especially when the rest of the cloak fell away to reveal scaled green skin that made it easy to believe it was some kind of reptile.

Except for the eyes. Those were puzzlingly human and stared at him like a man was trapped in the body of a monster.

"Yesssss....a sssssimple body for ssssimple tasks. Ussssseful, I suppossssse. But I have no intention to make thisssss eassssy for you, barbarian. One swipe of your ax and off comes a head, and yet..."

The body began to change and expand before his eyes. Skharr frowned as the figure transformed and altered itself. The snake grew to the size of most dragons, and although the creature had no wings, multiple heads emerged from the main body. A few were long enough to have bodies of their own and all fixed him with those annoyingly human eyes.

A handful of the heads jerked forward and Skharr jumped away to avoid the snapping jaws, which was likely intended to prevent them from trying to attack while the transformation was ongoing.

"There is nothing easy about a hydra," Sera whispered, drew her sword, and inspected the edge. "I assume you've fought one of these before."

"Never." His emphatic declaration seemed to surprise her.

"Oh. Well, avoid cutting the heads. Their blood is as deathly as their venom, and for each head removed, two more grow to make the creature more powerful."

"Then how the fuck do we kill it?"

She had no answer to that, but he had to admit that he did not either.

There was enough of a battle ahead for them to find out, however.

Surprisingly, another thought pushed for attention, seemingly determined to find resolution. "Before we're too busy, might I ask whether you're with child or not?"

"It's too early to tell. Don't you know how women's bodies work?"

He shrugged. "Some parts, yes. Other areas of my expertise are annoyingly lacking. It is why I ask."

"Well, I have no reason to believe I might not be carrying a little one." She sounded as if she hadn't considered it until now. "I did not carry, eat, or drink any preventative measures since fucking you was not what I expected to do any time soon. I might be, given all the folk who seem to think so. I suppose we'll have to wait and see, now won't we?"

Skharr nodded and glanced at her for a moment, although that was all they could spare as the creature's transformation appeared to reach its conclusion. It still tried to drive them back to the edge of the flat area, where a sheer cliff awaited them.

"There is no blame, of course," he told her. "But...I suppose you are the protection for our son now."

"Or daughter." She rolled her eyes at him. "Gods, we're already fighting like an old married couple."

"We've always fought, but never over the possible sex of our child." He turned to look at the hydra and realized that they had its full attention now. "I suppose I might even be a little angry. I'll protect you, and you protect—"

"I'll stop you right there," Sera snapped. "Neither of us will survive if we fight this creature on the defensive. There will be no protecting. We will attack and we will find a way to kill this piece of shit—although the six heads do present a challenging complication."

The barbarian laughed and focused on the creature as it began to slither closer to them. He had no issues with what she insisted on. Protecting and defending had never been what he was interested in either. When it attacked, they moved to different sides to force the beast to spread its focus.

Of course, the six heads indicated that someone had already tried to lop a head off, and he assumed there were a few very dead bastards out there who had thought for a moment that they had managed to kill the beast.

He would not follow in their footsteps, however. Skharr dove to the right as one of the heads lunged at him. Its fangs flashed in the weak sunlight and caught the rocks instead of him.

It was fast and he was careful to not risk giving it an easy target. The barbarian swung his ax and one of the heads jerked down and tried to intentionally be removed. He had expected it and angled over its body to inflict a shallow cut along its scales. Dark green liquid bubbled out and immediately filled the air with a noxious scent.

"I don't think we would be able to marry at this point," he shouted as the monster retreated and tried to cover its wound, which gave them a moment to talk again. "There are certain expectations of who a princess should marry and a barbarian is not among those."

"My bastard of a father turned my mother, my sister, and I out like lepers," she snapped. "Do you think I give a shit about what my position demands I do with my family life?"

"Well, no, but—"

"So, the only reason we could not be married is if you were to object to it. Which is your right, of course."

"I'd be a fool to not take you as a wife," he admitted and hefted his ax when the beast began to surge toward them. "You have my back in all things and are a warrior besides, but...the fact that you are related to the emperor is a complication."

"I can toss that title aside easily so I don't see why it should be."

Skharr did not want anything to do with making her any less than who she was.

"It is my problem to handle, Sera Ferat, not yours. You are as perfect as—"

"Oh, shut the fuck up, you big oaf." She twisted her blade and slashed at the snake to drive it back again. "Leave it as I'm perfect for now and we'll continue this conversation once the beast is dead, yes?"

He couldn't fault her logic and darted back as three of the heads aimed their attacks at him.

It certainly made sense to discuss it all later.

CHAPTER TWENTY-THREE

He'd always pictured a hydra as a massive, four-legged monster with a dozen or so heads that charged whatever was in front of it and overwhelmed them with attacks from the many heads. There was a reason for that, of course. Statues and pictures of them featured often in the history books since the swamplands used to be infested with the beasts, and killing them became a sign of great honor. Hunts were organized to kill them and the heads were stuffed and mounted in the homes of those who managed it.

Skharr always assumed they had been hunted to extinction, but there was some convincing evidence that their extinction had been wildly overstated. Then again, the creature they now battled was nothing like any of the pictures or the stories. It was a massive writhing snake about the size of the giant reptile he and Cassandra had battled not long before.

Each head attacked independently but did appear to strike in a coordinated fashion, which strongly suggested they were being directed by something central. It was, he thought, like a single brain kept all of them connected and allowed them to attack without needing to communicate.

It didn't matter. They battled a creature that could heal itself, bled venomous blood, and whose heads grew back double when removed.

"We need to find the center of it!" Skharr shouted.

"What?" Surprised, she snapped the question without looking at him.

"We can't kill it by striking the heads, but something that large must have a heart to pump all that blood. Something central."

She snorted, the sound both amused and scornful. "It's a magical fucking snake with heads that multiply. What makes you think there is anything resembling a regular creature in it?"

He scowled but directed it at the hydra. "Magic reflects nature. No matter how outlandish, it would still be a reflection of nature. There must be something that would enable us to kill it."

They had hacked and slashed at the creature repeatedly, and the beast's foul-smelling blood coated most of the ground. Every time, it retreated into the cave and appeared to heal itself before they could do any real damage to it.

"All right." Sera dropped to one knee and dragged a deep breath in. "I suppose you have a plan?"

"Not...not really. Do you happen to carry any explosives on you? We could bring the damn cave down on the fucker when it retreats in there."

She laughed and shook her head. "You know, I left all my explosives in my other alchemical pack."

For now, she looked like she was having fun, although it wouldn't be long before the fight for their lives grew a little more desperate.

Skharr grinned at her. "In that case, we need a distraction. Something to keep its mind occupied that would allow us to get close without having to bat any of the fucking snake heads away."

"You mean something like that?"

He turned to where she pointed at a rent that had appeared in the air on the path they had used to reach this point. It flared and flashed and a group of DeathEaters jumped out, their weapons in hand like they were ready for a battle. A group of Elites—from the look of their armor, at least—joined them, and the last one through before the tear closed was dressed in full paladin armor, her sword in hand as she shouted for the group to attack.

To their credit, they paused only for a moment in shock when they first saw the monster before they recovered their wits and immediately prepared themselves for combat.

"It's a hydra, which means don't cut the heads off," Cassandra warned. The barbarians knew better than to rush at anything that looked like a dragon and instead, began to draw their bows.

In moments, arrows streaked through the cold mountain air to pierce the hydra repeatedly and prompt a loud hiss from all the heads as the beast rushed out of the cavern to engage the newcomers.

"Yes," Skharr answered with a grin. "Something like that."

In all honesty, he doubted he would have been able to survive a trial like this with only one companion. All he could do was be thankful for the unexpected help and take advantage of it as decisively as possible.

"Come along then," he shouted and raced forward as the monster pushed forward to engage the newcomers directly. "We have a hydra to kill!"

The Elites lined up immediately to form a small shield wall that stood its ground against the snake heads. They were forced back almost immediately, but they bought time for the barbarians to continue to assail the beast with arrow after arrow.

Despite their efforts, it looked like it would drive them off the cliff edge but a cry went up from behind them.

"Theros!" Cassandra sprinted into the fight and forced the creature back a step. She stabbed her spear through one of the heads and pushed it into the ground. Two others attacked her but jerked back when they struck the armor.

Instead, the tails reached out like tentacles, wound around her leg, and pulled her back. She drew her sword, hacked the appendages off, and yanked herself free barely in time. To her surprise, even the tails began to regrow after a few seconds, and where one had been hacked off, two emerged and branched away from the creature.

"If we can hack enough pieces of it off, we might make it large enough that it'll be stuck in that fucking cave," Sera suggested.

"And in the meantime, we will be killed or trapped in there with it." Skharr shook his head. "The longer this fight lasts, the more likely it will be that we will be killed."

"What are you thinking?"

"I have no real plan as yet, but I have a feeling that if I get close enough to the center of it and begin to hack its internal organs, it will kill something or at least give the others the chance to kill something."

Her eyes widened. "That's a terrible plan."

"True. Do you have a better one?"

She scowled and finally shook her head. "Hack at internal organs it is."

"A truly barbarian plan."

He darted toward the creature and two of the heads suddenly snapped to focus on him. Sera stepped in to defend his back and knocked one of the tails away as it swept across the ground and tried to lash out at him.

The way it moved suggested there was no armor to it, but it was still fast and deft enough, and its wounds began to heal the moment they were inflicted. He had to find a way to kill it and do so quickly before it could heal again.

One of the heads snapped toward him almost faster than he could blink and he ducked and dove to the ground. He rolled over his shoulder and immediately regained his feet to push toward the mass of the creature ahead of him. Another head swung to try to attack him as he moved away from where Sera was able to block the rest of the attacks. He buried his ax deep into the central part of the creature's body.

The thick, noxious blood welled instantly from the wound, and Skharr realized that the blood healed the creature so quickly, although he doubted it would offer him a similar benefit.

He yanked the ax out again and turned to see the head advancing with its fangs exposed and aimed at him. With a twist, he moved the cheek of the ax to act like a shield and push the creature away from him. His blade was left with a slather of the creature's venom as he kicked it back.

Surprisingly, the venom suddenly disappeared into the blade like it was absorbed by the steel. He turned and used a moment of respite to hack into the flesh that was already healing from his first strike. The blood flowed again.

This time, however, there was no sign that the wound was being healed. There was no way to know why, although he had his suspicions and wouldn't question the effects. All that could be done now was to press the advantage.

It hissed in agony as the barbarian drew his ax out and powered it into its flesh again. The blow cut through bones and into something a little deeper that made the whole beast writhe in agony. Now, he had its attention.

He didn't see the tail until it was already on him and he sprawled heavily to leave the ax buried almost to the haft in the thickest part of the creature's body. The impact knocked the breath out of him, and he realized that the tails had begun to wind around his leg and squeeze tightly enough for him to feel like it attempted to force the life out of him.

Many serpents in the warmer parts of the world wrapped around their prey to squeeze them to death, but those had no venom in their fangs, which had often made him wonder why they had them at all.

This one had them as well but he could see the venom drip

from them as it leaned closer to finish him while the tails held him down.

"Fuck," Skharr whispered and strained to pull himself free from his binds.

In that moment, the head was gone and Sera stood beside him, her sword coated in the beast's blood.

That solved the immediate problem, and he managed to draw his dagger from his belt and stab it into the tails still wrapped around him. They sprang away, almost offended that he had dared to fight back.

"We don't have time to lay around all day," Cassandra shouted from where she and her group continued to try to distract the other heads. "We've got a damn hydra to kill!"

He couldn't argue with that. The barbarian pushed to his feet again and scowled at the head Sera had cut off. It began to grow again with a spare alongside it. They wouldn't be stopped without a little extra effort, and he had a feeling his ax was the weapon for the job. It hadn't been when they started, but it now seemed like it had been infused with the venom from the snake and altered enough to be able to kill it.

It was known that a snake's venom couldn't kill it, but dwarf handiwork and Theros' blessing were a crafty combination and gave him the opportunity to attack. He grasped his weapon and turned as both new heads—now fully grown—focused their attention on him and lunged in a joint attack.

Skharr drew a deep breath, watched the heads strike, and jumped to the side to move out of the way of the attacks at the right time. It was a gamble and if he lost, there would be two more heads for them to deal with.

Still, he was willing to take that risk. The first head that struck was already past and now tried to circle to complete the kill when the ax bit into its neck.

The head came off as easily as if the blade had struck only air and it tumbled to writhe and wriggle in the dirt.

Better yet, there was no indication that another head or two would grow from the stump.

That was a promising sign. The entire creature shivered at the strike and the other heads pulled away from their attack on the rest of the group and turned their attention to him. The tails immediately slithered toward him to try to constrict and bind him. They knew he was the source of the pain that it began to feel.

The others saw that as the signal for them to throw themselves into the attack. Skharr could appreciate their enthusiasm, but the whole hydra had begun to converge on him and ignore the efforts of his comrades. He was in the center of it all and this was enough to make any man start to think about what might wait for them on the other side.

Another of the heads struck but he was already in motion to avoid the tails that attempted to twist around him. Sera stood beside him and continued to cut and slash, but the hydra did not appear to pay her much mind despite her repeated assaults with her sword.

"Here!" Skharr shouted and tossed her the ax as he drew his sword. All the heads were still focused on him when the weapon changed hands. Perhaps it thought he was the only one who was able to cut it to pieces.

He was willing to take that risk.

She caught the ax without so much as missing a beat, snatched it out of the air, and immediately adjusted to grasp it a little higher than Skharr had to balance the weight as she attacked one of the heads that slithered in to strike at him instead of her.

The head was neatly severed and like the one before it, there was no sign that it would grow back.

The beast did not like that. The whole body writhed and any attempt to attack him suddenly ceased. There was a desperation to it. The creature did not think that it could be killed and was being introduced to the very real possibility that it would lose its life.

"Cassandra!" Skharr shouted as Sera broke into a run to escape the hydra that suddenly decided she had to die. "Spear!"

The paladin had her weapon already in hand and launched it to where he was. He appreciated that she hadn't thrown it directly at him.

It arced downward and the head buried into the rock as he ran toward it grasped it smoothly without a pause while Sera snapped her head around to remove another head from the creature as it struck without so much as breaking stride.

The blademasters certainly knew a thing or two about how to produce killers. He wondered if their child would have time for such training, either at her hand or at the hands of those who trained her.

Skharr would be happy to teach the child how to use the bow.

His hold on the spear tightened as he bounded to where he could see the wound he'd inflicted on the creature. He buried the spearhead quickly and deeply into the wound, then drove it deeper to where he could see precious and vital organs bulging through the blood.

That appeared to hurt too. Cutting heads off with a blessed ax was one way to kill the beast. Another was to impale the organs it could not grow back.

Pinning it in place was extremely useful as well. The rest of their group continued to rush in, cutting and slashing, while Sera attacked anything she could reach.

No single stroke would kill a beast like this. The barbarian knew that much, but watching it slowly be cut down was as gratifying as a fast kill.

It wasn't long before few pieces were left attached to the center. One head remained and the creature dragged itself pitifully over the ground and tried to move away.

Skharr could almost feel a little bad for it. Or he could have if it hadn't attempted to kill him and start a war.

"Will you do the honors?" Sera asked and handed him the ax.

"Aye." The barbarian approached the last remaining head, which looked at him.

It was already dead. If they left it behind, there was no way that a cold-blooded creature like it would survive in the cold mountain nights. Still, there was no point in leaving anything to chance at this point. He hefted the ax.

"You...mussssssst....know...that..."

The head fell in a single, smooth stroke.

"I have a feeling I do," he whispered and focused on the darkness that had begun to push out from inside the cavern.

It wasn't another creature, but Skharr assumed it was its master, who had hoped the hydra would be successful in its attempt to kill him.

The figure was almost as tall as he was but extremely thin. He looked like a man but only in a vague and general way. The limbs were too long and slender and the fingers ended in claws. He'd read of them before—the old evil men, creatures who were elevated during the wars—but most had been killed off. Like the hydra, it was said they were extinct.

This visage was what humans had been thousands of years earlier—or, at least, that was the claim.

"Do you know how difficult it was to find a hydra willing to fight for me?" the figure whispered as he approached. "They are honorable creatures, not prone to killing without cause."

"Am I to assume I am speaking to the Patron God of Assassins?" Skharr asked. "The Nameless One, I think you prefer to be called—is that correct?"

"And you called me by that many times in the past."

"No longer." It took effort but he maintained a cold, calm tone.

The god snorted. "And now? What? Do you think that killing my followers will redeem you?"

"No. I kill your followers because they tried to kill me. Because you tried to kill me. I thought the people you lead tend to succeed rather than try."

"Impudent whelp!"

The slap wasn't entirely a surprise. A bony hand connected with his cheek, hard enough to draw blood from the flesh over his cheekbone.

Still, it lacked the power he expected from a vengeful god. Skharr tilted his head and looked at the figure, whose slitted eyes stared at his hands.

More shadows appeared, this time to reveal another figure. He recognized Ahverna immediately. At least she wasn't passing herself off as a halfling anymore.

"My, my," she said. "It would appear that gods are not allowed to jump in like that. That's the way a bitch-assed demigod might act but it assumes there is room for a demigod assassin deity, and between you and me…I think not."

"What are you doing here?" the Nameless One whispered and took a step away from her.

She smiled with hard promise. "You. And I'll be doing you good."

That didn't seem to make any sense until she lunged and her fist careened off the skull of the Nameless One and he staggered back. He ducked away from her second strike but was lifted off his feet by the third and catapulted into the mountainside with a thunderous thud.

"You…can't…kill me, you pitiful shitstain!"

Ahverna smiled and withdrew something from her cloak. Skharr recognized the Scepter of Silvanius that he and Brahgen had collected from the trial vault. She twisted it firmly and shattered the exterior to reveal a sword within.

"Indeed I can." She fixed him with a gimlet glare.

His eyes widened and the Nameless One extended his arms and tried to draw the shadows on himself like a cloak. Ahverna was already in motion and lunged forward in the blink of an eye to impale him through the chest.

An inhuman scream echoed through the mountains, silenced finally when the blade came out the other side. A concussive blast hurled Skharr back a step. Ahverna pushed forward step by step until the blade was planted into the side of the mountain.

Finally, she released it. The world shifted like the sword was drawing in all the light and color from everything around it.

Another blast battered the barbarian off his feet and he landed hard. He scrambled up immediately, grasped his ax decisively, and waited for something to happen.

Instead, all he could see was the scepter planted in the mountain where the sword had been. It glowed with a bright golden light that was already starting to fade. Ahverna seemed unperturbed and brushed a few specks of dirt and dust carelessly from her cloak.

"If I were to guess, I would say there is a special reason why the scepter was placed in the Seven Trials," she said and patted it almost affectionately before she yanked it out of the rock. "Someone did not want such a dangerous weapon in the hands of the gods. It is a shame your follower was such an idiot, though. And speaking as a previous demigoddess, I did get my hands dirty from time to time. There is an abundance of skills to learn over the millennia. It is a great pity, however, that you will not have the opportunity to learn as I did."

Skharr approached her, his eyes narrowed. "Who the fuck are you talking to?"

"Gods do not die quickly. They...tend to linger for a while. I was saying my fond farewells." She turned and registered the look of shock on the faces of all those present. "What? I did not start this mess, but I think I did a damn good job of finishing it. And my brother would agree."

Theros leaned against the wall of the mountain. The barbarian didn't like how they appeared to simply materialize out of thin air all the time. It wasn't unusual for them by any means, but the fact that he was present for so many of those times had begun to annoy him.

"Yes." The old man sighed. "I suppose I would have to say that you did rather well."

Ahverna grinned and winked at Skharr. "Stay on the path, barbarian. It's not over."

"It isn't?" He looked around before he simply shrugged. "Well, I suppose I have a team to deal with whatever comes."

"No more lone adventures for you," Sera insisted and sheathed her sword. "You would have to tie me down for that to happen."

"I wouldn't dream of it, Captain Ferat," he answered. "It wouldn't do to leave the half-pint DeathEater without a father, now would it?"

"Good. I'd rather not have to tell stories about their dead father."

"Father?" Turan asked and raised an eyebrow.

"Everyone to the portal. We're heading back," Cassandra called before Skharr could answer, although he did note that she grinned at him while the others started to move through the portal.

"What?" He raised an eyebrow at her.

Her grin widened. "I always knew you had it in you."

"I didn't think that was ever in doubt."

The DeathEaters and the Elites were already through the gateway, which closed immediately when Cassandra joined them. They left Skharr and Sera alone on the mountain with Ahverna as Theros had disappeared as mysteriously as he had arrived.

"And then there were three," the goddess said. "Or…four, if the omens prove true. Forming a child, especially a DeathEater child, is never an easy task. I would avoid battle if at all possible."

"A DeathEater half-pint can stand a little excitement," Sera asserted with some confidence. "And fighting has always been in my blood as well."

"She is a suitable companion, Skharr," Ahverna admitted with a smile. "One hell of a path."

He nodded. "I always thought as much. What did you warn me of before Tryam came?"

"Ah. Yes." She cleared her throat. "Ascension has not been quite the smooth path I thought it would be, and I knew some other god would have to be torn down for me to rise. As it was never my intention to ascend until recently, it was never a problem. And yet, my followers—Brahgen and the others—deserved a real goddess. I had to find out who my competition was and lo and behold, I find that shit was already up to his conniving asshole tricks and trying to kill you."

"There was no real surprise on my side," he muttered. "I always seem to attract the attention of asshole gods wherever I go."

"Not for much longer, but...that is not for me to explain. Perhaps you should have a word with Sera's sister on that matter."

He rolled his eyes in mock horror. "Oh, gods. What is she up to this time?"

"That's 'oh, goddess' to you. And...well, Micah is perceptive."

"Too perceptive," Sera interjected.

"Well, perhaps someone should walk like they hadn't satiated their lust for each other on an altar for hours on end. How long did you two last in there? Time has always been a little...odd in these trials."

Sera made no attempt to answer that question. "I thought I hid that."

"Not well enough, I assure you. But I'm afraid it is time for this to end." Ahverna gestured and a portal appeared to provide them with a way off the mountain without having to travel for weeks on end. "And it is time for you two to leave. They don't need to see me."

"Duties?" Skharr asked.

"Constraints. Theros and I played rather loosely with the rules this time. It was a chance we could take, given that we were acting against one who was outright breaking the rules. For now, though, we will need to…obfuscate ourselves."

"Thank you." He extended his hand and she took it at the wrist. "I suppose the one thing that was stolen the most was my heart."

"Wait until the little one is born," Ahverna said with a grin. "If you think you fear for Sera's life now, wait until you hold that little one in those brutish hands of yours for the first time."

He smiled and turned as Sera took hold of one of his hands as they stepped through the portal.

It closed and Ahverna sighed and shook her head slowly.

"Well, I guess I'll have to ask Janus how he finds someone to share his bed now that my favorite companion will no longer join me."

CHAPTER TWENTY-FOUR

O f all the places she could have sent them, they emerged in the royal throne room. Skharr looked around with a scowl. "Fucking portals."

"Is there a problem?" Sera asked and wiped some blood from her cheek.

"Not really, although I would have appreciated a little privacy for when we returned. Time for a change of clothes and perhaps a bath."

She smirked. "That would have taken you...at least thirty minutes."

"I bathe quickly."

"I would have made sure that it took at least thirty minutes."

"Ah." Skharr nodded his understanding.

"Are...we interrupting something?" The emperor's voice surprised them both.

The barbarian looked around and realized that they shared the room with Tryam, Elric, Turan, and Micah, all of whom watched them intently.

"Because we could always leave and come back when the two of you are finished." Micah completed Tryam's thought for him.

"There is no point in that," Sera answered. "You are already here and the moment's ruined. We'll continue it some other time."

"Well, now that we have your full attention," the emperor stated with a smile, "we might as well return to business. The missing royal."

"I thought you had all three," Skharr noted.

"One was a decoy," Micah explained. "Well, a body double was sent instead of the third, who we assume already knew we suspected him and sent another. It was revealed under questioning. He is still in his castle and we assume he is building his defenses. From what we know of it, the castle is in the mountains and already a pain in the ass to attack, and it protects him from the occasional monster attacks from the pass near him. Reports say the gates are already closed and he has sent word out to levy more men for the defenses."

The barbarian nodded. "I can go and bring my fellow DeathEaters and we can arrive there before his force becomes substantial. We can climb the walls, open the gate, and allow the Emperor's Eagles led by Micah to retake it as your lawful representative."

"That…is a plan," Micah admitted.

"A barbarian plan," Sera agreed.

He turned to Turan, who showed no sign of liking or disliking the plan. "What say you?"

The chieftain scratched his beard for a moment and considered it carefully. "Would we be allowed to plunder the castle?"

"Gold and treasure only," Tryam told him. "I'll need the people to be on our side when I appoint another duke to take control of the region—one who represents my interests. I think…Sera would be the finest choice to maintain order in the region until she is relieved. What say you, sister?"

"Oh." She looked surprised that she was being considered at all and it appeared that she had not followed the conversation closely. "I suppose I can, but I would ask that it not last too long."

"Excellent." Tryam cleared his throat and glanced at Elric. "How long before they can leave?"

"Not long." The lord commander sounded certain enough that he probably had his men ready and waiting.

Micah cleared her throat softly. "If I may be excused? I need to check for additional evidence against the noble."

"Of course." The emperor motioned for her to go and she did so through a side door as he turned his attention to Elric again. "Well?"

"An expeditionary force could be ready to leave before the sun sets," the lord commander explained. "It should be enough to take the castle if the gates are opened and the defenses weakened by the barbarians. However, should such an incursion not be possible or should it fail, we would then have to arrange to blockade the castle to ensure that no additional forces or fortifications can be added before a proper siege can be mounted. By then, word will have spread that the duke is raising his levies without the emperor's sanction. Keeping the bastard in the castle will be the priority."

Tryam nodded. "Make it so."

Elric bowed stiffly. "Your Grace." With that, he hurried through the same side door Micah had exited through.

"As for the rest of you," the young ruler continued and focused on Skharr and Turan, "you should be ready to leave by nightfall as well. I do not want word to spread that you have left the palace, so you will travel in the dead of night."

"Your Grace," Skharr answered with a small grin as they assumed they were now dismissed from the emperor's presence.

He couldn't help a little pride at seeing that the young emperor was up to the tasks of his office.

CHAPTER TWENTY-FIVE

"Thoughts?" Skharr looked at his Clan chieftain.

Turan shrugged. "It's summer now. The walls shouldn't be too cold."

Skharr looked up, his head tilted as he studied the walls. They were far enough from the patrols and had made sure of that. Men moved across the ramparts every three hours, but they neglected it at night, especially the places that were elevated and on the other side of the gate.

It had been interesting to watch the barbarian in his element like this. Sera had hated to see him like a fish out of water when he was forced to deal with politics and civilized behavior. Lately, he'd had too few opportunities for him to shine as he did there.

Another one of the DeathEaters approached and remained low before he leaned against the wall. They knew how to move silently when they wished to and negotiating mountainous terrain was something that came naturally to all of them. They had done it since they were children.

"The Eagles are waiting on horseback just out of sight," he stated once they were sure no one could hear. "They'll wait for our signal, but we'll have to keep the gate open until they arrive. How are the walls?"

"Warm enough," Turan answered.

Sera shook her head. "Why...what is the relevance of the temperature of the walls?"

"DeathEaters scale sheer rock from the time we are children," Skharr explained. "A wall like this should be child's play, but nothing's worse on the fingers than ice-cold rock. Warm rock means easy climbing."

"Oh. Why don't you wear gloves?"

"Because you cannot climb sheer rock with gloves," the chieftain interjected. "If you cannot feel the rock, it means you could choose a treacherous grip and fall to your death. It's always better to climb with bare hands."

"Honestly," Micah interjected, "it's like those blademasters didn't teach you anything about climbing."

Her sister rolled her eyes. "They didn't. They're blademasters, not...climbingmasters."

Skharr grinned. Micah was at least dressed for the occasion in the leathers that seemed to disappear in the shadows, and she approached where he was pressed against the wall and spoke to him alone.

Her sister couldn't hear what was said but she could see even in the darkness that he narrowed his eyes. Finally, he nodded and seemed to agree to whatever she had suggested.

"Wonderful," she muttered. "Now my devious sister has reached an agreement with my devious barbarian on how to attack the castle."

"Is there a problem?" one of the barbarians asked when he heard her talking to herself.

"Only if you want to see any fighting."

Turan motioned for his people to be ready. They were and in moments, they began to climb the walls. Sera had no idea how they did it. Micah didn't surprise her much since she had done this kind of thing even when they were children, but Sera had always found climbing difficult. She could navigate regular buildings well enough but never anything like this.

The DeathEaters reached the top of the wall in moments, and Skharr lowered a rope for her to follow them up.

"That was impressive," she whispered once they were all together. "Now what?"

"We lower the drawbridge," he whispered and crouched in the shadows.

"You shouldn't have come," Micah told her sharply. "That's my niece you've got there, you know."

"Bite me. I won't be handled with soft gloves."

Skharr grinned and they began to approach the gatehouse. The DeathEaters entered first and climbed through windows. In moments, the doors opened and what soldiers were within were dead or otherwise disabled.

"The drawbridge should be easy enough," Turan whispered. "But we'll need to remain here and defend the gatehouse to ensure that they cannot lower the portcullis."

"It's only for a few minutes," Skharr told him. "Give the Eagles their signal and start with the gates. Hopefully, that will give them less time."

Turan nodded as he moved to the window of the gatehouse, took a torch from the wall, and waved it up and down twice before he returned it to the sconce.

"You will lower the drawbridge," Skharr signaled two DeathEaters, "and you will lift the portcullis. The rest, prepare to defend the gatehouse."

The barbarians responded with alacrity and set to work on the gates while the others held their bows in hand and arrows ready.

Less than a minute after the gates began to open, alarm bells were heard on the far side of the wall and they were quickly picked up by the rest of the castle.

"Those damn horsemen had better not be late," Turan muttered as the first of the castle guards appeared. An arrow materialized in the defender's chest and forced him over the wall's crenellations to splash into the moat below.

Two more men appeared but immediately dropped back, one with an arrow through his neck while the other managed to hide behind his comrade barely in time.

"How many?" the chieftain asked.

"Seventy in total," Skharr answered. "By the scout reports, at least. It might be more."

"There are certainly more."

Those who appeared next carried shields and blocked the three arrows that were launched at them as they approached two at a time.

Skharr grasped his ax tighter and drew a deep breath before he rushed out.

"Fucking...idiot." Sera hissed in frustration. He carried a shield as well and used it to deflect a couple of arrows launched at him before he swung his ax into the raised shield of the first of the approaching guards.

The blade cut the barrier in two like it was nothing and took the man's arm with it. He screamed in pain as his attacker battered him out of the way with his shield and tipped him over the wall as well before he hacked the head off the man beside him.

Without much thought, he leaned forward and kicked the shields behind to topple the group down the steps again.

He laughed as he raised his shield to block another two arrows fired at him.

"I am Skharr DeathEater!" he roared as the guards gathered themselves for another attempt. "My kin and I claim this castle in the name of the emperor. Come die at my hand if you dare!"

Those few who rushed forward despite the warning were quickly cut down by the arrows fired by the other DeathEaters.

Even so, Sera could see that they recognized his name and his appearance, and a handful had begun to back away.

Word of Skharr had certainly spread this far. From what they had been told, the duke claimed to be raising his army in the name of the emperor and to now discover that a known associate of Tryam's was there to cut them to pieces caused a sudden drop in morale.

"Come on you maggot-brained turds. Will you be turned away by mere word—" The captain who tried to rally his men was cut off when an arrow punched through his throat. It was a precise strike that highlighted the barbarians' impressive skills with their bows. By cutting down the officers and those brave enough to fight, it would take the heart from those who didn't want to fight in the first place.

Even better, the Eagles proved true to their name and already, hooves clattered over the drawbridge, through the gate, and into the courtyard. A handful of them carried bows as well and killed the men coming up the walls.

Some of the defenders had already begun to drop their weapons, and as more were ridden down by the Elites, others started to surrender. Many hurried to do so when they saw that the riders bore the crest of the Emperor's Eagles and confirmed in their mind that they were battling against the empire.

"Find the duke!" Sera called to the Eagles below.

The captain nodded and gestured for his men to follow him into the castle while a few remained outside to ensure that those who had surrendered stood by their word.

In minutes, the duke was removed from his quarters and looked very much like he had been dragged out of bed. Even the alarms hadn't been enough to wake him.

Sera drew her sword as the man was forced to his knees.

"Who are you?" he demanded and tried to pull free. "I'll have your heads for this treachery!"

"I am Captain Sera Ferat," she answered and rested her blade at his throat. "Sister to the emperor. In his name, I condemn you to death. Do you have any last words?"

"What...no, this must—"

It didn't appear that they would get anything of value or deserving of the history books from him , and she drew her blade back enough to give her the power she needed to cut his head away cleanly. It tumbled to lie still beside the fallen body.

"Put it on a spike outside the castle walls," she ordered.

The Eagle Captain placed his hand to his chest in salute before he took the head and turned to obey her order.

"The castle is yours," Skharr told her and wiped the blood from his ax.

"It was a good fight, that," Turan agreed. "And it worked up a nice appetite. I don't suppose we'll be allowed some food."

"I am sure the castle servants wouldn't mind rewarding you with a decent meal," Sera answered. "You're free to take what you can carry from the castle. I think you'll find that most of the treasure and jewels are in this dead bastard's room."

"You have our thanks." Turan grinned and hurried away to find his men.

"A little castle living should be interesting," Skharr commented.

"There are two more to deal with," Sera answered as she cleaned and sheathed her weapon. "Tryam wants some kind of assurance that no rebellion will start around here. I don't suppose we could count on your kin to help with that?"

He shrugged. "As long as you continue providing them with free food and ample coin, they'll be willing to kill almost anyone in your name. Or the emperor's, as it were."

CHAPTER TWENTY-SIX

"Y ou don't have to look so pleased with yourself over this."
Sera stared dubiously at her reflection.

"How could I not?" Micah answered and adjusted her sister's gown. "It's not every day that my sister is a proper duchess, after all. And to know I played a part in it. Given how quickly you took control of the region out there, I'm surprised we were able to arrange this in such a short time."

It had been an interesting few weeks with a great deal of traveling. There was no sign that she was with child yet—or, at least, none of the obvious signs. Her monthly time was already late by a week or so, and that was enough of an indication that everyone was right, but thankfully, none of the sickness or weakness that usually came with pregnancy had assailed her.

Which meant her gown did not need to be altered for her to wear it to the official ceremony.

"There," Micah whispered and smoothed her hand over the shoulder of the gown. "Are you ready?"

"About as ready as I'll ever be." The captain looked almost grimmer than she did going into battle.

"An interesting answer. I can guarantee that Skharr is feeling far more nervous than you are."

"Why?" Sera seemed genuinely surprised.

Micah's glance was wickedly teasing. "You've taken over three duchies in the span of a few weeks. He might be Tryam's personal confidant but as of this moment, you are a member of the gentry. A good deal higher than he is too."

"That's not what this is about."

"I'll wager you that he is thinking about it."

"Well, then he is..." Sera trailed off and shifted her gaze to look ahead.

Her sister laughed. "You intended to say he is a fool."

"Yes. Which...we already know he is, I suppose."

"Indeed. Come on. The emperor is already waiting for us."

Micah wore a gorgeous black gown that seemed to fit her new position as well. Sera had been outfitted in a dress in red and purple, the imperial colors. That was an intentional move on their younger brother's part, although she didn't know what he tried to tell the rest of the world.

It was a short walk to the throne room. The moment the guards saw them, they pushed the doors open to reveal that most of the gentry—landed or not—were present, whispering and talking as the two sisters entered.

There was no point in playing coy at this point. If Tryam wanted the world to know they were members of his family, it would happen regardless of what they did.

She straightened her back, rested her hand on the sword at her hip, and walked through the cleared center path to the throne where the emperor already waited. He wore red and purple as well, although with gold and silver mixed in. Perhaps this was an indication that while the sisters were his family, he was still the emperor.

The guards who flanked the pathway she walked down drew their swords and raised them above her head as a kind of salute as she approached the throne. Sera drew a deep breath and looked up the five steps leading to the royal seat. Elites stood between her and Tryam, and she could see Skharr at the base of the steps and a little to the side. He was likely meant to look like a bodyguard as well, although he winked as she came to a halt.

Palace manners had been ingrained in her from a young age and certain things would never be forgotten. She dropped into an appropriate curtsey and lowered her head carefully.

"Rise," Tryam commanded and stood from his throne, prompting all others in the room to do the same. "Decades ago, before I was even born, my father did the unspeakable. He sent his wife away and with her, two daughters—my sisters, who stand before you now."

Sera rose quickly and stood tall.

"I will not turn my back on my family as he did," the emperor announced as he reached the bottom of the steps, quickly joined by Elric who hovered at his side to ensure that his sisters had no machinations. "As you all know, there was an attempt made on the life of Skharr DeathEater in an attempt to provoke open war with our neighbors in Sareena. Captain Sera Ferat and Dame Micah Ferat were both instrumental in foiling this treachery and ensuring that the dukes responsible received their proper justice. Rewards are in order."

He turned to his scribe, who immediately began to pour hot wax over two documents, and the emperor pressed his seal into them.

"I hereby officially declare that Captain Sera Ferat and Dame Micah Ferat are members of my family, my blood, and my sisters. Furthermore, Dame Micah Ferat will be elevated to my personal council and will be known as Dame no more but Duchess Micah Ferat. She is further granted land and titles to the Bannar duchy. Captain Sera Ferat will be known as captain no more but Duchess Sera Ferat and is granted land and titles to the Briar duchy."

Not a word was spoken. No one in the room was surprised by this since it had been the talk of the city over the past month or so.

Even Sera, who had no idea what all this meant, was not surprised. She knew that by accepting the position in a temporary capacity, she would likely be called to do so more permanently, although she was relieved to find that she would only take the one. Even then, it felt like a daunting task. The Bessu Duchy, however, remained vacant.

She could only hope that someone competent would take on the role of its duke.

"Skharr DeathEater, step forward." Tryam's lip twitched slightly and belied the stern tone.

That caused a few tongues to wag behind them and even Skharr looked surprised that he was called forward. He likely expected that his role would mostly be about remaining silent and looking deadly.

The scribe already had a third sheaf of paper and began to pour wax on it as well.

"Oh...*fuck*," Sera whispered and watched her barbarian's face as the emperor continued.

"For your efforts in keeping the empire from open war and enacting the will of the Lord High God Theros, you will no longer be known as Skharr DeathEater, but Duke Skharr Death-Eater and I hereby grant you land and titles to the Bessu Duchy."

After a stunned silence, Tryam smirked. "The High Priest of Theros looks over these proceedings," he announced and motioned for the old man in priest's robes to take a step forward and study the documents. "What do the gods say of this?"

The priest inspected the papers closely and made sure the emperor's seal was setting and cooling correctly before he nodded. "The gods bless these endowments, Your Grace."

Micah leaned closer to whisper in Sera's ear. "It isn't every day

MICHAEL ANDERLE

that you get to marry a duke barbarian, now is it? I suppose that makes you the *real* barbarian princess."

There was no real answer to that and Sera bristled when she saw Elric struggle to not look amused at the surprise on Skharr's face.

"Wait," Sera whispered. "Marry? But he hasn't even asked me yet."

"Oh, has he not?"

Her sister looked a little too smug for all this, and she understood why when Skharr turned to face her and looked particularly nervous.

Her heart raced and she glanced at the old priest, who suddenly looked familiar. His form had changed and aged almost twenty years, but the eyes were very much the same. Theros smiled and winked at her as Skharr dropped to one knee.

"I—"

She flushed and tried to end this as quickly as possible. "Yes, you big fucking oaf."

He looked up with a confused frown. "I...think I have to...uh, say the words."

"Why? You know my answer."

"Well...official shit." He rolled his eyes when his grin disarmed her. If he could stand the attention, she could too.

"Oh. Right."

Skharr cleared his throat. "Duchess Sera Ferat...I have experienced a great many honors in my life, but none match that of fighting...at *your* side. If you...would you do me the honor of giving me your hand in marriage?" Theros deftly dropping a ring that Skharr had shown her he had taken...from the god's dungeon.

It was adorable that he had devised a proper-sounding proposal, even if he'd messed his lines up.

"Of course." She grinned, yanked him off his feet, and pressed her lips to his, although she needed to do it while he was still in the process of standing to ensure that he wasn't too tall for it. "Of course, I assume this means our lands will be joined and we'll both take the time to battle any monsters that might come out of the north, human or otherwise."

"That...uh, you...honor me, Duchess."

"Fuck off. And I want those two words as part of the official record for this." She gestured at the scribes, who nodded.

Skharr grinned from ear to ear and Elric approached and clapped them both on the shoulder.

"Well, I suppose those are two duchies that we won't have to worry about ever again," the lord commander commented. "Congratulations to you both."

"Three," Micah cut in. "I won't have much time to tend to my lands while I am officially a part of the emperor's council, so I would have to turn the care of the duchy over to my sister and soon-to-be brother-in-law."

"Our soon-to-be brother-in-law," Tryam said. "Officially now. Of course, I am a close friend of said brother-in-law, or she might have ambitions to become the next empress."

"I would suggest that whoever believes they will capture your heart had better not have any devious thoughts," Elric commented as the event officially ended and folk began to file out to where a feast was already prepared.

Sera noticed the barbarians already partaking in the food and drink. The group had rapidly become the toast of the city and were greeted by many of the nobles who filed out of the throne room.

"Why do you say that?" Tryam asked with a small smile.

"Because, unless I miss my guess, any who would have foul intentions toward you will start to go missing over the next few years. My job is about to become far more interesting."

"They aren't married yet," the emperor reminded him. "He's a barbarian and there's no telling what will come out of his mouth."

"Still, you might want to ready yourself for those who might not be happy to find themselves equals to a barbarian."

"Let us hope they are not in any great numbers, then." Tryam patted the man on the shoulder. "Now, come. A party needs to start, and I have a great need to drink until I am escorted out for fear that I might say or do something indecent."

"It's your right to be indecent," Skharr reminded him. "You're the emperor. It's the rest of us who need to be careful."

CHAPTER TWENTY-SEVEN

The chieftain of the Clan had a responsive audience. "I swear, he stepped out into the open, swung the ax, and started shouting about how he was Skharr DeathEater and all those who dared to fight him had better step up and do it. He held a shield up while archers tried to find a shot, and all the while, our men were shooting those who were shooting at him. If I thought the man had any brains to him, I would have assumed that he was deliberately distracting the bastards."

It had been a good few months. The Clan had previously struggled and with their new alliance with the empire, they had food and coin, which would facilitate trade with their dwarf allies under the mountains. The debts owed to them were being paid off quickly too.

Turan sipped the wine sent up with Tryam's compliments, which he shared with the rest of the Clan around the council fire. With a broad smile, he continued his tale.

"He's married now and his wife is pregnant, probably sporting a belly to show it too. Hells, Skharr probably has a belly of his own now. He's growing soft and lazy with servants there to feed him and tend to his every need every night."

The rest of the Clan laughed at the idea. It wasn't often that a DeathEater was allowed the opportunity to grow soft and fat and while some mockery was required, each and every one of them envied the man who could do it.

Shouting erupted outside and Turan looked up as people rushed in. Most of the Clan had gathered to partake in the wine, but a few were missing—scouts and guards, for the most part, who kept an eye on the roads and the ax.

The man guarding the ax rushed in and allowed the cold winter air in with him.

"Chief!" the youth shouted, red in the face and his eyes wide in fear. "Chief…the ax! It's gone!"

"Gone?" Turan fixed him with a hard look.

"It was there one moment and disappeared the next! There was two of us who saw it!"

"Where's the other?"

The young man's consternation flavored his response. "He's still there. We wanted to make sure to see it if the ax…well, reappeared."

Turan could tell that he expected to be berated and beaten for letting the weapon vanish from under his nose, but instead, the chieftain threw his head back and laughed loudly. He was quickly joined by the other five who had been with him on their travels.

He winked at the now thoroughly confused guard. "Bless my fucking beard, but Skharr is back to his old tricks again. I was a fool to assume otherwise. That damned boy couldn't stay away from trouble if he tried. Now! Who wants to be a part of a real DeathEater tale?"

The gathered Clan stood and roared their approval.

"Five will join me!" Turan declared loudly and stood from his seat. "We will find Skharr, help him, and bring the ax back when it is done. The world will be a great deal emptier and the afterlife will be a good deal fuller. Bring me my ax!"

Cassandra has fought alongside Skharr DeathEater, but will she be able to forge a new path alone?

When the former paladin turned Barbarian Princess is robbed while aiding travelers against brigands, she vows to find the miscreants. Will her search lead her to them or greater danger?

In the war-ravaged north-east of the continent, a new evil has arisen and begins to impose a rule of dark sorcery and fear on the small settlements.

Will she find the allies she needs in time to save a town? How will she know who she can trust in this evil hour?

Her quest will demand everything from her but she cannot turn away. Does she have sufficient skill, experience, and determination to defeat the rising malevolence?

She pits her steel and will against sorcery and its army and digs deep. This is what it means to be a Barbarian of Theros, but can she hope to survive?

With new allies at her side, Cassandra fights to turn the tide of darkness and fear.

This is her path—to smite evil and save innocents.

Grab your copy today at Amazon or Kindle Unlimited.

Thank you for not only reading this story about my loving and compassionate barbarian but these author notes as well.

THANK YOU SO MUCH for coming along on the Skharr Journey with me. While I wasn't sure WHAT the hell I was going to create when I told myself, 'I want to read some sword & sorcery stories.' I am really jazzed over Skharr. He's a guy I'll come back and read multiple times just to be with him. From that perspective, I like him more than Conan.

You can never give Robert E. Howard too much credit for creating Conan in my mind. His light was extinguished way too early in his life.

I have to admit I'm a little sad about the end of this part of Skharr's journey. Will we have the sales from these 8 books to invest in another Skharr DeathEater anytime soon? Or, will I just get a wild hair at some point and decide, 'screw it, I want another Skharr story' whether the sales are there to support the cost of another story or not?

Give me some time to think about it.

I have set up Skharr (and his wife, child, family) so that we can continue these stories into the future. Right now (as mentioned), we are spending a lot of time on the Myth of the Dragon series, and we have two other short trilogies here in Skharr's world.

Please, grab them all ;-)

Eventually, probably in the first quarter of 2022, I suspect I will need another Skharr story… Hell, just follow me on Amazon, and I think you will get a notice about a pre-order before the end of either December or March.

Because, who wouldn't want a story about a barbarian, his deadly wife, their child who would be protected by his aunt who (might) rule the underworld?

I know I do.

Shit… I think I just talked myself into making another story… Or three. Please, tell your friends to read these stories – I have a barbarian problem.

It's like a drug problem - only I get some money back and unfortunately GAIN weight as I read the books. In short, it isn't anything like a drug problem, I guess.

As a publisher who needs to make a profit… It is some kind of problem. ;-)

Have a fantastic week or weekend, whichever it is for you!

Ad Aeternitatem,

Michael Anderle

CONNECT WITH THE AUTHOR

Connect with Michael Anderle

Website: http://lmbpn.com

Email List: http://lmbpn.com/email/

https://www.facebook.com/LMBPNPublishing

https://twitter.com/MichaelAnderle

https://www.instagram.com/lmbpn_publishing/

https://www.bookbub.com/authors/michael-anderle

BOOKS BY MICHAEL ANDERLE

Sign up for the LMBPN email list to be notified of new releases and special deals!

https://lmbpn.com/email/

For a complete list of books by Michael Anderle, please visit:

www.lmbpn.com/ma-books/

www.ingramcontent.com/pod-product-compliance
Lightning Source LLC
Chambersburg PA
CBHW050527110726
47899CB00005B/1628